AMERICAN
PATHFINDER

Charles MacDonald
PATHFINDER BOOK I

FRANK MITCHELL

STORY MERCHANT BOOKS • LOS ANGELES • 2016

Story Merchant Books
400 S. Burnside Avenue #11B,
Los Angeles, CA 90036

http://www.storymerchantbooks.com

ISBN-13: 978-0-9969908-5-1

Author Website: http://PathfinderTales.com

Interior: Danielle Canfield, www.529Books.com

Cover Design: Dafeenah Jamal, www.IndieDesignz.com

I would like to dedicate this book to James O'Shea Wade, Steve Berry and James O. Born who were of great help in writing the final version.

OTHER BOOKS BY FRANK MITCHELL:

Attack at Khoda Bridge
An International Thriller
Gus Smith Book I
A 2015 Story Merchant Publication

Coming Soon:
Attempt in Tehran: Gus Smith Book II
Ambush at Mt. Gilead: Gus Smith Book III

Elizabeth Series: America at the Dawn of the 19th Century
Elizabeth's Journey: Book I
Whiskey Boys: Book II

Dr. Henry Ravenal Series: Reconstruction after the Civil War
Memminger Hoard: Book I

COMING SOON IN THE *PATHFINDER SERIES*:

AMERICAN
PATHFINDER

FRANCE

1798

CHAPTER

ONE

March 30ᵗʰ

ARTILLERY SCHOOL, CHÂLONS-SUR-MARNE, FRANCE

Sous-Lieutenant Charles MacDonald waited patiently in the martial arts training hall and watched as the two French swordsmen prepared to attack him simultaneously. Though standing absolutely still, he was actually tensing and releasing each muscle group as he mentally prepared for the next engagement.

He and his opponents were using the schools' unsharpened straight military swords with metal buttons-*fleurets* covering the point. All three were relying on the touch and not the cut or thrust that *sabreuse* normally used with their dulled practice sabres. Their master called this type of practice, *jeu d'épée*—game of swordsmanship.

He studied his opponents at the other end of the fencing *piste* and thought about what let him beat them every time. Since he was taller than any other student at the school he could extend his blade six inches further than any other cadet or junior officer.

After arriving last September, he had grown another inch. As he pulled on his tight gloves, he mentally noted that all of his uniforms and clothes were becoming too small. Lowering his mesh-mask, he raised his épée in salute. His two friends, Edmond and Quentin, both lowered their masks and saluted him in return.

He planned to attack for the next pass. This morning he had defended more than half-a-dozen times and attacked only four. He jumped forward in a false attack, remaining upright. He drew the attention of both fencers by stamping his foot on the sanded white oak floor. As he expected, Quentin attacked first.

Charles dropped low and lunged up and to the right at Quentin, under his half-inch rhombic blade, striking him in the center of his chest. Balancing with his left hand on the floor and pivoting to the left he dodged beneath Edmond's extending blade.

"*Touché*," Quentin said in a constrained voice as Charles counterattacked from his lowered position by using his arm and both feet to spring forward, using his blade to beat Edmond's up and then extending it to touch him on his chest.

"Touché," Edmond blurted. Charles realized that both must be frustrated from losing every match.

"*Merde*, Edmond and I never beat you," Quentin said in a mixture of French and broken English. "As a matter of fact, no one here at Châlons including the maître has ever touched the famous *Américain sauvage* with cold steel." Charles realized it was because he was too short.

Charles suspected that Quentin was using his birth in Virginia as an excuse for losing. He was ignoring the fact that for the last thirteen years he had been training in swordsmanship and other martial arts under a fencing-master in Paris.

He practiced every day. Charles had been fencing with the épée since he was six and he started sabre training when he was nine.

As he removed his fencing mask, a younger cadet called, "Charles and Quentin, the commandant wants to see you." After shaking hands, the three students went to their dormitory room.

As they crossed the caserne, Charles wondered if the reason the commandant had summoned them would delay him rejoining his graduate engineering classes in Paris. His two roommates would not graduate from Châlons until July.

Most of the students were among the almost a hundred cadets, *Élève Officiers* at the advanced French Artillery School. A dozen graduate students were already junior artillery officers taking advanced training. He and the younger Edmond Talley were among the three graduate engineering officers—and quite probably, he was the only American-born 2nd Lieutenant in the French army.

His father, General James MacDonald was a graduate engineer who worked for George Washington during the American Revolution. In Virginia he met and married Elizabeth Hancock where Charles and his sister were born.

Charles became a Sous-Lieutenant of Military Engineers-*l'Génie Militaire,* when he graduated with a bachelor's degree in Engineering from *L'École Polytechnique.* He then moved on to advanced classes at *L'École des Ponts & Chaussées,* the graduate engineering-demonstration school of bridges and roads. Génie meant Genius in Latin.

After the three reached their room, Edmond watched as Charles and Quentin changed into their dress uniforms. Charles' *nationale bleue* tailcoat with its black collar and cuffs had faded, and the lining had washed out to a dull puce rather than the fresh scarlet of the other cadet *habits.* His mother had converted his student *surtout* jacket into a second lieutenant's, but it no longer fit properly, everything was uncomfortably tight and way too short. His father lived on the disability pension from the National Convention and some consulting fees. Charles had to pay for his own expenses.

Edmond taunted his friends while they hurriedly dressed. "What have you done? Have you been breaking some of the sacred rules of this place?" Without bothering to respond, Charles and Quentin left the cadet barracks and rushed to the commandant's office.

Six students, four of them cadets and two graduate students who were already second lieutenants, knocked and entered the oversized office of the older Commandant of Cadets, Colonel DeWinter. Out of the corner of his eye, Charles noted that both assistant commandants and all six of the professors on the faculty were standing at the back of the room. What had they done to deserve this?

Anticipating the worst, he was surprised when Commandant DeWinter announced, "The faculty and I are pleased to award each cadet a graduation diploma and promotion to *Sous-Lieutenant* in the Artillery. The two graduate officers will each receive a diploma of qualifications in Advanced Artillery Ballistics." The commandant stood up and handed out parchment diplomas, ending with documents for Charles and Quentin.

"You are to take the mail coach to Paris early tomorrow morning starting a four week leave at home," DeWinter continued. "All six of you are to join the new Army of England— *L'armée d'Angleterre* in Toulon by the beginning of May."

"Pick up travel vouchers from the Adjutants Office to ride on the mail coach to Paris tomorrow morning. He will give you a three-month advance on your pay and an allowance to purchase uniforms and field equipment. The quartermaster has a selection of artillery officer uniforms and equipment that you can purchase with some of your stipend." Apparently, Charles was the only engineering officer ready to graduate three months early.

"You are finished with your education; it's time for the six of you to go to work. Turning to the two graduate officers he said, "Quentin Fermont, as the senior artillery graduate student, I am appointing you as a First Lieutenant in the Horse-Artillery. MacDonald, you are to appear before the Directeur-Général of the *Corps des Ponts* to receive your *la Maîtrise* Masters Diploma in Engineering. Then, you are to report to the War Depot. They will promote you to First Lieutenant in the Geographical Engineers. Neither of you will get the advance money or uniform allowance and I'm sorry but we don't have either special uniform in the commissary."

Charles was secretly relieved and delighted. As soon as he graduated from des ponts, he would be jumping from military engineering, to the *Corps des Ingénieurs Géographes.* Apparently, they were promoting him to full Lieutenant, Geographer-2nd Class. He was following his father, shadowing his footsteps as a geographical engineer.

The independent Corps of Geographical Engineers, usually called IG, were a specialized contingent of few more than three-dozen officers, all graduate engineers. Trained in mapmaking, navigation, and surveying, a select few of them were pathfinders who scouted ahead of the army with the advanced screen.

They collected intelligence and carried out field reconnaissance in advance of army operations. They were not a part of the regular army but rather they worked for the *Dépôt de la Guerre,* directly under the control of the Minister of War and the five-man *Directoire.*

As the six officers left, each of their professors shook their hands and wished them success in their endeavors. Even the crusty and austere math professor, Bonnard, offered a rare smile to the tall engineer.

CHAPTER

TWO

March 30ᵗʰ

PLACE DE LA VILLE, CHÂLONS-SUR-MARNE, FRANCE

At two in the morning, the cold mist rising off the Marne River was beginning to obscure the nearly full moon. Walking alongside the lower fortified wall enclosing the river and the extensive *cantonnement* of the Applied School of Artillery, the six youthful French officers walked through the southern postern gate in the main defensive wall and headed for the commune square.

Two of the first four teenagers pulled a baggage cart loaded with four trunks ahead of two more athletic looking young men pushing. However, all six were carrying bags slung over their shoulders. The trailing man was half-a-head taller than the other five.

The new officers were heading two blocks up to the main square fronting the city hall and the route national between Paris and the eastern frontier. The *diligence* or mail coach from the Germany to Paris stopped there at the tavern, sometime within the next hour or two.

Bright moonlight illuminated the layer of cold fog now creeping over the first few feet of the large plaza. The six officers could no longer see the bridge over the Marne or the ground floors of the riverfront buildings.

The two muscular senior-lieutenants went in and introduced themselves to the tavern-keeper who was also the ticket agent of the local *Messageries Nationales*. He told them to wait outside. He wouldn't know how many seats were available until the coach arrived.

The six young men watched him rush around getting ready for the arrival of the nighttime diligence. Charles knew it was nicknamed *turgotine,* for Robert Turgot, the minister who reformed the royal mail ten years previously.

A rumpled server took their order for drinks and toasted cheese bread. She said, "We have wine and beer, but no coffee or tea until breakfast. However, I could fix a pot of hot chocolate." When she realized that at least two of the officers wanted hot cocoa she mentioned, "It'll cost extra."

As she was inside fixing their food, the mail coach slid to a stop on the cold stones of the torch lit square, cattycorner to the city hall of Châlons-sur-Marne. It had a mail guard sitting on the baggage carrier holding a blunderbuss.

When he finished exchanging the mail pouches, the agent stepped back over to the two young officers and said, "I have room for two officers on top and two inside the turgotine."

Moving closer he said to Charles and Quentin in a low voice, "Since your travel vouchers to Paris are worth 75 francs each, I'll take them and pay both of you the value plus 25 francs extra to shuttle some post horses back toward Paris. Two army officers rode them here a couple of days ago, and continued toward the frontier on the turgotine. I'll even put your baggage in the boot of the mail coach. However, you won't get any free meals. You'll have to switch mounts at Reims, Château-Thierry, and Meaux on your way back, one-hundred seventy-five francs."

Thinking about the offer, Charles realized that he needed the extra money, although riding all the way to Paris would be a lot more strenuous than sitting in the coach. He was carrying some bread, fruit and a hunk of cheese from the militaire mess.

Quentin said, "We'll be exhausted by the time we arrive, but I can use the money. The Hussar uniforms of the Horse-Artillery cost twice as much as a standard tail-coat habit."

As Charles and his friend Quentin waited for their saddled horses, they sat next to the other four officers at the outside trestle table. As they ate their day-old toasted bread with melted cheese, several flambeaux projecting from the wall of the inn lit their table.

The young men talked and speculated about what the future had in store for them. Meanwhile, rather than talking, Charles was listening with one ear as he watched the two hostlers hitch up three-teams of six horses rather than two-teams of four. He wondered why they needed two postillion drivers and an extra team; the road to Reims was flat, not hilly.

Walking over to the *conducteur* he introduced himself. The official looked at the two thin red stripes on his shoulder boards. "I was promoted to first lieutenant yesterday afternoon," responded Charles."

Still curious, he asked him about the weight of their load and the conductor gruffly said, "It's none of your business." What a pig's ass, Charles thought, but refrained from flinging back a response to his elder.

Since they were riding the same route as the coach, Charles said to Quentin as he walked back to the table, "Both of us are good shots and we know how to use our sabres. I think that we should load our weapons and keep them available. Why don't you talk to the other lieutenants?"

Sitting on the torch-lit bench beside the doorway into the inn, Charles loaded his *dragon* pistol with a ball and three buckshots. It was a short-length oval-muzzled blunderbuss usually carried by cavalry dragoons.

He then loaded the rifled *carabine* he'd borrowed from his father for a boar hunt in the Ardennes forest last November. It was an elegantly finished officer's version of the new French army *Jäger* rifle designed for cavalrymen.

He took the wide black leather *bandolier* out of his bag, slung it over his shoulder, and buckled the matching *centurion* sword-belt around his waist. He then slid the loaded carabine into the ringed scabbard boot and muzzle thimble that caught it by the nose and at the lock. Then he snapped the rifle holster onto the bandolier hook.

Finally he removed his father's sabre from its travel case and exchanged it with his lighter officer's dress épée. After unpacking their weapons, holsters, and belts, Charles picked up their bags and ran over to put them with the luggage for the mail coach.

Quentin was just finished loading a pair of cavalry pistols. He started to hook up his light cavalry sabre to the straps hanging from his sword-belt. The conductor called for everyone to climb aboard the mail coach.

As they sat and waited, Charles told Quentin in a low voice that couldn't be overheard, "The turgotine is carrying an extra heavy load. I am certain that it must be carrying gold." Charles almost shivered with excitement.

"If it is, highwaymen or royalist-émigrés may attack. Let me know if you see any riders to our rear or to either side. One sign of attack would be a blockage in the road. We need to keep a sharp lookout."

"I warned the new sous-lieutenants, but none of them has bothered to load their weapons," Quentin said. "They are going to rely on the official guard to protect them."

After leaving Châlons, the mail coach clattered on its way, changing horses every couple of hours. As the morning wore on, low scudding clouds hid the rising sun. By the time they had ridden the twenty-eight miles to Reims, they were almost a half-league in front of the coach.

They both visited the outhouse and then washed and drank some cool water from the courtyard well while the hostler saddled their fresh set of horses. The passengers on the coach were entitled to a breakfast at the inn in Reims, but Charles and Quentin were not.

They planned to save money by finishing the loaf of bread, two apples and a slice of cheese Charles had picked up at the school in Châlons. Charles turned to Quentin and said, "It's getting windy and colder; a storm front will pass us in the next few hours. We need to put on our greatcoats, *bonnets* and gloves."

They stopped for a second change of horses in Château-Thierry and then a third change and dinner in Meaux at nearly three in the afternoon. The turgotine had arrived a few minutes ahead of them. Both he and Quentin were exhausted from their thirteen hours of riding, and the two officers agreed to buy hot food.

Inside, they both rested beside the fire as they ate their first real meal of the day, hot onion soup and a steaming mutton pie. During the last hours of the morning, it began sleeting and then turned to snow. They were glad to eat their dinner inside, out of the cold and sharp wind.

Just before dark, the coach was traveling through the *Bois de Claye-Souilly* on the route national from Reims to Paris and both young officers were riding just over a hundred yards behind.

The snow and sleet had stopped, but a cold wind swirled out of the northwest. The turgotine was passing patches of woods interspersed with snowy fields, some plowed and the rest too muddy to work. The peasants probably sowed winter wheat last fall over the then dryer harrowed fields. Looking across the farmland toward the setting sun, Charles could see a stream with a mill just beside the bending road. Trees bordered the stream on both sides.

Suddenly, an obstacle appeared, at the turn in the road. There was a wagon filled with sacks of grain sticking out into the post road. It had gotten stuck in the entrance to the yard of the mill when it turned in at too sharp an angle. Charles called out to Quentin, "*Alerte.*" The lead postillion driver slowed the turgotine teams to a walk to maneuver around the stranded wagon.

Unexpectedly, there was loud thwack followed by the bang of a shot from the mill yard. The second driver fell off the rear horse, carrying the reins with him.

The sound of the shot intermingled with the thump of the front wheel running over the postillion. As the coach rocked to a stop, half-a-dozen riders dressed in dark clothing rode out of the mill yard and started to surround the coach.

Charles slipped his rifled carabine out of its muzzle thimble and scabbard boot. He raised it to the ready position, cocking it as he brought it to his shoulder. He narrowed his vision to concentrate on his front sight, with the gaggle of highwaymen blurry in the distance.

His tired horse was still as he locked the front blade into the rear sight notch. He concentrated on the softened smear of the closest man furiously brandishing his sabre. He could see a white face between a dark scarf and a black hat a hundred yards away.

Blocking all outside distractions, Charles pulled the butt into the pocket of his shoulder as he lightly rested the forearm in his left hand. He closed his left eye and squinted through the narrow slit of his right, concentrating on keeping the front and rear sights aligned.

He slowly squeezed the trigger, ignoring the flash and sharp recoil as the short rifle fired. Although his horse jumped sideways with the sound, he was sure he had hit his target despite the movement and cloud of billowing smoke obscuring his vision.

As the smoke blew away, five mounted horsemen stared at Charles and Quentin instead of pointing their pistols at the coach; the sixth man was falling off his horse right in front of the other five.

Using both hands, Charles slipped the carabine back into the leather scabbard hooked to his bandolier. Suddenly, his horse bolted directly at the bandits.

He yanked at the loose reins as he yelled and spurred trying to gain control of his skittish horse. His post horse was wildly galloping directly at the highwaymen, straight into danger.

His left grabbing the leads, he used his right hand to begin pulling the dragon pistol from the centurion belt strapped outside his caped greatcoat.

Quickly approaching to within a dozen yards, he cocked and pointed it with a locked right wrist, and his right arm aiming the dragoon's pistol as one.

Squeezing the trigger, it discharged at the next closest rider, probably the leader. He saw the buckshot and ball puncture the black cloth of the brigand's riding coat as he recoiled from the impact. Nothing happened.

He realized that Quentin was following him just a few paces to his rear. No one on the coach was firing at the other highwaymen, but all five bandits were shooting at the two berserk officers.

Lead balls from Quentin's two cavalry pistols drove raiders back in their saddlery, but none fell off their mounts.

With a loud war cry, Charles tossed his empty pistol at the chief, causing him to duck. The high-strung post horse was turning to avoid a collision when he jerked the reins, pulling his head back to the left.

The rented horse crashed into the ringleaders mount, knocking him from his saddle and forcing him to drop his empty pistol. Charles grabbed his still strapped sabre scabbard in his left hand as he vaulted from his horse to confront the captain.

The leader rose and drew a dueling épée. He shouted in French, "This one's mine, get everybody off the coach." He was dressed in expensive looking dark clothing.

He spoke and moved like an experienced military officer as he saluted and said, "En Garde." Rather than controlling the passengers, three of the four bandits pulled back and started to reload while one waved his straight sabre at the conductor.

They were giving their boss room to fight. Charles was leading with his left side, the opposite of a normal right-handed fencing stance. He kept his still strapped scabbard raised horizontally, ready to parry.

He shouted out to Quentin, "They're wearing armor," as he distracted the brigand by stamping his left foot in the dirt, his *appel* ruse drawing an advance-lunge from the chief bandit.

He drew his sabre *laido* style with his left hand pulling the scabbard away from the blade and slinging it toward the bandit. Since the scabbard was still strapped to his sword belt, it fell down as he twisted his body like a matador avoiding the hurried thrust.

As he stepped backward with his leading left foot in an ungentlemanly cross over, he used his razor sharp blade to chop off the sword hand of his opponent. He heard the robber say, "*nique ta mere*" as his hand and épée fell to the ground in a spray of blood.

Redoubling his extension, Charles counter-attacked in a direct line to the center of the highwayman's chest, thrusting his sabre with both hands in a reverse backsword technique, as he exclaimed, "No, screw your mother."

The outlaw's final word was, "Merde," as the breath huffed out of his lungs. Under his waistcoat, the road agent was wearing a blackened steel cuirass.

The chisel point of the *tachi* blade drove through the steel breastplate and punched on out his back, stopping when the cross-guard indented the curved steel plate over an inch.

Planting his foot on the man's kneeling body to brace himself, he pushed him onto his back as he withdrew the blade from the bandit's breastplate. Gazing around Charles suddenly charged three steps toward the nearest highwayman with his sabre raised over his head.

All four hastily turned and rode away as fast as they could. He walked back, leaned over, wiped the blood off his sabre using the dark cloak of his opponent, and re-inserted it into his scabbard.

The threads of his right glove had split in three places, so he pulled it off and put it in his pocket. Luckily, his cavalry cloak covered the split seams of his threadbare jacket and the crotch of his poor breeches. He called out for Quentin and heard a moan in reply.

He looked over and saw Quentin lying in front of his horse with blood dripping from his leg. Charles climbed the rear wheel and grabbed his bag, opened it, took out a cotton towel and tied it around his friend's thigh with a tight knot.

The conductor was finished checking the dead postillion driver and had started asking the passengers if there were other wounded. Charles grabbed the conductor's arm and pulled him to the side.

"We need to head straight for Paris as quick as we can. If you're replacing the driver, whip the horses. My friend is wounded and bleeding, we've got to get to a doctor quick."

"Shouldn't we go to the next village and send for a doctor?" the conductor asked anxiously. "What are we going to do about the dead men and their horses? If we leave them here, their friends will retrieve the bodies. We'll have no evidence. Beside they now belong to you."

"Throw the two bandits bodies on the coach roof and tie all three horses to the rear," Charles ordered, "We need to go to the military hospital in Paris."

He ran over to the other body. His rifle shot had careened across his body, entering at the gap behind the armhole of his breastplate and crossing his chest to the other side. Hoisting the man's body on his shoulder, and grabbing the assassin's carabine, he collected the reins to the man's horse.

As he walked back to the turgotine he called out to the two sous-lieutenants on top, "Help me put this body on the roof." Turning to the official carrying the second body he said, "You can report to the *Gendarmerie Nationale* when we get to the *Terminus*." The conductor did not dispute Charles' orders.

After putting the driver's body in the front box, the conductor and the mail-guard tied both bodies on top of the coach while Charles tied the Quentin's post horses and both bandits' black horses to the rear. "Shouldn't I try and find a doctor?" the conductor asked once again. "Paris is seven leagues further, it'll take us almost two hours."

"No, let's push on. I'll take him to the military hospital at *Les Invalides*. The officer-*chirurgien* there will have more experience with gunshots." During the trip to Paris, he shouted through the window to two of the new artillery officers to clean Quentin's wound and stop the bleeding.

All four civilian passengers sat back on the seats watching them help Charles' friend. The pistol ball had passed through his leg muscle without hitting the large bone. The blood flowing from Quentin's wound was now oozing, so the urgency was somewhat diminished.

At the next stop, he bought a bottle of brandy to give to his friend. While talking with Charles the conductor explained that the horses, tack, weapons and anything in the bandits pockets belonged to the person who killed them. While the groom was hooking up fresh horses, he checked the pockets of the two dead highwaymen.

In his coat pocket, the leader had half-a-dozen gold coins and a letter from his mother in England. The address on the letter was to Captain Raoul Forté of the *Cuirassier d'Cheval Noir Regiment* with the Army of Condé.

Charles recalled that they were a royalist regiment whose officers had escaped the guillotine by emigrating across the German-French border. During a stop on the last leg into Paris, he realized that the passengers were armed. He asked the men, "Why didn't you shoot at the highwaymen?"

All four looked at him as if he was an idiot. One said, "Nobody interferes with highwaymen. They might get angry and retaliate. Did you notice that no one resisted, not even your four lieutenants, the mail-guard, or the conductor."

When the coach arrived at the nationalized Republic Messenger Terminus in Paris, Charles turned the two post horses over to hostlers and immediately engaged the driver of a *fiacre*, a two-wheeled, one-horse cabriolet.

With Quentin's leg propped on the mud apron, he took him to the military hospital, across the Seine. Before leaving the terminus, he tied both captured horses to the back of the cab. All four Sous-Lieutenants stayed since they were heading for their various homes, none in Paris.

He watched the senior doctor on night duty, Surgeon Major Dominique Larrey treat the new officer. First he flushed out his wounds with a brandy-water mixture and inserted felt plugs into both the in and out holes. He then tightly wrapped bandages around the wound.

He handed Charles a damp cloth to scrub the grime off his cheeks. During his ministrations, Larrey asked him many questions about the attempted robbery. "What did the bandits look like? How were they armed, and what kind of horses they were riding?"

After reading the letter from the dead man's mother he said, "The Black Horse Cuirassier officers are almost all royalist émigrés from the old King's Army. They seemed to disappear from Coblenz, Germany about two years ago. I thought that the regiment had disbanded."

The surgeon explained that he was asking these questions because he had to report the information to higher authority later that night. When Charles told him that both officers were supposed to be in Toulon at the beginning of May he said, "Lieutenant Fermont won't be joining the horse artillery, he needs to stay at home and heal for at least three months. I plugged the holes so the wound will heal from inside to outside."

"In the meantime, I will check on the status of your actual transfer into the geographical engineers. Come back tomorrow morning to visit your friend and I will see if we can handle the formalities here. What name should I have written on the new commission?"

"I am Charles Alexander MacDonald. Can I come here at twelve o'clock? I already have orders to report to the chief engineer at the *Corps des Ponts* at nine o'clock tomorrow morning." It was dark by the time he got walked home.

Downstairs, Jean the retired sergeant major who was his father's manservant and the cook greeted him with joy. They asked him a hundred questions while he cleaned the equipment and himself. Both of them commented on his torn uniform and Jean said, "Your father will want a full explanation of the diligence robbery and where you got the horses and guns. You'd better see if your mother could repair your uniform before tomorrow. She's upstairs. I guess she'll be happy to see you, your father will be too."

THREE

April 1ˢᵗ

MACDONALD TOWN HOUSE, AVENUE DE SAX, PARIS

C harles left his family's town house after an early breakfast and walked down the Rue de Sevres, turning east on the quai beside the Seine and on across the new bridge over the river to the narrow and congested Marias district of the right bank. He was wearing his grey wool manteau overcoat.

He finally reached the Hôtel Carnavalet, now housing the graduate school of bridges and roads, near the site of the old Bastille.

Beneath the wrong colored overcoat he was wearing his hastily repaired faded uniform of a second lieutenant in the military engineers with its black cuffs and collar, although it was still too tight. His mother had said, "It's too small and short, you need to buy a new one." His knee-high breeches gaped two inches above his old boots. It was worse if he had to sit down, since his stocking didn't span the gap.

Reporting to the office of the Directeur-Général, he knocked, entered and saluted. After a quarter-hour of small talk Gaspard De Prony said, "Based on your overall graduate studies, last year's apprenticeship with the mathematicians at the Bureau des Longitudes, and this year's studies of ballistics and theory at the advanced artillery school, I am pleased to award you a Master's Diploma in Engineering." He handed Charles a parchment diploma.

Charles glanced at his document and saw written on the bottom the words, *Summa cum laude* followed by *Très honorable avec félicitations du jury*.

De Prony said, "You are needed in the IG Corps much more than in the Corps of Bridges and Roads. Your family has a history as geographers and topographical engineers, and I think very highly of your father. Although you are graduating three months early, you are fully qualified. General-in-Chief Bonaparte and his new army require smart young officers. If you ever need anything, please call on me for help."

Just before noon, Charles arrived back on the left bank at the Invalides military hospital to visit Quentin. When he entered the ward, there were several officers, including two generals, surrounding his bed.

Seeing his tri-colored sash, Charles recognized the one talking to Surgeon Major Larrey as General-in-Chief Bonaparte. Bonaparte was a short, thin young man with a Roman nose, strong cheekbones and a chiseled jaw. His shoulder length lanky hair was styled like two dog's-ears. The second man was a major general, wearing a red and gold sash. The two generals were discussing the war and loot from Italy.

Charles approached and saluted. Dr. Larrey introduced him, "I want you to meet General-in-Chief Bonaparte and the director of the War Depot, General Jean Ernouf, who also commands the Ingé-nieurs-Geographes. General Bonaparte has come to congratulate both of you for your bravery and he wants to personally promote Lieutenant MacDonald."

Bonaparte shook Charles and Quentin's hands and remarked, "My friend, Major Larrey came to my house last night and told me all about your adventures during the diligence robbery. The ladies were enthralled listening to his description of your valor."

Charles had known General Bonaparte since he was a six-year-old American and the future general was a fifteen-year-old Corsican student at the Royal Military Academy in Paris.

Charles followed the older cadets everywhere, like a stray puppy. There's no way that he remembers me he thought, although young Bonaparte was one of my father's favorite students. He ate Sunday dinner with us more than a dozen times.

"I still have great respect for your father," Bonaparte said, completely astounding Charles. "He knows more about geographical engineering and pathfinding than any officer I have ever met. I also remember you from the École Militaire. I remember when you got lost and all of the cadets were called out to search for you."

Turning to the other officers Bonaparte said, "I found him marching behind the military band that was practicing on the Field of Mars. He wasn't lost, just busy."

"We called him the Américain Pathfinder since he acted like a wild Indian, spying on everything we did. General MacDonald, our new professor had explained about the Canadian pathfinders and mapmakers who had explored most of the North American continent with the help of the wild Indians."

Bonaparte smiled and said, "Charles was fluent in English and his nanny's Arabic, but when he spoke French, he had an American accent. He listened intently to everything we said, to improve his French."

Charles replied, "I still have a slight accent."

"There's nothing wrong with an accent. I still have an Italian one," Bonaparte responded. "What matters to me, lieutenant, is that in '84 and '85, I discovered that you had a real flair for mathematics."

"As a six year old, you already knew multiplication and were learning division. Since then, I have been getting reports of your progress in school. As a general-in-chief, I am responsible for your early graduation and commissioning. You are the only student with a perfect score on last fall's new Ingénieur-Geographe exam."

"I have reports that you are one of only half-a-dozen men in France who understands how to calculate longitude. The other five are old and fat. I am also aware that you are one of the better young swordsman and pistol shot in the army."

After the hospital he walked home. The townhouse was starting to look rundown, the once brilliant white paint was discolored from the extensive coal smoke that everyone was now using and two window panes were broken and patched, with another three cracked.

For Charles, the following four weeks were a whirlwind of activity. That first afternoon, he went for a twelve-mile run south of the city walls. From then on, he ran cross-country every morning, usually leaving around five o'clock. He wore old breeches, a loose shirt, knit socks and a pair of well-worn hobnailed infantry shoes. When it was cold, rainy or windy he wore his wool brown farm jacket.

He was resuming the exercise regimen that had been his daily routine since returning from Virginia, four years ago. On odd numbered days, he usually ran from ten to twenty miles and on even numbered days, he finished a shorter run of several miles and then exercised with his makeshift weight set in the coach-yard behind the town house.

On the second day, his father's dog Scout and his almost twelve-year old twin brothers, George and Benjamin, accompanied him on the shorter run. The boys as well as the dog needed water after running only two miles.

After they drank from a small, clear stream Charles explained to his brothers, "I'm counting French *toise*, the old Roman pace. Each time my left heel hits the ground; I add a count to measure how far we've gone. Father and I both use the old Legionnaire system of a *mille passus*, where 1,000 paces are a Roman mile, the same as an English mile."

"Why don't you count in meters?" George asked.

"Father, mother and I still think in miles, while most Frenchmen still use the old *Paris league*, twice as far. I do write distances in meters; however, right now the meter not yet an official measure. A few scientists are the only ones using the new unit. Most officers still use leagues and not kilometers. Maybe when De Borda's commission defines the final measurement, we'll all use it for work." He then showed them how he counted paces using colored beads on a leather thong.

Later that afternoon he set up a training regimen for both of his brothers that allowed them to run with him every other day. He went out to the naval armory and scrounged several smaller bar shot. There was a lighter set with three-pound balls on each end connected by a crossbar. He also got a heavier set with six-pound balls. These homemade dumbbells copied his expedient pairs of heavier bar shot that gave him training weights. He also had Jean build them a step so they could reach his pull-up bar or vault onto his wooden pommel horse.

During the late morning of his first week at home, Charles had visited Quentin in the hospital every day during the visiting hour. After the doctor released Quentin from the hospital, Charles borrowed his family's coach and helped him get to his family farm just south of the city.

On the fourth day of his leave, a determined investigator came to the house to ask him numerous questions about the turgotine robbery attempt.

Gendarme Lieutenant DuMayne asked to see the highwaymen's weapons and horses that Charles had brought home. Charles gave him the letter that the royalist officer had been carrying, but did not mention the gold in the bandit's pocket.

Everyone in Paris was talking about the attempt to rob three diligences. Most were talking about the one south of Senlis where the highwaymen had murdered seven escorts, not his attack or the one in Flanders the next day where the robbers weren't successful.

Charles was busy every day and time seemed to disappear. Starting on his second afternoon at home, he visited first one and then they sent to a number of shops to start to purchase new uniforms and equipment. His first visit was to a military tailor for the standard staff officer blue wool dress uniform and a plainer working uniform with a *surtout* jacket. He asked, but the tailor couldn't rework the old uniform just like his mother told him.

As an IG officer the collar, cuffs, and piping were now aurore colored velvet rather than the black of a génie. Aurore was a shade of orange meant to represent the rising sun. The tailor and his assistant measured him on his first visit and a week later for a second fitting. He got a final fitting and the uniforms during his third visit.

They furnished the blue wool uniforms but not the white linen items. Charles had to go to a seamstress shop for the white linen summer breeches, waistcoat, a loose shirt and two pairs of under-drawers.

He went to a cordwainer for his one new pair of riding boots, black with a tan top. The boot maker resoled and renovated his old boots. He also renewed his comfortable infantry hobnailed shoes, installing new laces and waterproofing the boot and shoe leather with a homemade mixture of beeswax and lampblack polish.

At the knitter's societe he got his wool and cotton stockings, and they sent him to a glove guild shop for a new pair of tight-fitting officers white kid gloves and heavier gauntleted field gloves.

He stopped at the hatter at least twice and purchased two different beaver felt hats, a fine folding dress hat stored in a triangular tin and a heavier field bicorne, both with aurore plumes.

He had to purchase accoutrements and other equipment at several different shops. For dress wear and parades, he had to buy a gold embroidered wide bandolier strap with a hussar cartouche box on the back with a matching centurion waistbelt with sabre straps. He also needed a plain black leather field set. He purchased a rectangular portmanteau, additional straps, and two portfolio-messenger bags. Everything was custom built by Maison Morel, leather malletier and bag makers.

The malitier sent him to a silversmith who furnished his Ingénieur-Geographe symbols to mount on the steel gorget, brass chest plate, and belt buckle and to rivet to the flaps of his bags.

For his last birthday, his father had written that he was giving Charles his two LePage over-and-under presentation pistols. During his leave, Citizen LaBoessiere his *maîtres d'armes* aided him in purchasing two plain belt holsters, a smaller hussar cartouche box and a larger 36-cartouche infantry giberne for both the pistols and the carabine. He then practiced with firing and reloading his firearms several hundred times.

He was running short of money and couldn't afford silk dress breeches, stockings and a waistcoat, or even buckled shoes, and horse tack. Everything was expensive and he needed to set aside 250 francs for the cost of the turgotine trip to Toulon.

Every few days his mother insisted he go out to evening entertainment. It seemed like she conspired with all the other mothers in
Paris who had daughters. In addition to her arranged, official escort
duties, he went to a ballet, two concerts, and an opera by himself.

He loved music and dearly wished he could play his violin better.
On these occasions, he saw a number of beautiful young ladies, but
he could only admire their loveliness from a distance. He was alone
and didn't know any young men that could properly introduce him.
He was too shy to introduce himself, besides it was against all social
rules.

His sister Barbara came home from Madame Campan's school at
St-Germain-en-Laye every ninth day for the weekend. For the first
two weekends, she brought her best friends. Barbara was disappoint-
ed when she couldn't get Charles to hold a civilized discussion with
either of them.

He had no trouble talking about war, or politics with the men.
He just became tongue-tied when he tried to speak with young ladies.
Apart from his mother and sister, Charles had spent little of his life
in the company of women.

The almost monastic existence that was a part of his years of
training and education in the military arts and sciences meant that he
was constantly in the company of men. Though the sight of beautiful
women filled him with ardent desire, he was, unlike most of his
fellow soldiers, still a virgin. A natural fastidiousness had kept him
from going whoring with his companions. Although he was skilled in
the art of war, he was a stranger to the more gentle war between the
sexes.

FOUR

Mid-April

FURLOUGH IN PARIS

Charles MacDonald didn't think of his father as being rich since his retirement on a modest pension. The family lived discreetly after the Austrians had blinded him in combat, although the National Convention voted unanimously to award him a farm and give him a modest disability pension for his retirement. The town house was paid for, they grew their own food and he earned a few francs every month as a consultant.

Charles needed every *sou* of the stipend that the Directory furnished engineering students and now the salary he received as a lieutenant. Therefore, he had no choice but to supplement his limited income.

Three times in the past three *décadi*, he had visited gentlemen's sporting clubs and fought in competition for cash prizes. These clandestine bouts allowed heavy betting among the gambling crowd on contests of *Savate de Rue,* street fighting among various fighters of the lower class who had nothing to lose.

He had fought in these matches several dozen times before he left Paris last year. At first, he lost many of his bouts. As he learned more, he started winning. However, just before he left in the summer of '97 an opponent broke his nose. It turned into a bloody mess, although he finally won the contest.

Because of the *Révolution Française*, his father and his educated, but unemployed, friends had tutored Charles at home until the start of the mass executions. It was too dangerous to attend a traditional religious school. During *la Terreur* Charles, his sister and a tutor fled to Virginia.

In the fall of '94 after he returned from eighteen months in America, Charles was impatient to join the army and go to war, although he was just sixteen. Even though he had an American college diploma in natural philosophy, his father wanted him to get a French *licence & maîtrise* in engineering.

Schools in America granted diplomas' based on informal testing and they were not as meticulous as the engineering schools in France. His father also thought he should learn more about duty, honor, fighting, and life.

However, the deciding factor was information from Nicolas Boëssière, the master at the *Salle d'Armes* of *Boëssière & fils*. He and his sons, Antoine and Joseph, had added savate and street fighting techniques to their athletic syllabus, joining sword fighting, haute école dressage, Greco-Roman wrestling, and shooting along with military cavalry movements.

During his two years at the new Polytechnique and his subsequent two years at graduate school, he had gone to Boëssière almost every afternoon to train in fighting.

He would change his clothes and run from either of the engineering schools to the indoor salle d' armes at No. 152 Rue Saint-Honore, just down the street from the Palais Royale.

Every other day he continued on several blocks west to No. 350 Rue Saint-Honore, opposite the Tuileries, where they hosted their outdoor French riding school and longer range shooting. In addition to mastering both epée and sabre, he had become very good at kickboxing, fist boxing, wrestling, and stick fighting. At home Jean helped teach him to fight with *no-holds-barred*, he always tried to win using any method; no restrictions, rules or conventions.

Over three weeks ago, he had fought in his first new bout. Most of the gamblers didn't remember him since he had been away for almost a year, and he was even bigger. His opponent was an older beef carcass porter and occasional butcher at the *Abattoir des Innocents*, the putrid meat market. He got lucky with his first move, a low hammer-kick that broke the shin of his adversary. Contestants wore old infantry shoes, socks, belted-breeches, and nothing else. He won almost two months pay, 200 francs. Six days later he fought a younger opponent who he beat with ease.

Last week he had faced a much more difficult competitor in front of a hundred sportsmen. He was fighting for a prize of 500 francs against one of the best fighters in Paris. He would earn an extra four month's pay if he won.

He moved around the pit stretching and exercising his arms and legs. Looking at his opponent, he saw a muscular, stocky thirty-year old former mariner from Toulon, named Marcel—known as *Le Matelot*, The Sailor. He was dark and hairy, and he had a number of scars on his face and arms.

Looking down at himself, Charles realized that he was half-a-foot taller than his opponent was. His reach with his arms and legs was even longer. His chest and arms were almost as muscular, but he was wiry and leaner. He was also a few pounds lighter. His only scar was his bent nose with its bump.

As the bout started, the sailor remained stationary while Charles began a slow circle to his left. Both men held their hands high. He decided he would try a fencing move. Jumping forward in a false attack, he stamped his feet on landing.

The shorter man reacted to the bogus attack and exploded with a *chassé italien*, a kick to his inner thigh. Charles avoided the kick by retreating backward a step and turning. He then rapidly advanced with a left-hand jab, making contact with Marcel's out-of-balance jaw. He immediately followed with a right-hand uppercut to his chin. The two solid hits rocked his opponent.

Charles quickly kicked with his left-foot in a hammer-like movement to Sailor's exposed thigh. He followed up with a roundhouse high whip-kick to his kidney with his right leg.

Stepping in close, he delivered a series of blows with his closed fist, targeting his adversary's stomach and head. He stepped back, as his opponent appeared to sag.

Instead of pausing, he dropped into a low sweeping kick to the ankles, dropping him to the floor. Jumping up Charles launched a series of kicks to his opponent's head and upper chest. The referee stopped the fight in less than two minutes.

Marcel was unconscious and Charles had won the prize money. His breeches and infantry shoes had drops of blood all over them. He wasn't bleeding. The only kick from the sailor had missed. After the match, he had to sneak into the house and up to his room. He was sure that his family would not approve of his extracurricular activities.

His last morning at home began with a final inspection of the equipment and clothes he planned to carry on his first military assignment. He would work on his weapons last. His sister Barbara had tearfully said her goodbyes' and gone back to school five days earlier. Under the new republican calendar with its ten-day weeks, she only got to come home once every décadi.

His mother came up to his room and helped him pack his bags, rolling his clothing tightly so it would not wrinkle and packing extra food in drawstring bags to keep the metal containers from rattling.

She gave him advice, in the English they used at home. She also scolded him for not carrying enough extra clothing. "There's no spare room in my bags," he explained. "I plan to wash my under-clothes every evening while I wear my extra set the next day." He agreed to take an extra shirt.

Later just after noon on his last day in Paris, Charles made himself sit at the large oak worktable in his garret room and finish letters to his friends. He realized that all his classmates were away from Paris except Quentin Fermont.

The public now called *L'École Polytechnique*, "*X*"—an appropriate way of using the math symbol to refer to an institution devoted to the technical aspects scientific learning. Whenever anyone listed military officers, even the newspapers inserted —*X* after their name if they were graduates of Polytechnique. Most of his colleagues from school were now in the army. After finishing the letters, he still needed to clean and oil his weapons.

The MacDonald family town house was in the southwestern suburbs near the old military school campus. It was well south of the aristocratic *Faubourg Saint-Germain*, but still within the city wall.

James MacDonald began building the town house in '84 at the start of his new assignment as the engineering, topography and geography professor at the Royal Military Academy.

After more than thirty years of active military and intelligence service, he had accumulated a little wealth, although he was a techni-cian rather than an aristocrat. He planned to teach for the next ten years before retiring and writing textbooks. Even though he was a colonel in the French Corps of Topographical Engineers, he was also a brigadier general in the American Army, promoted during the American Revolution.

The École Militaire closed at the end of '87 to save money and he was unemployed until late '91, when the French National Assembly promoted him to general for his support of the new French revolutionary armies.

The house was set back on the south side of the Avenue de Saxe by an iron spear-fenced courtyard with semi-circular stairs rising to the main entrance on the first floor. The walled property had a lawn and kitchen garden at the back and a coach house on the back alley. There was a side drive to bring the carriage from the stable block to the front courtyard. A rough stone wall enclosed the sides and back.

It was a typical bourgeoisie 48-foot square, four-story building. There were two-front and two-back rooms on either side of an 8-foot center hall and stairway. A service entrance was under the monumental stairs that led to the semi-basement ground storage rooms, workrooms and a kitchen. The first elevated floor, the *premiere étage,* had a reception room and a formal dining facing the street. At the back were a family dining room, and a library-office overlooking the garden. His parents, his sister Barbara and twin brothers had bedrooms on the next elevated floor.

In '86 toward the end of construction, his father had added a projecting back stairwell with a scullery sink and English water closets on the upper floors, and a bathtub off the attached tower down the hall from the bedrooms. The circular steps ran from the kitchen scullery to the attic.

The roof had a zinc storage tank that the private Paris Water Company filled by subscription. Water flowed through iron pipes from a 110-foot tower near the Quai d'Orsay, just a few hundred yards from L'Palais-Bourbon.

Charles remembered when the students at X studied *Louise*, the steam engine pump from Birmingham that lifted Seine water to the top of the tall storage tower. When the residents of the Ecole Militaire neighborhood subscribed to the water service, so did his father. He also purchased shares of the La Compagnie des Eaux de Paris.

Charles had persuaded his father to combine the two attic rooms facing the wide boulevard into one 48-foot long fencing salle with his sleeping and study spaces tucked into the dormers. Servants and his father's old sergeant major Jean Dulcos occupied the other garret rooms.

Over the past three weeks, his father helped him secure the paraphernalia he needed in the field. They had to refinish or repair many of the items that dated from over the past four decades. Charles also had to buy a few accessories to replace damaged or missing items from the weapons and campaign equipment his father was lending him. He was aware that his father and Jean both knew more about soldiering than he ever hoped to learn.

He started cleaning, oiling, and inspecting the various weapons and equipment he was taking to his first posting. Almost four weeks ago, he had cleaned his father's short-barreled carabine and blunderbuss pistol in the downstairs workroom using boiling water from the kitchen. Father made him clean and oil his equipment and scrub himself before he could come upstairs. To combat rust he was carrying a tin of rock oil and another of olive oil for cooking.

After reloading with a ball and buckshot, Jean took the pistol and put it in father's bedside table drawer. At school, they taught him not to load a gun until just before use but father insisted on keeping a loaded pistol in his drawer.

He re-checked the cleanliness of the carabine, and then checked the pair of double-barreled military pistols he was taking to war. He had decided to reload the carabine and pistols tomorrow, just before he left.

Sewn into the right shaft his new riding boots was a scabbard for his father's five-inch blade *skean-achlais*. The Scots dagger was almost ten-inches long and double-edged rather than single like a shorter *skean-dhu* eating utensil. The boot maker made the leather shaft of his right boot larger to allow for the knife sheath. It had a Damascus blade, a small bolster, no quillion and a *skull-crusher* pommel. The blade was dark from blood reacting with the iron over the past century and the bog oak haft was black with age. He also had a sleeve scabbard for it.

General MacDonald had carried his father's knife since escaping from Scotland in '46. He was one of the exiled Jacobite Scots who served as technical officers in the French army.

A graduate engineer, he had spent 40 years in the French Ingé-nieurs-Geographes. Although an explorer, pathfinder, and geographer, he had also been an intelligence agent for the French king's *Secret du Roi*.

During the American Revolution, he was one of several secret agents who went to America with the Marquis de Lafayette. There he met and married Elizabeth Hancock from Charlottesville.

Charles had grown-up in America moving to France when he was six. During the *Paris Terror* he and his sister went back to Virginia where he spent a year-and-a-half in college. Charles returned to France to help his father, blinded during the French Revolution cannonade of Valmy.

One of his new gusseted portfolio bags had two loops to hold the captured Mohawk tomahawk his father had brought back from

America. He sharpened and oiled the knife, hatchet, his own dueling épée and father's unique sabre.

There was a knock at the doorframe and he turned and saw it was his father. He guided him to a chair next to the worktable. Charles spoke to him in English, saying, "As you asked, I mentally reviewed my actions during the mail coach robbery and I think I made several major errors." Charles started explaining with his slightly American accent.

"First, I fired at the highwayman from the back of an untrained horse. Second, I fired the dragon pistol at the leader's center of mass instead of his head or shooting his horse. Third, I really wasn't in control when my horse collided with his, so I exposed myself to the fire of five riders. I was saved by his shout calling off the other highwaymen."

General MacDonald patted his knee and said with a slight Scots accent, "You're right, you should not have fired from the back of a rental horse that you hadn't trained to stand still at the sound. You're lucky you hit anything. Shooting your dragon pistol at the chest of the first rider was not wrong. There was no way for you to know he was wearing a steel cuirass. Steering your horse into a collision also wasn't a mistake. You should always immediately attack the most dangerous person without waiting or warning, don't follow the *Code Duello*."

"And bear this in mind, dueling is stupid," he added. "There is no need to prove your manhood or your courage. You are never to challenge anyone to a duel." He paused thoughtfully and then continued, "I've always refused to kill fellow officers in a duel."

Father is right Charles thought I've killed men in combat. I don't have to prove my valor. Thinking that he was leaving home and no longer have his father's tutelage he suddenly said, "Father, you're the smartest man I know. I hope I'll be half as good a soldier."

General MacDonald nodded and asked Charles to hand him his weapons one at a time. Starting with the carabine, he felt their weight and balance and then cocked each and released the trigger, catching the cock before it struck the frizzen. He felt the sabre and slightly drew it from the scabbard. "Even though the sabre is made from a Japanese war blade, I had a artisan make a removable basket hilt that resembles a Scottish claymore. Its incredibly sharp blade is sheathed in the original magnolia wood scabbard, overlaid with enameled steel alternating the polished black lacquer with an engraved dark bronze throat, then two matching bronze lockets with rings and finally a matching drag."

After pausing while he felt the sword, he then said. "After the war in Canada, I took your grandfathers broadsword claymore and pistols back to Scotland and gave them to your cousin Richard, Chief of the MacDonalds of Keppoch. Did you have the accessory strap made for carrying your sabre over-the-shoulder?" his father asked. When Charles said he had done so, his father slowly exhaled and said, "I am giving you all of my weapons, campaign accessories and engineering equipment. I have similar paraphernalia on order for the twins next birthday."

Charles stood up and hugged him while thanking him for his generosity. He then escorted his father downstairs for an early dinner.

FIVE

April 24ᵗʰ

IMPORTANT VISITORS AT THE MACDONALD TOWN HOUSE

At six o'clock, Charles heard a carriage and escort arriving in the cobblestoned courtyard and then a visitor at the front door asking Jean Dulcos to see General MacDonald. Minutes later, as Charles was dressing in his field surtout, another guest arrived on horseback with an escort. Shortly after that, his father sent Jean up to his room to ask him to come down and meet his guests. Entering the first floor reception room, he re-closed the double pocket doors behind him.

The first visitor was a large, distinguished-looking gentleman, with curly dark hair. The second was General Bonaparte.

Speaking in French his father said, "Charles I would like you to meet Paul Barras, twice the Président and one of the original members of the Executive Directory of the Republic."

Charles advanced and shook Barras' hand. Then General Mac-Donald added, "Of course you have met General Bonaparte."

Since he was wearing his uniform, Charles saluted.

"My visitors asked for you to be present," his father explained. "They were impressed by your recent actions defending the turgotine. Why don't we all sit and continue our discussion?"

Charles took his father's arm and helped him to a neo-classical armchair, one of the upholstered pieces facing the carved stone fireplace. He then added some coal to the cast iron insert and stoked up the fire.

He sat next to his father while Bonaparte sat opposite and Barras sat on a sofa. Barras turned and said to his father, "We came to ask your opinion about something that General Bonaparte and I have been arguing for the past week. James, you and I both served in India, twice. You in the first Anglo-Mysore war, while both of us were in the second." He paused to catch his breath.

"We also want to discuss your two expeditions to Egypt, particularly since you are one of the few men to cross from India back through Egypt. Tippu, the Sultan of Mysore has asked for our support against the British. I think that we should send a naval expedition around the cape with additional support for the Sultan. Your former student General Bonaparte thinks differently. Tonight, we came here to find out if you have any additional information or private diaries about these journeys."

Bonaparte broke in and said, "I need to know about conditions in Egypt during the summer, military fortifications around Alexandria and Cairo, tactics used by the Mamluk military, and animals used for transportation across the desert."

"You can see that Bonaparte wants to conquer Egypt on his way to India," Barras added. "To do that, he'll also need information about trails across the Sinai isthmus and onward travel to southern India." There was a pause in the conversation.

"On my first expedition to Egypt," General MacDonald responded, "I was a young Scots-born, French engineering student who assisted in the surveying. I did keep personal journals during my two-year apprenticeship in Egypt. I have additional journals from my years in India in the sixties, again in '82 and my later journey back through Egypt in early '84."

There was a knock at the door and Jean entered carrying a large silver tray with a coffee set, a pitcher of warm au lait and a china plate of cookies. "Jean was with me when I crossed the desert in 1784, he should stay and answerer some of your questions."

Charles' mother entered carrying a smaller silver tray with a de-canter of Cognac and a set of small Venetian glass goblets. As Elizabeth MacDonald served brandy to her husband's guests, General MacDonald introduced her to Paul Barras and reintroduced her to General Bonaparte. The young general was eating one of the macaroon cookie. He turned to Elizabeth and said, "My mother made the same almond macaroons back in Corsica. In fact she also used buttercream filing for special occasions, it tasted the same." His mother did not pour Charles a Cognac. Elizabeth MacDonald then left, leaving Jean beside the closed door. Charles stood and poured himself a large glass full of brandy.

Setting down his cup of sugared coffee, Bonaparte stood and cautioned them, "This is highly secret information. The five-man Directory has encouraged me to develop a plan to invade Egypt, and later send support to Mysore in India. We are leaving next month with almost 54,000 soldiers, about 150 savants, scholars, naturalist and other scientists. We will sail on more than 400 ships from five ports in the south. It's the largest invasion in history. Fewer than forty people know of our plans."

Looking directly at Paul Barras, he continued, "The Executive Directory has approved the operation as long as I take care of the extra funding. They insist that I go with the expedition to Egypt. My plan is to send at least two divisions on to India from there. Director Barras has doubts that we can defeat the Mamluks and still furnish troops to help India."

Barras calmly answered, "I feel that this adventure is ill-advised although the other directors approve. It will take too many resources that we need here in France. It would be cheaper to just send a few demi-brigades to India around the cape."

"Egypt is a tempting prize for us because it's just across the Mediterranean." Stomping the wood floor for emphasis, Bonaparte said, "The British naval blockade in the Atlantic has destroyed trade with our colonies in the Caribbean. They can easily defeat any fleet we send out into the Atlantic. Our soldiers will never make it past the British occupied Cape of Good Hope."

"By invading Egypt, we can replace the lost commerce and cut a major Anglo-Indian trade route, it's their only alternate to the long trip around the southern tip of Africa." He moved back and forth gesturing wildly with both arms. "The English will have a hard time maintaining a blockade of the eastern Mediterranean from their only naval base at Gibraltar."

He calmed down and sipped from his glass of brandy, "Egypt is rich. The Nile valley produces enough food for all of France. River trade on the Nile is our major source of coffee, spices, ivory, gold, and other commodities from central Africa. French and Italian ships carry most of the cargo to and from Europe. Their only competition is the Levant Company, in English ships." He sat down, swallowed the rest of his brandy, and poured himself a second cup of coffee.

Charles was overwhelmed by what he had just heard. Since childhood, he had been dreaming about following in the footsteps of Alexander the Great through Egypt, across the Middle East and into India. When General Bonaparte drained his goblet, he also took a deep drink of brandy and almost coughed it out.

General MacDonald assured Bonaparte, "I can give my journals to Charles. He can study them while traveling to Toulon and on across the Mediterranean. He can read the other journals about India and the Orient as he gets the time. He should be thoroughly familiar with my observations when you arrive in Egypt."

As he drained his glass and held it out to Charles, asking for a refill, Barras said, "The Directory has no extra money for this expedition. General Bonaparte has been extracting funds from the bankers in Rome, the Swiss cantons, the Rhineland, and the Hapsburg Netherlands to finance this risky venture. He has already spent the money he secured in Italy on some of the costs such as renting ships and buying supplies."

Barras took another sip and continued, "There have been other incidents since Charles drove off the highwaymen. Barras turned to Charles and said, "It's a secret but your coach was carrying a gold shipment from the Rothschild and Warburg banks in Frankfurt am Main, in Hessia. You have undoubtedly heard that bandits robbed another mail coach the same day. You may not have heard that it was carrying the annual indemnity payment from the new Batavian Republic; they got over three million francs worth of gold and killed all of the men on board. The next day there was an attempt by brigands to rob the mail coach carrying a similar shipment of gold from bankers in Brussels. Luckily, a troop of cavalry that was following the diligence surprised the highwaymen just as they were stopping the mail coach. The robbers were probably former soldiers. Our countryside is infested with deserters stealing everything." Barras paused to catch his breath.

"An informer told us that a British agent planned all the robberies," Bonaparte jumped up almost shouting. "We also found proof that an émigré cavalry unit was responsible. There are English agents everywhere. I still need to ship all the gold we have collected here in Paris on to Toulon. In addition, there are other gold shipments going straight to the Mediterranean ports."

"Last week highwaymen robbed half-a-million francs from a diligence in Baden, near the French border," sitting down, he picked up his coffee cup. "Two days ago, someone shot at me with a rifle as I was riding in the Bois. The British Secret Service has wormed its way into activities here in Paris, but I just can't prove it. There have been several other attempts to assassinate me over the past month. Twice more, someone has shot at me as I was riding, and a woman tried to poison me. Suspicious looking men regularly follow me."

As he put his cup down, Bonaparte said to Charles's father, "I know you have extensive experience crossing swords with the British Secret Service. I suspect they have discovered our plans and will try to disrupt any attempt by France to compete with the British East India Company. They are ignoring the rumors of our mounting an invasion of England or Ireland."

Bonaparte smiled ruefully, "I wonder if the French rumors of our invasion of England are competing with the British rumors of our invasion of America. The United States signed the Jay Treaty with England that has led to a naval quasi-war with France."

"The main cause was Alexander Hamilton's refusal to pay their Revolutionary War debts to France; mainly motivated by the execution of King Louis XVI. The secondary reason was the British Secret Service rumors coming from their agent in Prussia that we plan to invade the United States through Louisiana and Florida. In any case, we must discover how the English are getting their information. I cannot afford to lose any more gold on its way to Toulon."

He then touched the arm of Charles' blind father, "General MacDonald, do you have any ideas of how to ferret out these spies? Will you help me?"

MacDonald replied thoughtfully, "With over 150 civilians and 400 ships involved, some of your associates must suspect your destination. They have probably bragged to their friends about their suspicions. You said there are fewer than forty who know the target of the expedition. Most of them have probably told their colleagues or their wives where they are going." Bonaparte grimaced and looked a bit embarrassed. Everyone knew that his wife, Josephine, couldn't keep a secret.

"You must proceed as if the English have knowledge of your plans," General MacDonald insisted. "You need to appoint an experienced investigator here in Paris to question everyone under suspicion of aiding the British, someone who will act ruthlessly and unsparingly."

"There was a gendarme officer assigned to investigate the robberies," Bonaparte responded. "I heard that he has arrested three royalist-émigrés. However, I haven't been able to find him to ask about his discoveries. He has disappeared. I wanted him to investigate the new robbery in Baden."

"A gendarme, Lieutenant DuMayne questioned me here at the *maison*," Charles said. "He seemed very competent. You're probably referring to him."

His father turned his head directly toward Bonaparte and said firmly, "You must make every effort to protect the movement of money, equipment and personnel to the southern ports. You should make every attempt to disguise the movement of your fleet. If you can make a feint with the fleet and temporarily stop in someplace like Sicily, Malta, or Crete, you should carry out a tactical diversion."

"What wrong with Malta," said Jean, breaking his silence.

"In fact, Malta would be perfect," agreed the old general. "It is small. The Knights of St. John do not have a large military force. They do have a large treasury, and they have a considerable number of Muslim slaves. You could free the slaves and carry them to Egypt. Releasing those galley slaves would impress the Muslim Arabs."

"They must be convinced that you have no intention of conquering the Islamic people or attacking their religion. Malta would also make a perfect southern base for the French fleet. Without Malta the only option for the British would be to establish stronger relationships with the Barbary pirates so their ships could land and re-water in Algiers, Tunis or Tripoli."   General MacDonald showed no hesitation about talking so frankly to a much younger general, who had become the most promising, and the prickliest, senior military officer in the forces of France.

Bonaparte made no response but turned and asked Charles, "Do you still speak Arabic?"

"Oui, mon générale. Our horse trainer and I have been speaking Arabic to each other for the past fourteen years. I first learned it from my nanny in Virginia, a slave from the Sudan in upper Egypt."

Bonaparte nodded and said, "Based on what I have heard about your fighting ability, I will assign you to my Corps of Guides as their geographical engineer. You will always be near at hand to discuss topographical information. If I send you out in advance of the army as a pathfinder, a scouting party of the guide's *éclaireurs* can accompany you."   He paused and then asked, "When are you leaving for Toulon? I was told you were going tomorrow."

"I leave by mail coach tomorrow morning. It is scheduled to leave shortly after two o'clock."

Bonaparte glanced at Barras; "We are shipping 600,000 francs worth of gold by coach tomorrow. We are hoping to keep the shipment secret by letting regular passengers travel on the coach. It has no special guard or escort. Fewer than five people know about this shipment. However, one of my old sergeant majors is the conductor and knows about the gold. I have faith in the mail guard on top, also a former soldier. You could be a third unexpected defender. There is nobody here in Paris I can trust to send with my old sergeant major. I want someone who is untouched by the corruption here. I want someone who is the son of a man in whom I have confidence." Napoleon went on to explain that he wanted his men to fight and overcome any resistance.

"I will give you a pass for your travel on the mail coach to Toulon and I will write a letter of appointment outlining your authority and responsibilities as the officer in charge of the cargo."

Charles opened the pocket doors and stepped out to get some writing material from the library next door. Returning he placed a military style mahogany writing box on the card table between the front windows. Bonaparte opened it and used the scissors from an upper pockets to divide the heavy watermarked paper into two half sheets. He then began to write the pass and letter with a quill pen dipped into the quartz inkwell in the top compartment, signing each document with his last name in the Italian style with a flourish sweeping underneath. General Bonaparte then handed both documents to Paul Barras for his countersignature.

"I'll keep my ears and eyes open for any suspicious activities," Charles promised. He also realized he could use a free ride. The cost of the coach to Toulon was more than a month's pay. After spending everything he had accumulated on uniforms and equipment, he had just over 250 francs left, the cost of a coach ride plus food.

After escorting the guests and his father to the hallway and saying goodbye. He walked his father upstairs to his room. He then went back and ate all of the remaining cookies. To wash them down he poured and drank another glass of brandy.

SIX

April 25th

LEAVING HOME, AVENUE DE SAXE

After tossing and turning then finally dozing off, Charles was jolted awake from his restless sleep by a noise from downstairs. He had a dry mouth and a sore head.

Picking up his Bréguet chronometer from the side table and holding it by the safety chain, he opened the gold cover and turned its face to the light coming through the dormer window from the streetlamp on their front gatepost, it was mandated by the commune. He saw it was half past midnight on the dial.

He had slept for fewer than four hours. He shivered and realized it was April 25th and he would be leaving on the first part of his long odyssey to Egypt in two hours.

He opened the window finding it was cool, misty and quiet outside. The pungent odors of Paris floated into his room where he could smell sewer gas and animal manure overlaid by the river. While he was gazing out the window, his mother knocked on the door and whispered, "Charles, it's time."

Charles had to dress and collect his things for the ride to the turgotine terminus. He closed the window, pulled off his nightshirt and washed his face in cold water poured from a ewer into a basin and then put on his new field uniform.

Since it was still April, he wore the blue wool-breeches and long-sleeved matching waistcoat rather than the sleeveless bleached linen summer uniform set his mother had rolled up in his kit bag. He pulled on his comfortable old boots, inserting his father's knife in its scabbard built into the shaft. Then he wrapped a black kerchief stock around his neck.

He clasped the buckle plate of his black leather waist belt over his waistcoat. As a sign that he was an officer, his sabre had a woven leather lanyard with a sword knot made from the leather and gold bullion.

Since he wasn't the duty officer, he kept his steel gorget packed. The field outfit included a matching longer-waisted blue surtout, with tails but no lapels. The front fastened with a single row of nine gilt buttons that went all the way up to the high orange collar.

It, the cuffs, lining and edge piping were the same aurore colored linen rather than velvet cloth. His black field bicorne had a short aurore colored plume and a tricolor cockade.

He had already packed his dress uniform, including the double-breasted tailcoat habit with velvet turn-backs and lining, folding chapeau, white linen waistcoat and breeches. He had strapped the case with his dress epée to the outside of his kit bag, the leather portmanteau.

Next to it he strapped the rolled gray manteau-capote. He first got his caped greatcoat as a cadet at X. Originally felted wool; it was now as comfortable as a blanket. It's black kersey lining was still in good shape; his only change had been to replace the student horn buttons with new gilt ones.

Picking up his baggage, weapons and the equipment for his new assignment Charles quietly went down three flights of stairs so he wouldn't wake his brothers.

Waiting in the ground floor corridor were his father and Scout. Standing beside them was Jean Dulcos. His mother was in the kitchen fixing something to eat. His father said, "Jean says that your guns aren't loaded, why not?"

"For safety we were taught to not load our firearms until we were in the field."

His father quietly said, "Bollocks. Always keep your weapons loaded, check your priming regularly, and make sure that cold steel is within reach. Never give up your skean-achlais. You should even wear it in church, or if you're bedding a woman. At all times have a plan to use them."

Jean said, "Give me your rifle and pistols. I'll load 'em."

Charles unclasped his waist belt and sabre, "My guns and holsters are with my messenger bags," he told Jean. "After you load the pistols, can you attach the holsters to my waist belt?"

"Based on my experience with the British Secret Service," General MacDonald told Charles as they stood in the hallway, "They are thorough and unrelenting. They will do anything necessary to crush any attempt to interrupt their trade with India. I have fought against them over the last forty years and they have never failed to plan the destruction of their enemies. They will kill anyone who gets in their way."

Charles's mother called everyone into the kitchen for a pot of coffee and slices of brioche she had toasted with cheese. To his surprise, his brothers George and Benjamin were sitting at the table. The upstairs hall clock struck a single chime for one o'clock as he helped his blind father to his kitchen chair.

"If Bonaparte suspects the British know of his plans to invade Egypt, you can be sure that they know all about them," General MacDonald warned. "The British have espionage organizations throughout France. They have spy rings in most of the major port cities and along the strategic roads. They have Paris covered with operatives and they have agents in most major cities. In addition, they have bribed important local people all over France to get information and help. Of course they also have the support of many of the former aristocrats who have stayed in France hiding under false identities."

Elizabeth filled everyone's cup. She poured black coffee for James and Charles, and hot cocoa for herself and the twins. Charles emulated his father and drank his coffee without sugar or milk. Jean brought Charles' rifle and pistols and set them down in the flagstone hallway running down the center of the ground floor. He poked his head into the kitchen and said, "I'll hitch two horses to the carriage to save us time." Charles collected his weapons and carried them to the ground floor entrance. He heard the first farmer's cart arriving outside on the Avenue de Saxe for the weekly market.

Walking back to the kitchen he grabbed another slice of toasted bread and cheese and gave half to the dog Scout. He then began to say farewell to his family. He felt a sudden pang of sadness. How much he would miss them all.

Charles hugged his father and his mother. George shook his hand while Benjamin grabbed him and gave him a hug as he held back a tear. His mother held him out with both hands and said, "You are so handsome. Everyone will be impressed."

"You mean the harem girls," he said with a smile. His mother gave him a bag of food for the trip. He peeked into it and saw a small ham, liver pate, cheese and a roast chicken. There were biscuits, fruit preserves from their farm, and a brioche inside. Next to the bag, his mother had filled his Spanish goatskin with red wine.

As he turned to leave, his mother rushed into the hall and said, "Don't forget to wear your greatcoat, it can get cold in April."

"I'm too excited to be cold. I would burn up wearing it."

Benjamin gave him another big hug and began to sniffle as George formally wished him good luck. Jean was waiting outside with the MacDonald town calash. He had hitched two horses to the light carriage with the hood folded open. The family had a larger four-wheel road coach for long trips.

Charles handed Jean his travel bag, messenger bags and other equipment to place on the driver's seat. He buckled his centurion with its two sabre straps hanging down, and now carrying both pistols over his waistcoat just below his surtout. Slinging the bandolier over his left shoulder, he snapped the leather scabbard boot into place and put his carabine on the seat. He then turned and gave hugs to both his mother and father and kissed their cheeks. The twins, who had remained under the service arch, waved goodbye.

Jean traveled east on the Avenue de Saxe and then turned on Rue de Sevres, trotting northeast toward the Seine. The carriage was moving through streets with Saint-Germain-des-Prés on the left and the beginning of the Latin Quarter on the right.

They rode past great empty churches, high-walled monasteries and convents either abandoned or repurposed, and aristocratic palaces, now either boarded-up or occupied by rich contractors.

As they neared the left bank of the river, they passed side streets with narrow crowded tenement buildings and enormous potholes full of water. Most of the streets were missing half their limestone pavers, which the rabble pried up to form barricades. Any riffraff with a hammer could fragment the stones into shards to throw at soldiers.

He could hear and smell the essence of Paris. Occasionally they passed the stench rising from a clogged sewer. Scores of tenement residents threw their garbage out the window to rot in the street.

The occasional public building still had luminaries burning; but the private gatepost lamps usually ran out of oil or wax just after midnight. The few feeble lights and the half-visible moon helped Jean navigate through the darkness.

After half-an-hour of travel, they crossed a bridge over the Seine, the Pont National. At the far end of the bridge, a military sentry stopped them and the duty corporal asked for his papers. He showed him his authorization from General Bonaparte. The corporal read the note and signature, saluted him and said, "Pass."

They drove past the enormous Palais des Tuileries on the right with the Louvre Palace further on behind it. Continuing north, they passed the arcade and shops lining the Palais Royal.

The carriage turned east just beyond the enormous pleasure palace and zigzagged down several narrow streets. At three-quarters past one o'clock they finally arrived at the Messageries Nationales Terminus of Paris just off the Rue Notre Dame des Victoires.

Mail coaches arrive in Paris from all over the Republic every afternoon and early evening. Workers cleaned and repaired them, then sent them back out on their return journeys between two and four o'clock every morning. The company timed the early departures to avoid the congested morning traffic in the narrow streets of Paris.

Charles entered the passage onto the courtyard of the 150-foot long two-storied National Courier Company building. There were four large and two smaller mail coaches in the plaza and the hostlers were hitching up four and six horse teams to each coach.

The large turgotines were wooden-framed with lower mahogany panels painted forest green and hard leather upper black panels with a crimson stripe between. There were two large rear wheels and two smaller front wheels that turned with the singletree and horse team. The window openings had leather curtains.

Passengers could sit inside, on a six-foot wide front or rear-cushioned seat. Baggage was loaded into a rear wicker compartment with excess bags strapped on top. There was a five-foot wide forward facing spring-bench for additional passengers on top. Some of the coaches carried an armed mail-guard sitting on a short spring-seat on top of the wicker baggage compartment. At the front, there was a coupé-box and protective dashboard where the conductor and an additional defender could sit on a sheltered bench.

The regular coach route from Paris to Toulon took five days, with one overnight stop in Lyon. The coach would stop for a few minutes to change teams of horses at private inns or government post houses that were spaced about two hours apart. Coaches averaged six miles-per-hour over the entire route. Twice per day, there would be a 45-minute stop for food at a post inn, breakfast at about ten o'clock and dinner at about three o'clock.

Normally four horses would pull the coach at a trot. The driver rode postillion on the left rear horse since he could better control the reins of all four horses. Where the stage would encounter hills or heavy loads, they would use three pairs of horses. Three teams required a second driver on the left lead horse. Every three or four-post houses, drivers were relieved. The conductor and mail-guard usually traveled one leg of the route, such as Paris to Lyon, and returned after a days' rest. On this trip, the conductor and guard were the ex-military sergeants who General Bonaparte trusted so they would stay with the gold for the entire trip from Paris to Toulon.

Stepping out of the calash, Charles checked his weapons and snapped his carabine and sabre into place as he inspected each vehicle and attendants to make sure he choose the correct turgotine. He then walked over to the front wheel of the newest coach and introduced himself to the most likely ex-military supervisor. He gave him his pass for travel and Bonaparte's private note. After reading the note, the conductor studied the signature and the counter signature. He then inspected Charles up and down. He took particular notice of his two holsters, his sabre and his carabine.

"Where do you want to sit?" the conductor asked.

"Beside you in the conductor's box," Charles replied.

"Are your weapons loaded?"

"Yes, of course," Charles was suddenly glad that Jean had loaded his weapons.

"I served under your father in America. My name is Paul Forgeron, *Ex-Adjudant-Chef* to General Bonaparte."

Jean Dulcos walked up with the baggage. The two former sergeant majors instantly recognized each other and embraced. Jean turned to Charles and said, "We served together under your father in America." The two old companions moved off together to help the hostler check the horses and commenced an intense conversation, waving their arms and slapping each other on the back.

When Forgeron broke away and came back over to the coach, he said to Charles, "You'll do. Call me Paul," as he climbed up to check something on top the coach.

Charles, uncertain of the etiquette, edged over to Jean and whispered. "Father taught me to show great respect to senior sergeants. Is it proper to address him by his Christian name?"

"You call me Jean when we're alone or with the family," Jean responded in a soft voice. "You should call Conductor Forgeron, Paul in private. You can call him by his last name when others can hear you. Don't forget what I taught you about shooting two pistols with each hand. Always aim either the right or the left one, no shooting from the waist."

Charles turned and said to Paul as he climbed back down, "D'accord! You can call me Charles. Paul nodded and then beckoned another man to join him, "This is the mail-guard, Raoul Pelle. He was also a former sergeant under General Bonaparte in Italy. You can call him Raoul."

A military wagon with four armed soldiers in the back and a paymaster captain sitting next to the driver pulled up beside the coach. The captain stepped off and said, "Conductor Forgeron I have your special cargo. You must sign for it."

Pointing to Charles, Forgeron said, "This officer has been appointed as the person in charge of the shipment." The paymaster asked to see Charles' written authority.

He countersigned it while Forgeron supervised the soldiers as they unloaded ten heavy ironbound boxes and placed four of them in the foot well of the conductor's coupé-box. The other six were stowed in the lowest layer of the rear storage compartment of the coach. Forgeron covered all of the boxes with canvas. Two porters and the guard started loading passengers' baggage on top of the cargo in the rear compartment.

The paymaster turned to Charles and said, "Each box weighs over 45 pounds."

SEVEN

April 25ᵗʰ

TURGOTINE TERMINUS, PARIS

C harles watched as Conductor Forgeron pulled a gnarled black pipe from his pocket, packed it with tobacco from a leather pouch, placed a piece of fluffy tinder on top and lit it with a small flint snap-cock. He sucked the smoke in through a short brown mouthpiece.

His clothing was typical of first class conductors and consisted of short stout boots with hobnails, bottle-green velveteen trousers, and a waistcoat of the same material. Over this, he wore a nationale bleue long coat with no turned back tails. The coat had red colored embroidery on the collar, shoulder straps and cuffs.

He still seemed very much the soldier in his bearing and manner even though he had left the Army for a career in the mail coaches. Forgeron was a large muscular man about 50-years old. His shape reminded Charles of a sturdy wine barrel. His short hair was grizzled gray and beginning to thin at the front with a bald spot at the back. His nose had been broken multiple times and he had fighting scars on his face and hands. Raoul, the mail-guard looked like him, only fifteen years younger.

Jean helped him load his luggage and messenger bags onto the top of the coach. Placing his rifle, sabre and waistbelt with holsters in the conductor's box, he noticed Forgeron had two pistols and a blunderbuss with a 17-inch long barrel in holsters attached to the right side of the coupé. Putting his weapons and the bag of food from his mother on the left, Charles reached up to get his canteen and wineskin and placed them next to the food.

Forgeron came up and said, "The rest of the arriving Lyon passengers are being asked to sit inside at the table to the left of the fireplace. You need to show your travel pass to the clerk at the desk." Charles suddenly noticed a short, pudgy, pear-shaped infantry major walking out the door of the terminus building. He strutted up to Forgeron and asked, "Is the gold here yet?"

"Why do you want to know?"

"I am *Chef de Bataillon* Pierre Menou. I am on the staff of General Jacques Menou. I am in charge of the gold shipments."

"We just loaded it on the turgotine," Forgeron responded.

Major Menou was an overweight and slovenly middle-aged man. He was going bald and looked more like a shopkeeper than the way an infantry officer should look. He was wearing a short lightweight dress sword that would be useless in combat. He turned to Charles and asked, "Who are you? Why are you putting your things in the conductor's box?"

Charles calmly answered, "I've been appointed as the officer in charge of this shipment." From the outside, he seemed calm; however, he was very uncomfortable with these questions.

Major Menou spluttered, "Who said you are the officer in charge, I outrank you. I am in charge. You will take your orders from me."

Conductor Forgeron said, "I've seen his orders and I'm satisfied. Why don't you show them to the major?"

Charles slowly reached into his leather bag and removed the letter and handed it to the plump little officer, "Here is my authorization and authority from General-in-Chief Bonaparte; you'll notice that it is countersigned by Paul Barras. My designation as officer in charge is clear." Suddenly, Charles thought to act a little like his father, "Can I see a copy of your orders?"

He felt an instantaneous dislike for this officious little major. Menou thrust the letter back at Charles, turned, and waddled back into the main room of the terminus.

Forgeron grinned at Charles as he said, "I imagine General Menou assigned his cousin to this detail in order to get him out from under his feet."

Going inside, Charles presented the travel warrant to the clerk. As he laboriously entered the information in his register, Charles turned to survey the fifty or so people eating and drinking in the large, low ceilinged room. There was an extremely large limestone fireplace opposite the door. Many of those inside were smoking pipes; some were eating bread and most were drinking wine. The smell of fresh bread was overpowered by the odor of smoke and stale wine.

The table to the left of the fireplace had nine chairs pulled out. There was a family of four with their backs to him, two of them boys around ten or twelve years of age.

A navy commander and Major Menou were smoking clay pipes and talking beside the fireplace, while an army captain and a lieutenant were sitting beside a beautiful young lady who was probably the young captain's wife or fiancé. Both of the latter two men were wearing the orange collar and cuffs of Ingénieurs-Geographes. That was very unusual since Charles knew that there were less than three-dozen IG officers in France.

Peering more closely Charles realized he knew the young captain. Horace Say had shared his garret while they attended the new national *L'École Polytechnique* together. Charles's father, along with dozens of others had taken in the unhoused rural students as a favor to their Masonic friends. Approaching the table, he touched his friend's shoulder, "Horace, we're on the same mail coach."

Horace stood, grabbed him, kissed him on both cheeks and asked, "Charles, how are you? I thought you were still a graduate student at *X-Ponts*. I went by the house and your mother told me you were away studying at Châlons. Where are you going?"

"I was recently commissioned and have been assigned to Bonaparte's guides in Toulon. We're probably going to the same place. I wrote you a letter yesterday. It's probably with the mail pouch we're carrying. What are you doing in Paris? I'd heard you were assigned to General Caffarelli."

"I've been working at the War Depot since January," Say replied, "I married my Lyonnais sweetheart just before Christmas." Taking the hand of the young lady he said, "Dear, I would like you to meet our American savage, Charles MacDonald, my roommate from *X*. Charles, I would like to introduce you to my wife, Alphonsine Delaroche Say."

Charles took 's hand, kissed it and said, "Enchante, madame."

"We're on our honeymoon," Say continued. "Although I've been working at the topographical bureau, I've been running all over town collecting information and maps for General Caffarelli. I'm his chief aide." Opening his leather messenger bag, he displayed the contents to Charles, "As you see, I have many of your fathers' maps and reports."

Charles noticed one of his father's reports about Egypt. He suspected the bag contained many more maps or reports on that distant country.

Say gazed at the single red stripe on Charles' gold epaulette and contra-epaulette and asked, "Why aren't you a sous-lieutenant with two thin stripes? Who appointed you a full lieutenant?"

Charles, careful not to reveal the details about his mission, explained that he had been fortunate enough to graduate early and receive an appointment in the geographical engineers. He did not mention the attempted robbery, his friend Quentin's wounds or this mission guarding the gold shipment.

Horace asked after the health of Charles' parents, sister and brothers. "Everybody's in good health," Charles replied. "Barbara spends eight and half days at school just down from the farm, and the twins are following my new training regimen. Mother never told me that you'd gotten married or that you had stopped by. I've only been home for the past three weeks. If I had known you were in town, I would have come for a visit. All our friends are away with the army."

Horace then introduced him to the older lieutenant, "Charles, this is newly-promoted Lieutenant Jean Faurie. He's been an assistant in the Geographical-Engineers for the past twenty years. I believe he knew your father and was his draftsman drawing several maps."

Lieutenant Faurie was a thin man in his late 30's. He did not have the appearance of a warrior. Horace asked him for the date of his rank as a full lieutenant. Charles replied, "April first of this year."

"Then you are senior," Horace said, "Jean was promoted yesterday."

Glancing at Major Menou, Charles noticed he was taking great interest in their conversation. The major, he decided, was a bit too curious about matters that did not concern him. At that moment the clerk called out, "All passengers for Lyon, the mail coach is ready for loading."

The naval officer at the table stood and introduced himself to Charles. "I am Renee Duval, commander of the frigate *Peregrine*." The nine passengers began to drift outside to take their places on the coach. Moving to the front of the coupé, Charles buckled on his waistbelt with both holsters.

Adding the new second long strap to his sabre sling, he slung it down his back like a haversack with the hilt extending above his right shoulder. The scabbard hung between his shoulder blades. The curve of the scabbard positioned the tip just behind his left hip. His father had suggested he adopt this unusual oriental style carry while he was walking or seated on the coach. Horace came up and asked, "Where are you sitting?"

Motioning to the coupé-box, Charles replied, "Up there on the left seat."

Inside seats on the mail coach were more expensive than seats for the "monkeys" on top. The two boys and Lieutenant Faurie were climbing up to the roof deck. The boys' parents got into the coach and sat on the left and middle back seat, facing forward. Commander Duval sat in the back right and Major Menou sat across from him in the front right seat, which left two rear-facing seats for Horace and Alphonsine. The six-foot wide benches were tight with three people on each. Commander Duval didn't offer the preferred forward facing seat to Madam Say.

Charles followed Paul after the conductor had settled into position in their coupé. They both arranged their equipment, weapons and seating cushions. Charles was sitting on his folded cloak to cushion his butt against the hard wooden plank of his seat. The mail-guard was arranging several mailbags in the compartment at his feet.

The postillion driver mounted the nearside wheel horse, directly in front of him, and slapped the reins, shouting, "Hue!"

EIGHT

April 25th

PARIS TO MELUN

Leaving the Paris terminus the mail coach carried Charles east through the sleeping city. After crossing the Place de la Bastille, they turned toward the eastern tax barrier.

There were a few farm carts and heavy wagons on the streets. There was little other traffic and they were making good time, traveling about three miles-per-hour leaving Paris.

Even though many of the side streets were narrow and difficult to maneuver, the route they were taking was clear. The turgotine would not be crossing the upstream section of the Seine until they were further east.

The bridge at Montereau was under repair, making it necessary to detour and cross the Seine over the stone bridge at Melun. After showing their papers, they left the old *Barrière du Trône* of Paris. Everyone leaving or entering the city had to identify himself.

The diligence took the route national to the east through the Vincennes Wood. It was a favorite place for highwaymen to attack since it lay just outside the tax wall and the bandits could disappear back into the city slums.

Their path followed the old road through Fontainebleau and then rejoined the route national postal road rising up the valley of the Yonne River to a high point just beyond Auxerre.

The road then ran downhill to join the valley of the Saone River just beyond Beaune and down the Saone to Lyon where it joined the Rhone. From there it was a straight run south beside the Rhone River to Avignon. Traveling on to Aix, they would take the hilly coast road to Toulon, the major French Naval Base on the Mediterranean.

Everyone would have to sleep as best they could while sitting in the rocking and bouncing coach. Leather straps and curved springs supported the body, absorbing some of the movement.

Inside they could unfold a footrest and stretch out. On the top, there was no room to sleep unless you stretched out on the baggage. In the conductors box you could only wedge yourself into a corner. Passengers who were willing to take the extra time and pay the extra cost could stop overnight at an inn and continue on with the next day's coach.

Because he imagined danger from highwaymen at every turn, Charles became alert when he saw or felt anything. His body stiffened and he picked up the rifled carabine. Paul Forgeron would notice Charles preparing to defend the coach and pick up his blunderbuss. They crossed the first major bridge over the Marne River, the Pont de Charenton, shortly before their first change of horses.

During the changeover, Paul said, "Relax, calm down, you're driving me crazy. You're over-reacting to everything. Most conductors and guards don't even load their guns; they just give the government money to the highwaymen. Be prepared, but rely on your instincts and only react if you think something looks wrong. I trust your judgment if anything happens." Paul went on to explain the rules of the *Administration des Messageries*.

Charles started to calm down and actually study things. He watched the sunrise on his side of the coach just before the second change of horses as they traveled through villages and extensive farmland.

I used to smoke clay pipes," Conductor Forgeron started talking as he lit another pipe full. "I broke several of them each day. A few years ago I was a sergeant major with the Artillery and I bought a briar root burl along the southern coast and carved it myself, it's almost fireproof. The mouthpiece is real amber from the Baltic and the tobacco is from Virginia."

They talked some more. As soon as the light allowed, he pulled the gold watch out of his vest pocket and wound it using the key attached to its safety chain. His pocket chronometer had five movements. The single large hand pointed to the calendar day. The Roman numeral clock face was set to Paris time and the Arabic numeral one to local solar time. There was a second hand movement and a lunar dial for astronomical observations.

Every week he corrected it to the Paris meridian by adding a minute. When he could calibrate accurate longitude measurements, he checked his *ad hoc* chronometer corrections.

As soon as it was light enough, he took out his father's first journal and tried to read. He was too excited to follow the faded handwriting. He kept reading the same page, repeatedly. Finally, he put the journal back into his bag.

Between the first and the third stage, as they rode through several different forests he began thinking through his various strategies.

If British agents knew about the gold, they would send news ahead to a waiting gang. Since they couldn't be sure until they saw the strongboxes, a messenger would have to be riding just ahead of the coach. At each stage, he got down and asked the *hostler* if a rider had come through earlier that morning. By the third stage, after receiving another negative response, he started to rethink.

If a British agent knew about the gold shipment, he could have already set up the ambush. He would be sending word of the shipment using one of the passengers. He proceeded to keep an eye on the behavior of his fellow travelers. He was certain he could trust Horace Say, Conductor Forgeron and Mailguard Pelle. He couldn't trust anyone else. He decided to ask Forgeron what he thought about the various passengers.

Within the hour, they would to arrive in Melun, the fourth stage. There they would stop for the first of the two daily meals. The postillion would change over for a new driver. Across the Seine from Melun was the beginning of the Forest of Fontainebleau, a dense and hilly hunting forest. His father had warned him this area was one of the centers of royalist activities.

He turned to Paul and asked, "Do you have any reason to suspect that a British agent is one of our passengers?"

"No," Paul replied, "But if we're carrying a spy, we'll find out soon enough. A few leagues beyond Fontainebleau, the roadway opens up as we go on up the valley. No one will try and rob us there. Any robbery will happen while we're still in the forest, just before or after the royal hunting palace."

The mail coach drove into the town of Melun shortly after ten o'clock. The inn was set fifty feet off the main street with a rectangular courtyard behind it. There was enough room for the coach to pull off parallel to the buildings. The inn was at the intersection of two different stage routes.

Charles had stopped at this inn twice during his field survey duties for the Bureau des Longitudes. Last spring, he rode alone through Germany, Switzerland, and back through northern Italy. He was recording the lunar-celestial angles while calculating the longitude at each stop by reducing the lunar distances and checking the accuracy of his new experimental pocket chronometer.

The main structure was a two-story limestone inn. The innkeeper came out, opened the coach door, and said, "The *table d'hôte* is inside on the right. This morning we have eggs, bread, ham, duck, and several local cheeses."

Raoul Pelle threw the mailbag down to the innkeeper for sorting. As Paul and Charles climbed down from the conductor's box Charles asked, "Should one of us stay with the coach? I'll go inside and bring out food for both of us and for Raoul." The mail-guard was now sitting on top peering in all directions and holding his blunderbuss in a ready position.

Leaving his carabine in the box on the way inside, Charles adjusted his sabre to hang at his hip. The doorway was only 6 feet high and he had to remove his bicorne and duck his head.

Entering the common room, he approached the innkeeper and quietly asked, "Have any horsemen passed this morning?"

"Four men rode up to the stables earlier this morning and they have been sitting in the corner for the past two hours," he replied as he nodded his head at four tough looking men drinking from mugs at a corner table. Two of them were whispering to a third one who seemed to be the leader. He was slender, with curly dark hair, turning grey on the sides. He had black eyebrows and a graying Dutch style beard and mustachios.

Charles noticed that he was wearing an older, rapier style épée with an elaborate cupped hilt and basket, a classic dueling sword. Sitting in the corner, the middle-aged man was covertly surveying the passengers from the coach. Charles was almost certain he had seen the man before, but he could not remember where or when.

He walked to the host's table reserved for the mail coach passengers. The other travelers were already sitting down and eating. He kept an eye on the four strangers while he filled three plates with food.

He kept trying to remember where he had seen the bearded man. The other three also looked like fighting men. All were wearing dark colored civilian clothing. The leader glanced away when he realized that Charles was aware of his interest.

He was studying Charles' unusual sabre with its elegant swept-hilt guard shaped like a twisting and looped cobra with its hood flared into a striking position instead of an upper cross guard. In the place of a standard pommel, the haft extended two inches forming a short two-handed grip, two fingers resting on either side of the serpents looped tail. Nicholas-Noël Boutet the artiste at Versailles fitted the Japanese blade and carved the entire hand-guard from dark bronze that matched the original scabbard fittings.

Suddenly the leader of the quartet stood up, put some coins on the table and left, followed by the others. They went out the back entrance, which probably led to the stable yard.

As they left, Charles wondered why the bearded man had peered so intently at his father's sabre. General MacDonald seldom wore the custom war blade, preferring a plainer dress épée. After he lost his eyesight, he no longer wore a sword but carried a blackthorn cane with a concealed blade.

Going outside through the front door, Charles carried the food to Paul and then excused himself to go to the privy outhouse in the rear yard. After finishing his business, he walked to the washstand to wash his hands.

Glancing through the courtyard stable doors, he observed the four riders getting ready to mount their horses. He also noticed Major Menou talking to the presumed leader, who towered over the short officer. Charles estimated his height to be about six feet, only a few inches shorter than he was.

He also noted that all four men had saddle holsters and scabbards with carabines or blunderbusses. They mounted and rode out the far stable door. He walked back through the sally port and watched as they turned left and rode down the street toward the bridge over the Seine. As they reached the corner, he noticed an additional two riders joining them. Major Menou did not seem to be aware of Charles's scrutiny.

Walking up to the coach, Paul gave him the plate of food he had been keeping for him and asked, "Are there any problems!" Charles briefly described what he had seen and added; "I think we need to be especially careful for the next couple of stages."

Paul nodded toward the new second driver and said, "I have been conductor on this route for the past three years. I know all the lead drivers but I have never seen this postillion before. From the way he speaks and the quality of his clothes, he's not from same class as most of our drivers." He went into the inn and called for the passengers to reboard.

Charles stopped Horace Say on his way out and said, "There may be an attempt by highwaymen to stop and rob the coach."

"Where and why would they try and rob the coach?" Say asked.

"We are carrying special material for General Bonaparte. Did you notice the four men in the corner who left shortly after we arrived?"

"Yes. What can I do to help?"

"Protect Alphonsine first. Keep your eyes and ears open. Pay special attention to Major Menou, I do not think he will be of any help in a fight. If anything happens, try to keep everybody inside the coach, out of danger."

He turned and went up to Lieutenant Faurie and said, "On this section, if we get attacked by highwaymen, make sure you and the boys lay flat on the baggage *couvrir*. Also warn me if any riders approach from our rear."

He calculated that he had one rifle and four pistol balls, Paul's load of buckshot plus two pistol balls. Raoul the mail-guard carried the same weapons. That gave them eleven shots for six riders. There would be no time to reload. He might have to use his sabre. Turning to Paul, he asked, "Do you have any other weapons?"

"I have two .69 caliber musketoons under the seat."

"Get them out, check their loads and give one to Raoul. We may need both. They'll give us thirteen shots for six bandits. We can't afford to miss."

NINE

April 25ᵗʰ

FOREST OF FONTAINEBLEAU

The coach pulled out of the inn and started across the bridge over the Seine. A short distance after crossing the river they entered the forest of Fontainebleau. Their route took them through eight miles of spreading oaks adjoined by patches of tall pines or dense and dark groups of beech trees. The forest was also inhabited by peculiar rock formations that looked like grotesque animals in the filtered light. When they passed they should reach the open fields leading to the inn at the foot of the Palace de Fontainebleau.

"The town of Fontainebleau had a brigade of mounted gendarmes patrolling the forest. Beyond the town is another twelve miles of forest before rejoining the route national just south of Montereau. The road through the former royal hunting forest has some potholes and needs repair after the hard winter." Paul explained.

After traveling about 45 minutes, the coach began climbing up a hill. There was a slight drop off to the right and about halfway up the hill, a mass of boulders began rising on their left. The coach started slowing down for the rise in the road. As the coach reached the stone bulwark, they slowed even more.

We are going too slowly, Charles thought. He suddenly felt a faint prickling of the hair on his neck. He saw movement near the top of a crag, about 75 feet away.

Suddenly he recognized two eyes under a shapeless hat and the straight barrel of a rifle shifting to aim directly at him.

In one motion, he cocked and raised his own carbine. He was aiming with his half-closed right eye, while his left eye was almost shut.

His vision focused as if he was peering into a tunnel. Concentrating on the front sight blade and seeing the whiter slashes of the widening eyes, he squeezed the trigger as the rear sight notch came into alignment.

Through the smoke and flash, he saw the floppy hat jump several feet into the air. Simultaneously he felt his bicorne hat jerk off his head. The bandit had also fired his rifle, but too hastily.

The lead driver stopped the horses. At the same time, three riders came charging over the hill. In the background, he heard Lieutenant Faurie shout, "Beware, riders from behind!"

He dropped his carbine into the box. He drew both his pistols and cocked the flint hammers to each upper barrel.

Paul grabbed his musketoon from where it was leaning against the box. The first rider stopped 25 feet away at the lead outside horse, while the second and third riders rode closer on the right.

With his left pistol, Charles aimed at the bandit grabbing for the bridle of the lead horse. He fired and the bandit recoiled back in his saddle.

However, he didn't fall. Charles noticed that the highwayman, like his companions, had a scarf pulled up around his face. The best target was the shiny white of his eyes and forehead.

Squinting through his right eye and locking his wrist, he squeezed the rear trigger of his right pistol.

His bullet punched through his head and the bandit dropped off his horse like a sack of coal from a wagon. He saw movement out of the corner of his eye and watched as the rear postillion-the new man, fired a shot into the back of the lead coach team rider.

The closest robber, the leader was swinging his leg over his slowing horse while he shouted, "Stop, drop your weapons, give up the boxes."

Charles swung his attention to the second road agent, 10 feet away. This bandit was also wearing a scarf. As he watched, the rider flew off the back of his horse with a huge clang, like a bell. Paul had fired his musketoon at him and hit him in the center of his chest.

He shifted his vision to the dismounting leader while cocking the second lock on each of his pistols.

Seconds later Paul pushed Charles back with his hand while shouting, "Look out!" The rear driver had drawn a second pistol, swiveled and fired it at where Charles was sitting. The driver's shot hit Paul in his left hand. Blood splattered onto Charles' face. Paul raised his short blunderbuss with his right hand and shot the driver in the back.

The lead highwayman was out of sight, somewhere near the coach door. Charles was now holding two newly cocked pistols with charged lower barrels and no target.

Hearing shots to his right, he stepped on the seat, boosted himself to the top of the coach and peered over the right side. Both boys were beneath the spring seat and Faurie was prone, aiming his small pistol.

The two riders from below were holding pistols pointed at the coach door from fewer than 10 feet. Raoul aimed and shot his musketoon ball into the stomach of the furthermost bandit. The shot knocked him off his horse. Faurie fired his pistol charge into the closer rider with little effect.

Raoul shouted as he dropped the short musket. He pulled the blunderbuss hooked to his baldric and fired his shot charge into the near rider. Charles glimpsed the rolled steel collar of a breastplate as the buckshot drove the rider sideways. He shouted, "They're wearing armor. Shoot for their heads."

He could hear Major Menou screaming, "Don't resist. Give them the gold. Drop your weapons. They'll kill us all."

He raised both pistols and fired, first the right and then the left. One shot hit the rider on the right in his neck sending a jet of blood into the air.

The dismounted leader, who was shouting orders, was quickly turning when Charles fired his left pistol but missed him.

As the ringleader was drawing his sword, Charles jumped from the roof of the coach directly onto the highwayman, shouting the Keppoch clan war cry, "Lochaber." His jump knocked the bandit to his knees.

Recovering, the leader stood and turned toward him. He hesitated as he stared directly into his eyes. Instead of thrusting, he began sweeping his rapier blade in a cutting arc.

Charles realized that his lozenge shaped blade had a longer reach, and sharpened edges. It was a killing blade.

He tossed both empty pistols at the swordsman and stepped forward inside the sweep of the oncoming blade. He parried it with the metal covered scabbard hanging down his back, then drew his sabre and cut horizontally into the space between the rolled collar of the cuirass and the ringleaders' hat in one lightning draw stroke.

The tachi blade decapitated the leader. He gazed for a moment at the man's body thinking, why did he hesitate to thrust. A straight thrust would have wounded me, although I still might have won. It just would have taken me several more moves.

He knelt and wiped the blood off his blade with the bandit's black cloak. As he turned around, he saw everyone in the coach was looking at him. Some faces had an expression of horror, some of amazement. The two boys were jumping just like monkeys' and shouting from the coach top. Lieutenant Faurie had drawn his small sword.

Charles noticed one of the boys pointing at the bandit lying on the ground at the rear of the coach. He glanced over and realized he was still alive. Raoul's shot had hit the bottom of his steel breastplate and penetrated his groin, leaving the man writhing in agony.

He started toward the bandit needing some questions answered. Suddenly Commander Duval fired a dueling pistol out the rear window and hit the bandit in the head.

Paul was trying to climb down from the conductor's box using only one hand. Giving him some help, Charles asked, "Where are you wounded?"

"The driver shot off my little finger and the other bandit shot me between my arm and ribs."

Going to the coach door and opening it, he asked, "Is everyone all right? Is anyone wounded?" The three officers climbed out. The civilian man followed them.

"Check on our driver," Charles asked Horace. The father shouted at the yelling boys, "Quiet down! Are you hurt?" The boys were still yelling about what they had seen. All the men began to ask questions of Conductor Forgeron, pestering him as he was trying to wrap a kerchief around his hand.

Horace was shaking his head back and forth, as he returned from the driver. He joined Charles as he moved from one body to the next, examining them for any signs of life. As Charles removed the silk scarf from the head of the leader, he recognized who he was.

He said in a low voice to Horace and Paul, "It's Colonel DeVillars, the father of my late friend Hector. After my sister and I left for Virginia in '93, I got a letter from a neighbor letting me know the Committee of Public Safety had arrested and guillotined Hector and his mother. The colonel was in Germany with a royalist unit. His family lived near us on the Avenue de Saxe and we shared tutors and fencing classes for eight years. DeVillars must have seen my father's Japanese bladed sabre before. He must have recognized me as his son's best friend."

He removed the highwaymen's weapons and went through their pockets looking for clues about their identity. He also unwound the scarves covering the rest of their faces. DeVillars had a dozen gold coins in one pocket and a gold pocket watch in the other.

Charles looked behind him and saw the two boys had climbed down from the coach roof and were inspecting each body. He ordered Raoul to collect the horses and tie them to the back of the coach. Only one of the well-trained cavalry mounts had run off for a short distance. Four of the dark horses were mares. DeVillars horse was a black stallion.

He reloaded his carabine after he made sure that the spurious driver was dead and then climbed up the rock face searching for the seventh highwayman. When he found the body, Charles confirmed that his shot had hit the man in the face.

Studying the area, he discovered a German Jäger rifle and the man's dark gelding, tied next to a pair of mares hitched to a two-wheeled cart. Picking up the body, he hoisted it into the cart and started back down to the coach.

TEN

April 25ᵗʰ

EVIDENCE OF THE HOLD-UP

As Charles led the cart back down the hill a group of passengers came up to him and peppered him with questions.

He raised his hand. "I can only answer one question at a time."

Commander Duval asked, "Who were they and why did they attack us?"

"We were worried that a royalist unit might attack us, I was assigned to act as an extra guard. They must have known this coach was carrying a special cargo for the army in Toulon. The nearest Gendarmerie barracks is in Fontainebleau, we need to report the attempted robbery."

"Why didn't you just give them what they wanted?" Major Menou questioned. Charles didn't answer.

Raoul was bringing the horses to the back of the coach, one at a time. "Can you get the black horse, I can't catch him? I'm not very good with horses." He asked Charles.

DeVillars' horse was a young but well trained black Andalusian stallion. Charles whistled and he raised his head and stood still. In addition to black saddlery and holsters, there was a set of three matching leather bags attached to the cantle. He removed them to put them in the pile of other material although the hanging bags must be full of lead. Opening both pouches he saw paper tubes of gold coins on each side. There must be a thousand British guineas, each one worth almost 27 francs. He moved if to the floor of the coupé.

With the help of several others, they put the bodies into the cart and tied three horses to it and the other three to the turgotine. He wrapped the loose head in the black silk scarf and tied it to the body with his sword belt. Horace checked the reins to make sure that the boys had securely knotted them to the back of the cart and the coach while Charles boosted the body of the dead postillion driver up to Raoul, who tied him to the roof of the coach. He made sure all of the papers, material, and weapons he had collected were in the foot of the coupé – the conductors' compartment.

Madame Jonchere, the mother of the two boys, got out some bandages and a bread poultice. She gave them to him to wrap Paul's hand and stop the bleeding from his missing finger while he sat on a rock.

Checking his other wound, Charles found that DeVillars had fired his first pistol shot at Paul and the ball had gone between his left arm and side. There was a slice of skin missing from both areas. After wounding Paul, the pistol ball must have missed Charles by only inches.

Paul asked him in a low voice as he was wrapping his hand, "Light my pipe for me." After Charles got it lit, he asked, "How many men have you killed in combat? It's obvious that you have more experience than the earlier turgotine robbery attempt."

"When I was a fifteen-year-old boy in Virginia, I was on a one-week hunting trip into the Appalachian Mountains with an old friend of my grandfathers. There was a harvest break from college classes at Liberty Hall Academy near Lexington." He finished bandaging

Paul's hand and told him to remove his coat and shirt so that he could inspect the wound in his side. The bleeding had slowed.

"We were attacked by three Chickamauga Cherokee Indians escaping south on the Great Warrior Path after their defeat at the battle of Fallen Timbers. My mentor, Eli Smith was an old pathfinder, a long hunter and trapper. He was teaching me to hunt, scout and explore the mountains. After a long stalk, I shot a large buck. Eli had taught me to reload my rifle immediately. Before we moved up to bleed the deer and collect the meat for the boys at school."

He started wrapping a cloth around the poultice on Paul's wounded side as he said, "The three Indian warriors had heard my shot and came to check out the noise. One Cherokee fired and wounded Eli, while the second shot hit me in the buttocks. The three Indians then charged with tomahawks yelling in hellish war whoops. Eli shot one and I shot another. Subsequently, the third Indian was hatcheting Eli in the head. I turned, drew my long knife and stabbed him in the side, through his liver and up into his chest cavity."

Paul asked, "What happened?"

"Eli was seriously wounded in the head and side. I cut two poles, using blankets, and leather belts I made a litter and attached it to his horse. The Canadian *coureur des bois* call it a *travois*. Walking, I led both horses. With my wound, I could not sit in a saddle. Dragging Eli behind his horse for fourteen hours, we arrived back on the school campus at Mulberry Hill.

Eli eventually recovered. The bullet that hit me in the ass was a grazing wound, just like the one on your rib cage. I still have that old long knife. Eli made it out of an old file and the tang wasn't long enough. It's not very well balanced. I left all the captured Cherokee weapons in Virginia." Charles' story was interrupted by Duval as he passed them and went to help boost the buttocks of the major back into the coach.

Horace Say took Paul's place in the conductor's box, while Lieutenant Faurie drove the two-wheeled cart with the seven bodies. Both boys squeezed in beside their mother. Raoul reloaded his weapons and re-took the rear seat.

After taking a few minutes to reload the rifle and all four barrels of his pistols, he placed them back into their waistbelt holsters. Charles put on the reinforced right boot shaft of the dead rider and took the rear postillion position. With his damaged bicorne hat still sitting on the front seat, they proceeded to the post inn at Fontainebleau.

As he directed the six horse team he was thinking, "The conductor from my earlier encounter told me that I get to keep the plunder from the men I killed." He recalled that Paul had just told him. "That's the rule of the government owned Messengers Nationale, you get to keep anything the bandits have including horses and weapons." Then he remembered that he had overheard General Bonaparte say, "I'm changing the rules we had in Italy, my men spent more time looting rather than fighting. Any booty they get in the future must be turned in to the paymaster to draw from their future pay. Hoarding will be punishable by flogging."

Thinking of the report he needed to send to the General he thought, "I'm worried about writing my very first dispatch to General Bonaparte. Maybe if I send it to my father, he and my mother can correct my mistakes before delivering it to the General-in-Chief." Suddenly coughing he thought, "I also need to send my father everything that can help the investigation. I know I want to send the highwaymen's horses, equipment, papers and any money back to Paris, maybe I can find some one to hold it until we get it back."

He started thinking about his note, "I'll ask him to send our horse master Mahamoud, and a farmworker on the next coach to retrieve the horses, the unique rapier and other material that he can use in questioning hostlers and innkeepers in Paris. Maybe we should sell the slower horses and plain equipment to the *Messageries* or one of the local businesses. I'm keeping DeVillars two pistols for myself. In addition I want to include a few extra swords and pistols for our protection. Maybe we should carry the extra rifle and both blunder-busses."

CHAPTER

ELEVEN

April 25th

FONTAINEBLEAU, ÎLE-DE-FRANCE

Entering the town of Fontainebleau, Charles was relieved to see the inn immediately inside the city gate. Riding the inside wheel horse he was not comfortable handling the reins of six coach horses while towing a cavalcade of others.

Pulling the mail coach up in front of the proprietor, he asked, "Where is the nearest Gendarmerie?" The innkeeper first noticed his uniform, and then saw the officer sitting in the conductor's box and finally the two-horse cart and extra horses tied to the rear of both vehicles. He overcame his astonishment and said, "They're just down the street. I'll run and get them."

While the turgotine hostlers began to unhitch the teams, all of the passengers began getting down from the coach compartment. The first out of the coach was Paul Forgeron, who walked up to Charles and said, "I feel like shit."

Charles told him, "All the way here I have been thinking about what we need to do. I definitely need to send reports back to Paris. What about you, do you have to send back a report to Paris or just tell the next company agent?"

Paul interrupted, "All the way here I have been thinking about getting something to drink. Light my pipe for me."

Charles took the pipe and tobacco and started packing the bowl as requested. "I have also been thinking of how we can divide the spoils of war. I want everything from Colonel DeVillars while we can divide up the rest of the booty. His rapier and papers need to go to Paris; my father can send his man to get the horses and equipment."

Paul stared at Charles and said, "Fine with me. I am going to keep smoking my pipe and get something to drink that will kill this pain." He looked at Charles and grinned, "You need to scrub that smudge of gunpowder fouling off your face." Paul turned to Raoul and said, "Our *Officer-in-Charge* wants to keep all the loot from DeVillars while we get to divide up the booty from the highwaymen, do you have any objection? Move the postillion driver's body to the back stable yard and find a trestle to lay him out."

A gendarme corporal arrived with the innkeeper. He was adjusting his blue uniform coat over his buff trousers and vest. He breathlessly told Paul, "I've sent for the lieutenant. In the meantime tell me what happened." The innkeeper had begun herding the passengers into the inn and offering them a drink of wine and other refreshment. Paul called out, "Bring me a brandy, immediately."

While the gendarme was talking to Conductor Forgeron, Charles walked to the back of the coach, untied a pair of horses, and retied them to the first hitching post along the front wall. He continued until he had all eight horses tied to three posts. Five of them were younger and more spirited while three were older and slower.

He then carefully removed each body from the cart and organized them in a row, arranging DeVillars head in a natural position. He then brought the weapons stored in the mail coach and placed them next to each body. Several of the guns were unfired, so he dumped the powder out of the flash pans. When he was finished, he sat on a mounting block and examined the papers each man carried. He left the saddlebags loaded with gold on the floor of the conductor's box.

His search of each man's pockets yielded a number of papers and personal items in addition to two score silver and a dozen gold coins; their shoulder bags had more papers. The highwaymen were carrying two diaries, several letters and one Prussian passport among the items in their clothing and saddlebags. It was clear that they were royalists. He noted everything in his journal.

DeVillars pockets and cantle bags held several work-pages and messages in code and a common prayer book. Setting the money aside, Charles climbed to the coach roof with the papers in a bag and tied it to his rectangular campaign kit bag. He then stepped down into the conductor's box and retrieved his carabine and portfolio containing his documents and the note from Bonaparte. As he was climbing down from the box, four more gendarmes came running down the street. An energetic gendarme lieutenant was leading the parade. He questioned the corporal and Paul for several minutes and then turned to Charles.

As the gendarme officer's eyes widened in recognition, Charles said, "Lieutenant DuMayne, we meet again. Once again it's about the robbery of a diligence." Gesturing at the seven bodies lying in a row he told DuMayne, "These royalist highwaymen and their commander Honore DeVillars attempted to steal gold worth hundred of thousands of francs from the Republic."

"What are you doing on this coach?" DuMayne asked.

"If you read this letter from General Bonaparte, you will see my appointment and authority."

The gendarme lieutenant read the note. When he realized Paul Barras, *pour le Président du Directoire Exécutif de la République Française,* had countersigned it, he saluted and asked. "What do you need me to do?"

"Conductor Forgeron needs a doctor to dress his wounds. Please place a second guard on the coach. Have your men take care of the driver's body. After finishing out here, we should go inside and write up our reports. In addition, I need to write an independent report to send to my father in Paris. He'll send someone to collect the material we have captured." Charles paused long enough to catch his breath.

"Our mail coach is already behind schedule," he continued. "So we need to finish the investigations as soon as possible. You and any locals who may have knowledge should try and identify the dead highwaymen. I have already identified the first body as Honore DeVillars, a grandson of Marshal Duc de Villars. I believe he owned a nearby chateau." Once again Charles caught a quick breath.

"I also collected and inspected most of the papers they were carrying." He continued. "We may be able to identify some of the individuals from their documents. There were a large number of British guineas with DeVillars and his men had a few coins. He also had a prayer book and several pages in code. There is no question that this attempted robbery was a part of a British Secret Service plot to intercept official gold shipments."

"Why do you think it was the British?" asked Lieutenant DuMayne. "It would have been better if you'd not disturbed the evidence."

"Director Barras and General Bonaparte described what the British were planning when they asked my father, General MacDonald to help with uncovering their conspiracy," Charles responded. "I believe you met my father when you came to question me three weeks ago. I am sending some of the horses and equipment back with the documents and gold."

Charles then listed additional instructions for the gendarme lieutenant, "Conductor Forgeron, Mail-Guard Pelle, and I plan to divide the proceeds as the spoils of war." Charles paused to catch his breath and suddenly wondered. "Am I talking too much? I'm doing all the talking and this gendarme lieutenant isn't saying anything. He realized that his father wouldn't ramble on; he would listen twice as much as he talked."

"I have no problem with your plans so far," Lieutenant DuMayne said. "However, I still need to complete an official investigation."

"I'm talking too much," Charles responded. "Please ignore everything that I have said. Let's discuss any reports that you need to send back to Paris. You're in charge. It's just that I don't know who may be involved in this plot. I don't want your reports going to the wrong people. I'll write my father and request that General Bonaparte assign a trusted member of the Gendarmerie Nationale to help him in further inquiries. You can send your reports directly to him." Charles stopped talking but he could see that DuMayne was thinking about something.

"What do you think?" Charles said. "Be aware there will be additional shipments of gold to the ports on the Mediterranean over the next month. I doubt there are any more royalist fighting forces in this area, but the British may try and send in extra men."

As they walked away from the inn, Lieutenant DuMayne finally said to Charles that his colonel had assigned him to command the 24-man peloton in Fontainebleau only two weeks ago. "I was the *chef investigateur* for the 17th Gendarme Division in the *Île-de-France*-the Paris region. I led a small team working out of the Caserne de Gendarmerie on the northeastern perimeter wall. We took care of manor crimes within the entire region."

"I thought that the Paris Commune furnished policemen, night watchmen, firemen and spies within the city walls." Charles responded.

"My responsibilities for the last six months were to investigate corruption and British payments to members of the Directory and Ministers of the Republic." Lieutenant DuMayne responded. "One of the few honest men in the government, François de Neufchâteau-Minister of the Interior who was responsible for the Gendarmerie and the new Bureau Central of the National Police entrusted me with this task. I was already investigating other French traitors. My last assignment before exile to Fontainebleau was to investigate the gold robbery of the turgotine from Amsterdam in March and the other attempted mail coach holdups."

Charles told him. "Last night General-in-Chief Bonaparte was looking for the Gendarme Lieutenant who was investigating the diligence holdups. Apparently there was a new gold robbery in Baden, so I gave him your name. I had no idea that you had been transferred."

"Three different groups of royalist cavalry robbed the diligences. I think that the same seven dead men here robbed the mail coach of millions in gold just south of Senlis." DuMayne said.

"How do you know they were involved?" Charles asked. "Is it a fact?"

"During my investigation several eyewitnesses gave me the following facts. There were seven highwaymen in Senlis and six more on the Reims route. They were riding black or dark bay horses. Most of them had mustachios or Van Dyke chin hair. They were all wearing dark clothing. All of them were wearing black steel cuirasses under their waistcoats. The leader had an ornate rapier. Of course, you identified one of the dead highwaymen in your Reims group as a captain in the Black Horse Cuirassiers of the Army of Conté. Colonel DeVillars was the commander of that royalist regiment."

"Lots of men wear mustaches, ride dark horses or wear dark clothing." Charles said. "Of course not many wear steel breastplates or carry elaborate rapiers. Especially since the rapier is out of style except for the few assassins still challenging republicans to fight duels."

Lieutenant DuMayne shocked him when he said; "I arrested three royalist-émigrés who took part in the robberies. I suspect that the Minister of Police, a creature of several directors, exiled me because of that fact. I was on the verge of discovering too much about the corruption and there was too great a chance I would identify the rest of the gold robbers. I swear that two of the three men I arrested a fortnight ago are among the dead men laid out here. Someone released them after their arrest and my transfer." DuMayne then continued in a whisper.

"Your father can't trust anyone in Paris. I would love to work with him in uncovering this plot against the Republic. I think I should take the next coach to Paris. I could carry your letter, the evidence and the gold. No one will try and steal from an armed gendarme officer."

DuMayne added, "I could meet with your father and brief him on what my earlier investigations had uncovered. I need someone powerful to ask for my help before the colonel will reassign me back to Paris. I must use the influence of someone like General MacDonald to insist that I be a part of the continuing investigation. I will leave instructions that the horses and other equipment be turned over to your man when he arrives."

As the two officers walked back toward the inn, Charles decided that he must learn to listen carefully, like DuMayne, rather than talk too much. He realized that he'd been acting like a braying ass. During the ride after the ambuscade, all he could think about was what he needed to do. When he first talked to DuMayne, he had acted as if he were in charge of the investigation.

"General Bonaparte put me in charge of the gold shipment because he thought that I was free from corruption," he told DuMayne. "He didn't put my father in charge of anything, although he did ask him to help. I think that my father would make a great analyst of the available material. He could sift through all of the incoming intelligence, in multiple languages and make some sense out of the deluge of incoming data." Charles thought that it was obvious this gendarme officer had a lot more experience in these matters than he did. He would be wise to defer to him.

While Lieutenant DuMayne went to question the other passengers, Charles sat alone at a table by the fire and started to write his report and letters. When the innkeeper came up, he asked, "Could you get me a cup of black coffee?" Meanwhile, Conductor Forgeron was sitting at the next table by the fireplace drinking straight from a bottle of brandy, and furiously smoking his pipe.

Throughout the afternoon, Charles finished his official report and letters. He then entered his thoughts in his journal. Noticing Horace and Alphonsine sitting together in the afternoon light streaming through a west window, he started a drawing of the young couple. Later he went over to Lieutenant DuMayne and they discussed plans and methods for setting up a new team that could begin investigating British activities.

As he opened his pouch, packed tobacco into a disposable clay pipe and lit it with a straw from the fireplace DuMayne said, "Please call me Tristan." He went into some of the details of his reassignment.

He speculated why, after such a thorough investigation of the mail coach robberies, they had reassigned him. Was the Minister of

Police or the 17th Military District of the Gendarmerie Nationale responsible for his exile? Did they get their orders from a higher authority? Charles began to gain respect and confidence in the abilities of Tristan DuMayne.

He discovered that Tristan had graduated with a licence and maîtrise from the Faculty of Arts at the Sorbonne. He had finished his three years of law studies and been awarded a *doctorate* from the Faculty of Civil Laws at the University of Paris just weeks before the revolutionaries abolished the profession of advocate in '93.

Tristan was a muscular and athletic looking man. He was a handspan shorter than Charles was, with short brown hair, and unremarkable features. When he looked at him closely, he could see that Tristan looked as hard as nails.

He realized that DuMayne could wear any uniform or civilian habit and no one would notice. He wouldn't stand out from other men unless you looked into his eyes. He moved with economical gracefulness; it was clear that he was more than capable of defending himself and would be a good man to have at one's side in combat.

In Paris, Charles thought, my father would be the best leader of the investigation. The Executive Directory, the Council of Five Hundred, the Council of Ancients, and the various Ministers of the Republic universally respected and trusted him. They also weren't afraid of a blind man.

He could build up a detailed picture of the spider-web of British agents and activities. Father will need expert investigative officers working for him in the field. He believed that Tristan might be the best man for the lead detective position.

After writing out their investigative proposal, he had gone outside and sketched the faces of all seven men on sheets of drawing paper, which he gave to Tristan to carry to Paris along with copies of all his notes. The coach was now almost eight hours late. Even though the inn at Fontainebleau was not a normal food stop, the innkeeper had produced an excellent dinner. The coach was going to leave just before dark.

The northbound Paris mail coach would pass through in the early morning. Tristan purchased a ticket and then returned to the gendarme barracks to pack his belongings. Although he was almost 30 and still single, when he was in Paris Tristan lived with his parents and sisters. After reassignment to Fontainebleau two weeks earlier, he lived in the barracks with his men.

Charles kept 112 of the gold guineas, more than 15-month's salary. It weighed almost two pounds. He gave Tristan the other nine hundred coins, along with his report, letters, and the rapier to carry to his father in Paris.

The pay of a first lieutenant in the Ingénieurs-Geographes was 2,400 francs per year with additional allowances for horses, equipment, and supplies, a regular lieutenant made only 2,000. His spoils were worth over thirteen years of pay as a lieutenant. In addition to the money, Charles had also decided to keep the rifle, two blunderbusses and two horse pistols to carry in the coach for future protection.

After inspecting DeVillars two long-barreled dueling pistols, he realized that they were made by a famous London gunsmith, Joseph Manton. He decided to keep them. There was a leather covered wood-case in his cantle bag with a complete set of tools for the pistols.

During the afternoon, inn workers brought all the baggage into the common room while they cleaned the coach. They stacked the gold in the corner with a gendarme guarding it.

Horace Say came over and asked him in a low voice, "Where is your saddle? All the officers and cavalrymen are supposed to bring their tack. We're going to acquire horses in Egypt. You need to keep

DeVillars' English style hunting saddle, his cantle-bags and the matching pistol holsters." Horace then mentioned, "You can have an IG saddlecloth made at a shop in Lyon to fit under the leather skirts. I have one that is padded wool covered with national blue silk with two gold silk stripes around the perimeter. At the back corner on both sides is the symbol of the Ingénieurs-Geographes, on a large round orange-red patch with compasses and a square embroidered inside."

Conductor Forgeron sold the two heavy geldings and the two older mares to the innkeeper for the National Messenger Company. After setting aside two sets of tack for Mahamoud, he also sold the remainder of the saddlery, weapons and equipment. Selling the extra horses, equipment and weapons, Paul, Raoul and Charles divided over 4,200 francs in small coins between themselves. Commander Duval did not want any of the money even though he had shot the last bandit.

Before leaving Paris, General MacDonald had given him his linen multi-pocket under-vest, to wear beneath his waistcoat. He finally told Charles the story about why he had sewn this vest to smuggle valuables back from India in '84. "Sergeant Dulcos and I were stuck on a small dhow after escaping from our raid on the British East India Company fortress in Bombay. The boat had a spare set of light canvas sails, needles and thread. In order to avoid the danger of rescuers discovering our treasure, we both sewed vests as we sailed all the way to Batavia on the island of Java. Each had buttons up the front and laces at the back and sides. There were 50 pockets on each of the four panels suspended from our shoulders."

This story was Charles' first indication that his father was not poor, just hiding his wealth from the John Company at the East India House in Leadenhall Street, London.

Charles reviewed his current financial situation with satisfaction. When he had left Paris, he had only 250 francs. Most of them were silver and copper coins. With the warrant from General Bonaparte, he saved 200 francs for the fare and another 50 francs for food expenses. Adding the new gold coins and the silver coins from his share of the booty, he now had a total of 4,674 francs. However, his vest now weighed several pounds.

In the private letter to his father, Charles had asked him to use the 24,000 francs in gold to help purchase *Belle-Vue-Rivère*, the 150-acre estate and chateau adjoining their farm in Bougival. He now suspected that his father still had a lot of treasure left from his adventures in the Orient. Over the last four years, they had discussed purchasing the land next door and opening a horse stud, although Charles had no idea where the money was coming from. He thought that his father was dreaming.

The only delay was the legal dispute between the revolutionary government in Paris and the local commune in Bougival. Charles and his father had discussed the price that the commune would ask and they knew that the cash price would be one-quarter the amount that Bougival had to ask for depreciated notes, bonds or a paper loan from the central government. Assignats and mandats were worthless. He wrote to his father that the four horses he was sending back would constitute a core of cavalry horses when added to the horses that were already working at the farm.

CHAPTER

TWELEVE

April 25th

NIGHT TURGOTINE THROUGH YONNE

It was turning dark when the passengers boarded the mail coach for the continuation of the journey to Lyon. Earlier, Conductor Forgeron had told the two boys to sit inside the coach. Lieutenant Faurie still rode on top but he now carried one of the blunderbusses and a second pistol. Captain Say carried the other blunderbuss and pistol inside the coach. All of the officers were wearing their swords and Major Menou had unpacked and loaded a small muff pistol. Charles had drawn the charges from his weapons and cleaned them in hot water. He then oiled and reloaded them. He also cleaned and oiled his sabre, but it was too dim to check the edge and resharpen it.

As he mounted the conductor's box and settled into position, Paul knocked the ashes out of his pipe and put it in his coat pocket. Charles observed that he was a little unsteady. A new postillion driver mounted the left hand wheel horse and cracked a short whip when the hostler released the lead horse's bridle. The rushing mail coach passed the royal palace and its extensive gardens as it left Fontainebleau in the approaching dusk.

Earlier that afternoon, Alphonsine had told Charles that the rifle ball from the first shot had passed just over her head before exiting the back of the coach. When the second shot penetrated the compartment, she was on the floor. It passed directly through the spot where she had been sitting. Everyone was extremely lucky, except the dead driver and the poor plume on Charles' bicorne hat. It had been new before the rifle ball sheared it off along with several strands of his hair. The once new orange plume was now four-inches shorter.

Because of the eight-hour delay, the schedule had changed. A regular post messenger had passed through in the afternoon and carried word of the delay on down the line of post houses. They would arrive in Lyon on Friday morning for a late breakfast and stay overnight. They would leave on Saturday morning, a day late.

Paul had been drinking strong spirits for most of the afternoon to dull the pain from his wounds. He had bought a large stoneware jug of Brandywine to bring with him on the trip, and he had already taken several copious swallows. After it became completely dark, Charles turned to him and said, "Paul, why don't we divide up the watches. The last quarter moon won't rise until midnight. You try and sleep now while I watch. When the driver changes at the fourth stage, we can change duty. You'll have more light then."

"Are you trying to say I am blind?" Paul asked. He took another pull at the jug, coughed and spit over the side, and then grumpily settled into his corner, pulling his cape up to his chin.

It was dark on the road even though the driver had lit two coach lamps on either side of the conductor's box. Charles thought, it's a good thing the driver knows this route. I hope the horses know where they're going too. In order to stay alert, he started to plan what to do next. Lyon had been the center of a royalist uprising in '94 and the Committee of Public Safety had gone to great lengths to crush the revolt. Charles began to speculate on the possibilities of Royalists partisans in the area who might pose a potential threat. During the layover in Lyon, he thought, I should enlist the local Gendarmerie to help Raoul guard the gold during the stop. He recalled that the *caserne de gendarmerie* was in an old fortress on the peninsula between the two rivers. Maybe they had a strong room. This would free up both Paul and him to follow potential suspects. During the stop in Fontainebleau, he had dismissed Jonchere family as suspects. Their trip ended in Auxerre.

He also had a brief conversation with Commander Duval, who was traveling to Toulon to take command of the frigate *Peregrine*. For the past four years, he had been the Deputy-Chief of the Naval Office of Commerce and Consulates. His section was responsible for correspondence and naval support for all overseas French consulates. Well into the American Revolution, he had been in fleet combat as a young lieutenant aboard a ship that caught fire and exploded. He had subsequently been a prisoner of war for several years. His father was a French naval officer who had served during the Seven Years War. Duval was fully aware of the plans for action in Egypt since he had written the secret orders for the battle ships in the expedition. In fact, he was carrying over a dozen secret instructions in his shoulder bag. He was also responsible for correspondence with the foreign consulates in Leghorn, Naples, Malta, Crete, Istanbul, Alexandria, and Cairo. He worked with the Minister of Foreign Affairs, Citizen Talleyrand-Perigord. Although Duval seemed very well informed, he told Charles that he was not aware of any gold shipments or the collection of gold in Paris. Charles concluded that he was probably trustworthy, but something the naval officer had said or done earlier continued to bother him, although he could not remember what it was.

Horace Say and his new wife, however, were totally reliable. Since '94, he and Horace had become best friends. He was convinced;

there was no way that Horace could be involved in any double-dealing. His friend did admit that during their early morning travel, he had told all the passengers about Charles' prowess with a sword, pistol and rifle bragging that he might be the best young warrior in the French army.

He would talk to Major Menou and Lieutenant Faurie tomorrow at one of the meal stops. He was extremely suspicious of Menou, having seen him talking with DeVillars at the stables in Melun. He recalled what the major had shouted out at the beginning of the holdup. Did Menou know a robbery was going to happen? Horace said that Menou was on the floor before Alphonsine got there. Did he warn the highwaymen that Charles was an expert with gun and sabre? Did he know someone would be shooting to kill both men in the conductor's box? The floor would offer more protection from stray bullets than the front seat. Maybe he shouldn't question Major Menou; only listen. He and Paul could follow him everywhere in Lyon.

Charles then began thinking about what he was going to be carrying to Egypt. DeVillars black horse gear included an excellent quality English-style lightweight hunting saddle with matching cantle and saddlebags and holsters. The standard Bock cavalry device had a birch-wood frame and a laced leather hammock seat. It was ugly and required a saddle blanket to protect the horse and a *shabraque* to protect the rider's butt. It sat high above the horses back, adding another four inches to a rider's height; great for short cavalrymen. Charles decided he would buy a saddlecloth in Lyon like the one Horace described. If the saddlecloth maker can't finish it in one day, Horace will bring it with him. His leave in Lyon did not expire for another five days. As the coach was leaving the next stop, he saw that Paul was fully awake.

"What have you been thinking about?" Paul asked.

He thought that he should be truthful. "I have been thinking about the equipment that I am taking to Egypt."

"I have seen your rectangular leather kit bag, and your messenger bags. If you're on foot, you won't be able to carry everything. I heard Captain Say tell you that you will not have a horse until we conquer Egypt. Do you have much field equipment?"

"I have some of father's equipment such as his old copper field kitchen." Before I left, father told me, "Food is the single most important thing for a soldier. You can always find a common soldier to help you with cooking and carrying."

Paul laughed and said, "In America, I was your father's *ordonnance*, his common soldier who did his cooking; the Americans called me a batman. Jean Dulcos, who is ten years older than me, was his official sergeant and I was his cook, packsaddle and bodyguard. Geographical engineers receive a monthly allowance to pay for horses, assistants, interpreters and a batman. Lieutenants get enough money for one horse. The higher your rank, the more horses and servants you can afford. Your father, by then a brigadier general in the American army had a lieutenant aide-de-camp, a sergeant and me."

Paul then asked, "Do you have his oval copper kettle and fry pan with the nested coffee, tea and storage pots inside?"

"Yes. I had the inside re-plated before I left. Mother sewed silk drawstring bags and filled them with green coffee beans, hard wheat grain, dried beans and peas. She also made smaller packets with spices, sugar, salt, and tea, even a tin of cooking oil. She packed everything in the storage containers and pots to keep them from rattling."

"She always pays more attention to detail than anyone I know," Paul said. "In the field you'll need all of those things. You'll also need more oil, coffee, sugar and spices. I always ran out of those first."

"I also bought some new items like a water canteen, a *Quinquet* lantern with a bullseye lens, and a leather *nécessaire* kit with razors, brushes, a tortoise comb and soaps. I have father's engineering and surveying instruments in one of the portfolio bags. In the other shoulder bag are the items I will need on a day-to-day basis. I attached father's old hatchet to one of the messenger bags. "

"Be prepared to carry everything you need on your back for weeks at a time. When you get to Egypt, you need to buy a donkey and cart and pay one of the privates to cook and watch your equipment. Are you keeping DeVillars saddlebags?"

"Yes. When I get a horse, I can carry more equipment. My father told me to travel as light as possible. Therefore, I packed only my spare dress uniform and a single extra set of underclothing; my spare stockings are hot-weather cotton. My mother wanted me to carry another bag with several more changes of clothes. But, I am carrying too much equipment already. I must cut back," he then changed the subject. "My father and his aide were in Charlottesville, Virginia when I was born in '78. Were you there?"

"Of course, General Washington had given your father leave during the winter encampment. I remember going in to see you about an hour after you were born. You were all red and wrinkled. You were crying like the devil was sticking you with a pin."

"Three years later, right after the battle of Yorktown, your father and Jean were sent on a special mission to India to support Hyder Ali in Mysore. You father left me to help your mother. I returned to France with the family in '84. As a new professor at the Military School, your father could keep only Jean as his aide. He got me assigned to the artillery school at Auxonne. I was one of the first sergeants to graduate from the school."

"For the past day, I kept thinking I knew you from somewhere, I can remember some things about you from the trip from Virginia to

France," Charles told him. "I don't recollect much of you in Virginia."

"That's because I wasn't around you much. I spent most of my time in the field. I do remember that you didn't get seasick and you climbed the masts constantly, even though you weren't even six. I hate heights but your mother made me climb up and bring you down."

Somewhat disconcerted by Paul's image of him climbing in the rigging like a little monkey, Charles changed the subject. "I am pleased with the performance of my weapons. Under pressure, I reloaded my rifled carabine in less than a half-minute. It took over a minute to load both pistols, but that was for four barrels and four flash pans."

"Tell me about your various firearms," Paul said.

"Father gave me all of them. In addition to the short cavalry rifle, a model *1793 Carabine de Versailles*, I'm carrying two Le Page double barrel pistols in belt holsters. When I first started shooting father's carabine, it took me forever to reload. I was using a wooden mallet to hammer the standard French army over-sized *boulette* into the muzzle for each shot. Father suggested that I follow Daniel Morgan's Virginia riflemen and try a lead ball cast smaller than the bore diameter, and wrapped with a lubricated patch. A .52 caliber bullet and a cloth patch coated with lard are devastatingly accurate in the .54 caliber rifle. I can fire about 30 of the patched rounds before I have to worry about fouling. My two Le Page's and the new Manton pistols use the same size patched bullet."

Swinging the officer's cartouche box attached to the back of his bandolier strap into view, Charles lifted the flap and said, "This hussar *giberne* has twenty holes, in which I carry ten paper rifle cartridges and twenty doubled pistol rounds. Since my pistols' powder charge is half the carabine's, I fit two in each hole. I carry a second larger infantry cartouche box in my portfolio bag for additional shots. Attached to one of my shoulder bags I carry a small flask of superfine powder, and in it are a dozen knapped flints, a folding pocketknife, steel, tools and tinder. I strap father's old hatchet to the same bag. In my main rectangular kit bag are a large powder flask, a small pot for melting lead, a can of oil and my lead ball mold."

"Why are you carrying the hatchet?" Paul asked. "Wait a minute, is it the Mohawk tomahawk your father carried during the French and Indian war and again in the American Revolution."

"I guess." Charles said. "It has a straight handle with a narrow blade on one side and a hammer poll on the other. I brought it along to chop wood when I need to start a campfire."

"It's designed to kill men," Paul said bluntly. "It is one of the Indians best hand-to-hand or throwing weapons. Have you practiced throwing your hawk?"

"No, I didn't think I needed more weapons," Charles replied. "In Egypt, I plan to have one rifle and six pistol shots before reloading. Charles paused, and then added, "I am also carrying my father's sabre; I doubt if you had a chance to inspect it. In 1783, the Dutch Governor of Java sent my father and Jean to Japan to avoid arrest by the English East India Company authorities. With the end of the Fourth Anglo-Dutch war he was expecting them to arrive in Batavia any day."

"Why did the English want to arrest Jean and your father?"

"It had something to do with their raid on the John Company castle in Bombay during '82. For almost a year, they trained Japanese scholars in calculus, longitude and latitude, while learning the Japanese style of martial arts. The Emperor of Japan presented him a three-blade sword set that included a long war sword, a tachi. The translator told him that Masamune, a famous 14th century sword-smith made it. Back in France the artisan Boutet remounted the blade as a sabre with a serpentine shaped hand guard, a striking cobra cross guard and a short extended pommel for balance and for him to use two-handed. It's now the same length as a regular light cavalry sabre, but the weight is better concentrated. The curve of the blade is less severe than a Hungarian sabre making it a more effective thrusting blade. Because of its polished finish and fine edge, it will cut through almost anything. I sharpen it every day on a set of water stones—very carefully!"

THIRTEEN

April 26ᵗʰ

BREAKFAST IN AUXERRE

Through the night, the coach continued with its monotonous motion. Paul went back to sleep. After sleeping through the third stop and more than an hour and a half beyond, they pulled up to the fourth stage stop for a change of horses and drivers. Charles woke Paul; it was like poking a bear out of hibernation.

During the stop, he got out the package his mother had given him the morning before. His mother had packed his folding campaign utensils in the field kitchen wrapped in a cleaning cloth; unfortunately it was in his bag in the back. Using his cavalry sketch board to cut, he sliced the brioche into four pieces and then halved them with his skean-achlais. He then cut up the chicken and spread some of the pate and cheese on the bread. He offered Paul his choice of food. Paul gobbled down three of the four thick quarters of bread loaded with goodies as he was eating his one slice. He offered the wine skin to Paul after taking a drink. Paul said, "No, I'll have some more of this wonderful Brandywine." He then swallowed about a half pint of pure brandy. It was quite likely that he was indeed, as the expression goes, well on his way to feeling no pain. He cleaned his fighting dagger as the coach pulled out of the courtyard with two drivers and a six-horse team, for the long uphill grade. They passed the Paris-bound coach coming downhill. While Paul took up the watch, Charles nestled into his caped cloak, wedged himself into the corner of the conductor's box, and drifted off to sleep.

Although interrupted by the horse team changes every few hours, he managed to sleep for almost six hours before the rising sun started flickering into his eyes through the trees lining the road. He sat up straight as the coach pulled into the town of Auxerre for a breakfast stop. From the moment he woke up, he had been considering ways to collect more information about Major Menou.

He began discussing his options with Paul for the next quarter hour, as they maneuvered through the narrow streets. Paul also had misgivings about Major Menou and his actions during the coach holdup. Paul agreed the highwaymen seemed to be shooting to kill both of them without warning. He agreed to help him keep Major Menou under surveillance at the various stops, especially in Lyon.

"Paul, we're not getting any information while we sit here up front," Charles said. "We need to listen in on any talk in the coach."

"I can ride in the back until the next driver change by claiming to need for rest because of my wounds." Paul told him.

"That is a great idea. I can ask Horace Say to ride up front with me. He and I can discuss my suspicions. I can ask him what they've been talking about in the coach."

"Do you trust Horace Say?" Paul asked.

"We were best friends together at school. I know him better than I know my brothers. He collected a good bit of booty during the campaigns in Italy and has no need for extra money. He and his wife have no royalist sympathies."

He then asked Paul, "What's your impression of Commander Duval? Can he be trusted? I could talk to him and ask his advice.

Do you think it would be a good idea? Could he get additional information about Major Menou?"

"I don't know him but he probably has many important contacts," Paul said thoughtfully. "Duval strikes me as an experienced and capable officer. I can see how he could get information from Major Menou about the gold shipments. It can't hurt; maybe he can get some answers."

As the horse team pulled up to the hostler and the coach rocked to a stop, he and Paul climbed down. They both stretched and Charles adjusted his sabre.

"Why don't you talk to Commander Duval while I talk to Horace and Lieutenant Faurie," Charles suggested. "You and Raoul go and eat first. I'll eat when you come out."

The Jonchere family collected their baggage with the help of a local porter. Most of the passengers went around the back of the building. They were visiting the privy and washing up after the overnight journey. Charles peeked into the main room and saw there were fireplaces at each end of the room. There were a half dozen small tables seating from four to six. The food was set out on a trestle against the wall.

Walking back to the coach, he asked the innkeeper, "Have many riders came through over the past twelve hours."

"Only the postal messenger," the man told him.

Paul came around the corner of the building with Commander Duval. They walked up to him and Paul said, "Lieutenant, I've talked to Commander Duval and he has some questions for you."

"Yes sir, what do you want to know?"

Commander Duval asked, "I understand you have suspicions about Major Menou. On what information do you base this belief?"

Charles explained his reasoning, "I observed Major Menou meeting with the highwaymen in the stables at Melun. Later, I heard

Major Menou shouting out for everyone to surrender when the bandits approached. Finally, I heard him shout to give up the gold. Why did he shout about giving up the gold? He told me earlier he was in charge of the gold shipments."

Duval stared at Charles, and then said, "Major Menou told me that General Menou asked him to take over the responsibility for collecting the gold and shipping it onward to Toulon. Major Menou took over as the staff officer responsible for all correspondence and scheduling the gold shipments."

"As the officer in command, he outranks you, even though you may have been appointed as the officer in charge of this first shipment. You should report to him and follow his orders. He is on his way to Toulon with the first southbound shipment to ensure they are ready to receive more cargo in Toulon. Finally, based on the description of his work as an aide to General Menou in the Vendée, I believe he is a staunch anti-royalist."

After Commander Duval left to eat breakfast, Charles asked Paul, "Wasn't General Menou charged with treason for his failures in the Vendée, and when the charges were dismissed, wasn't there suspicion he had paid off the judges?"

"I was in the Vendée," Paul replied. "One of the reasons I retired was my disgust with General Menou. I thought he was a Royalist and a British agent. Before the revolution, all the members of his family were aristocrats. At the time, he was the Baron de Boussay. If he isn't an aristocrat, he is an incompetent idiot." After expressing his opinion, Paul also went in to breakfast.

A few minutes later, Paul came out with two plates of food and said, "You should go and get breakfast. You can sit with Captain Say and his wife. Commander Duval is sitting with Major Menou. I don't think we should ask him to help us watch Menou, in fact, I think we should keep an eye on both of them." He then handed a full plate up to Raoul. Charles suddenly remembered what had been bothering him all night. He explained to Paul how something had been nagging at the back of his mind, "I saw Commander Duval, whispering to Major Menou when I first entered the common room of the terminus in Paris. They were standing by the fireplace, away from the other passengers. When they saw me looking, they broke apart and moved to their seats at the common table. I'll bet that Menou was telling Duval about my presence." Charles left to get his breakfast.

He filled his plate with the scraps of food left on the side table and asked Horace and Alphonsine if he could join them. Lieutenant Faurie was also sitting at the table. Charles pulled the fourth chair out and sat down.

"Last night I was thinking of the supplies I still should buy for the expedition. Do you know of any shops in Lyon that sell flour, sugar, green coffee beans, and dried spices?" he asked Alphonsine. "Conductor Forgeron suggested that I buy more of those items." Then he added, "I need to get at least one set of white silk dress stockings, shoes, breeches and a waistcoat. I also want to order the saddlecloth Horace mentioned."

Alphonsine stared at Charles with astonishment since he had hardly spoken to her so far. "Lyon is the center of French silk manufacturing. Horace will know where you can get uniforms. I do know of a few shops, but our family cook will know where to get the cooking supplies. Why do you want flour and sugar?"

"I have a sourdough sponge for making fresh yeast in my cook kit," Charles hesitantly replied. "I need to add water and flour to re-proof it every time I remove some yeast to make bread. I can also use the sugar to occasionally make cinnamon rolls for dinner guests."

Alphonsine laughed and said, "So you are a famous chef. What else do you do?"

"I love to sketch and paint in watercolors." He immediately replied

"Let me see your sketch book." He paused for a moment.

"I have too many unfinished drawings. I will show it to you when we get to Lyon," he said, smiling shyly at her. "I love to try and play my violin, but I'm not very good. I wish I had brought it with me, but it's still in Paris. Maybe after I have a batman to take care of my baggage, I can bring it into the field to play at night. My mother made me practice while I lived at home. For the last six months at Châlons, I played a few times a week with my two roommates." He smiled again at Alphonsine and blushed.

Alphonsine laughed and asked, "Can you play Beethoven's *Piano Trio Number 3, Opus One?*"

"I tried to play it three-weeks ago after attending a performance in Paris. My mother even bought me a copy of the score and another for my 16-year old sister. I'm not very good, even though it's now one of my favorite pieces."

"My best friend and I have been practicing the Trio for months," Alphonsine told him. "Our violinist is her younger brother. He is leaving for the University of Bologna after the summer. Maybe during the stop in Lyon you could come for dinner and we could play it for you."

"Yes. That sounds wonderful."

Turning to Horace, Charles said, "Conductor Forgeron needs more rest. He's drinking too much for the pain and he needs to sleep. Could you change places with him and ride beside me until the next driver change? After that you could trade places with Lieutenant Faurie"

"Of course I'll sit with you, as long as it is all right with Alphonsine." After securing her approval, he and his companions at

106

the table rose and began to move outside to get on the coach with the rest of the passengers.

FOURTEEN

April 26ᵗʰ

MACDONALD TOWN HOUSE, AVENUE DE SAXE, PARIS

Gendarme Lieutenant Tristan DuMayne stood in front of the MacDonald home; it was five o'clock in the afternoon of Thursday, the 26ᵗʰ and he was finishing his pipeful of tobacco. No one in the MacDonald household smoked and he didn't want to offend anyone. Earlier that afternoon he had arrived on the Lyon to Paris mail coach at the terminus on the north side of the Seine. He had collected his baggage and walked south, crossing the Pont Neuf to the Latin Quarter on the left bank.

He stopped at his parent's apartment on the top floor of a five-story building in the crowded Montagne district. His father was a magistrate for the people in the district. After greeting his parents, he left his extra baggage and continued on to initiate his new investigation.

Finishing his pipe, he went up the main steps and knocked on the red door. A gruff and grizzled man of about sixty-five opened the door and asked whom he wanted to see. He announced, "I am Lieutenant de Gendarmes DuMayne. I need to see General Mac-Donald with a letter from Lieutenant Charles MacDonald."

Tristan was dressed in his officer's uniform of a scarlet-faced blue coatee, and chamois-colored waistcoat and breeches. He was wearing his sabre. His bicorne was worn *en bataille*, cross-wise. He had a large heavy bag with a long rapier style épée strapped to the top handle.

"Wait here," the man at the door said. "I'll ask if the General can meet with you."

A moment later, the general appeared. He was a tall-distinguished looking man in his late sixties, wearing a lounging coat. Tristan remembered him from his last visit.

General MacDonald said, "Come in to the reception room." Then DuMayne saw the huge tan and black guard dog. The dog began to growl and turned toward him as he started to follow General MacDonald. He was not comfortable with dogs, and this one sensed his fear.

General MacDonald said, "No, Scout," without turning his head. Entering the reception room, he took a seat on the sofa facing the fireplace. He didn't feel with his hands, he just stuck one out at the last minute and touched the sofa as he maneuvered around to a seat. Tristan followed into a twenty by twenty-four foot parlor with a seating arrangement fronting the fireplace. At the inside corner there were a harpsichord, cases for a violin and cello and a card table and chairs. Tristan sat in a chair facing the general, and the dog, settling at his feet.

"Scout will never bother a guest," said General MacDonald. "He is here to guide me and protect the family. He looks quite fierce because he is descended from Roman Legion guard dogs. He's from Rottweil, just over the German border. My doctor in Metz arranged for me to get a puppy from a litter born to dogs who guided blind men in Germany."

Tristan relaxed, slightly, and said, "The Lyon mail coach was attacked in the Forest of Fontainebleau, and a driver was killed. Lieutenant MacDonald killed four of the seven highwaymen. Conductor Forgeron, a passenger and the mail-guard killed the other three." He placed his packages on the low table in front of the couch. He opened the first package and said, "I have a letter and a report for you from Charles, the highwaymen's papers, some of their belongings and equipment. I also have bags with 900 gold British guineas. After you hear the information I've brought, we need to discuss what Charles and I think should be done."

"Conductor Forgeron, what is his full name and position?" General MacDonald asked.

Glancing down for the correct name Tristan said, "Conductor Paul Forgeron is an ex-sergeant major who is trusted by General Bonaparte. He is about forty-five years of age and has been a conductor for the Messageries Nationales since '94."

"He served under me during the war in America." General MacDonald told DuMayne, "I trust him. I'm glad he's travelling with Charles."

An attractive lady with wavy blond hair came in and asked, "Dear, what's happened?"

After introducing his wife to Lieutenant DuMayne, General MacDonald reassured her, "Charles is safe and unwounded. He is travelling with Paul Forgeron as the conductor of the diligence. I'll let you read his letter later. We need this meeting to be private, so please keep the children out."

After the general finished listening to DuMayne's recitation of the report and letter from Charles, he insisted on getting a full account of what Tristan's investigation had turned up. DuMayne was concluding his report when Jean Dulcos entered the reception room.

"Jean, it's too late to send Mahamoud to Fontainebleau. Take care of that first thing in the morning."

"Right now, go and hitch up the horses to the Calash. We are going to General Bonaparte's house as soon as I change. Lieutenant DuMayne, you wait here."

Before carrying out the general's order, Dulcos walked into the hall and opened a closet beside the front door. He removed a hat and cloak, and then slipped a catch in the closet wall exposing a concealed gun rack with two pistols and a blunderbuss. As he went downstairs carrying the blunderbuss, he slipped the two pistols into pockets of the cloak.

A quarter-hour later, General MacDonald came back down, helped by his wife and wearing the uniform of a general. He told Tristan, "Bring everything but the gold. Put the bags in the drawer over there. I need you to be my eyes—and I want those eyes to be sharp and miss nothing." Just then, Tristan noticed the general lift his head and listen. He suddenly heard the wheels of the carriage crunching gravel alongside the house and pull into the paved front courtyard.

After a three quarter hour carriage ride across the Seine and to the northeast, they arrived at Bonaparte's house on the Rue de la Victoire. The carriage stopped at the outer gate. As Jean hopped down and controlled the horse, DuMayne helped General MacDonald get out and they walked down a long and narrow gravel drive framed by linden trees. DuMayne held the general's arm and guided him. When they arrived at the main entrance, he knocked on the double-oak doors. When a footman opened it, MacDonald asked to see General Bonaparte. Looking beyond the footman's shoulder, DuMayne could see that a dinner party was nearing an end in the oval dining room on the left and the guests were moving across the foyer to the drawing room.

Bonaparte came to the door and was surprised to see General MacDonald. "There's been an attempt to rob the gold coach to Lyon." MacDonald informed him. "We need to talk in private about information this officer has brought from Fontainebleau."

Bonaparte turned and said, "Follow me." He crossed the foyer, up a staircase and led them into his study, closing the door after they entered.

The study had a simple writing table as a desk. Attractive green wallpaper and matching green curtains gave the room a tranquil feeling. The leather upholstery on the sofas and chairs complemented the green color scheme. Maps of Egypt and Malta were pinned to most of the open spaces on the walls. The bookcases on either side of the fireplace were made of light maple. Books, maps and papers covered almost every available space. DuMayne carefully noted everything in the room. He wanted to describe the scene to General MacDonald after they left.

After DuMayne helped him to a sofa, General MacDonald said, "This is Gendarme Lieutenant DuMayne. He has brought reports and information about the attack. He is also acquainted with the facts here in Paris leading to the attempted holdup. My son Charles wrote me I should place trust in the lieutenant; together, they have worked out plans to uncover this conspiracy."

Bonaparte said, "Tell me what happened."

Tristan proceeded to describe the coach and passengers and the actions that took place in the Forest of Fontainebleau. Bonaparte interrupted him frequently and asked a great many questions. At the conclusion of his description of the action, DuMayne said, "After shooting three bandits, Lieutenant MacDonald jumped on the leader and cut off his head with his sabre during the ensuing swordfight. It was the infamous royalist swordsman, Colonel Honore DeVillars.”

General MacDonald interrupted, “Colonel DeVillars’ son, Hector was Charles’ best friend, until he was guillotined. Charles recognized the colonel only after the swordfight.

“The conductor, the mail-guard and an officer in the coach shot three of the seven highwaymen. Six of them were wearing steel armor and the seventh had taken the place and uniform of a postil-lion.” With that bit of information, Tristan concluded his report on the hold-up.

General Bonaparte smiled and said, “I knew Charles was a talent-ed fencer. However, I didn’t know how lucky a fighter he is. Any one of those brigands could have killed him. I guess that I’d rather have a lucky officer working for me than an unlucky one.”

Bonaparte examined the report, papers, coded messages and fi-nally the drawings of the seven dead highwaymen. He immediately recognized DeVillars when he saw the sketches and said, “I’ve seen him a number of times. I think he’s occasionally been following me the last few months. I also think I have seen one or two of the others. My men tell me that someone follows me almost every day.”

DuMayne then gave an account of what he had been trying to discover about bribery of high officials in the Republic and corrupt members of the Executive Directory.

“I was the investigating officer for the robbery of the diligence from Amsterdam to Paris and the murder of its seven escorts. I was also reviewing the two other attempted gold robberies.”

“I’ve been looking for the officer-in-charge of the investigation for the last month,” Bonaparte told him. “Tell me about your promotion to lieutenant. Who is your mentor?”

DuMayne mentioned his father, the respected magistrate, and described his education at the Sorbonne and the University of Paris.

"As a student I became an idealist and supporter of the *Rights of Man* and equal citizenship. In 1793, I defended my final théses before the faculty. Later that year, the National Convention suppressed the Faculty of Law. One of my father's best friends, the director François Neufchâteau, helped me to get a position with the Gendarmerie Nationale since I couldn't work as an advocate. I was promoted to lieutenant within the year by Interior Minister DJ Garat, because of my performance." He then mentioned that when Citizen Neufchâteau took over the ministry, he asked his friend's son to investigate all the politicians.

"I was warned to keep my investigation secret," DuMayne explained. "My team questioned everyone in the general area. We had two descriptions of more than a dozen men dressed in dark clothes and riding dark horses. One description mentioned that the heavily armed riders were wearing cuirasses and both described the leader's curious rapier hilt."

He showed Bonaparte the rapier taken from DeVillars; "We also had reports of a heavy transport wagon escorted by eight dark riders on the route national from the north, turning west just before the Paris walls. One of my informers told me about some strangers living at an abandoned church a few leagues outside the north tax wall. My men and I raided the property and arrested three men. When we moved from ordinary to extraordinary questioning there at the church, one admitted that they were royalist-émigrés who had been heavy cavalrymen in Condé's army. I brought them in to the *Bureau Central* for further questioning. That evening, I gave the information directly to the Minister of Police, Nicolas Dondeau. I also let him know that two members of the Executive Directory were spreading new British *spade* guineas around town. Someone transferred me to Fontainebleau the next morning. The men Charles MacDonald killed outside Fontainebleau must have been the robbers of the Amsterdam mail coach in March. Two of the dead men were among the three I arrested north of Paris." He then continued to explain how he and Charles MacDonald had discussed setting up a special group led by General MacDonald to root out the conspiracy.

General Bonaparte had been pacing back and forth during this recital. He stopped directly in front of DuMayne. "I am promoting you to Captain of Gendarmes and assigning you to work directly for General MacDonald. I will notify Colonel Ackler, the Commander of the Gendarmerie for the 17th Military Division that I am reassigning you from Fontainebleau and that you will be under my direct control. I want a copy of your report about the two directors and the mail coach robbery."

Turning to General MacDonald he said, "You are recalled to active duty as a Major General. I appoint you to head this new *Section d'Investigation Spécial d'Gendarmerie Nationale*. You will keep your efforts secret. The British are bribing groups of politicians in the French government to oppose my efforts. We have to make sure that they do not find out about our investigation. I trust François Letourneau, the current interior minister. He is leaving office in June and I will get him replaced by my friend and your supporter François Neufchâteau. There is no easy way for me to fight a nationwide conspiracy of royalist and British agents. There are half-dozen different agencies, each with its own agenda. Of course, all twenty-eight Gendarmerie divisions operate in the countryside, outside most cities and report jointly to the interior and war ministers. There are a few company-sized special units still attached to the National Gendarmerie and I propose that the new *SIS* will be another one. You will report directly to me. You will have full investigative authority throughout France, including Paris. I also control the Ile-de-France division, the 17th that is responsible for all of the province and its eleven sub-provinces except Paris. The new Minister of General Police, the

National Guard and the Municipal Guard of Paris also report to the interior minister, however they maintain their independence. Several units are notorious for their royalist connections." Bonaparte continued pacing back and forth while he thought.

"You should work out of your home. I will assign several additional officers to work for you. They'll be there tomorrow and bring a letter of authorization for the new SIS section and enough money to fund the operation. The officers will bring any additional information I have about the British Secret Service."

"I'll become their new target," MacDonald said. "As soon as they identify my house, they'll attack. I have a peculiar and personal history with the British that dates to my time in India. They will want to search my house. During our meeting a few days ago, you mentioned assassination attempts. Have they tried to attack you at home?"

General Bonaparte paused, looked at the general and slowly answered, "A woman was caught trying to poison my food. During the day, I have my Guides to protect me. There have been several attempts to shoot me while I was out riding."

"They will attack your house if you don't have lookouts throughout the night," MacDonald warned him. "Assign a platoon of guides to 24-hour *picquet* duty. When they find out their robbery failed, they will try and kill you again."

"I will send the encoded letters directly to Eliza Rossignol, the granddaughter of Antoine-Bonaventure Rossignol," Bonaparte said. "She is a *nightingale* like her grandfather, father, mother, and sister, a codebreaker for the *Cabinet Noir*. She may be able to help us. I need to get the current Minister of Police fired. The only national police I trust is the small subsection called the *Sûreté* under Jacques Henry. One of your new men is a detective from his section. I don't trust anyone from the rest of that ministry or from the National Guard, which the old Paris commune controls. You must be discrete since you will be investigating the Executive Directory."

"Finally, I think I must also promote Charles MacDonald to Captain of Ingénieurs-Geographes. I will send a message to Colonel Bessières, chief of the guides and to General Caffarelli, Chief of Engineers to notify them. I need young officers who are quick thinking, quick shooting and quick acting. Also, they must be lucky."

After the meeting with Bonaparte, as General MacDonald and now Captain DuMayne were getting into the carriage, MacDonald said to the new captain, "I like the new name for our unit, but it tells the enemy who we are; we will call ourselves the *SIS*. Congratulations on your promotion. Can I drop you off at your parent's apartment? I do not think you should stay at the Gendarmerie barracks in the caserne. Tomorrow I will have Jean get an extra horse and several outfits of clothing for your work. You can keep the horse at my house. I think you will occasionally need to disguise yourself as a shopkeeper, a student, a common worker, and maybe a farmer. In his letter, Charles said you could pass for any man. Is he right?"

"I do have a rather average appearance," DuMayne said. "I will need to change from uniform to civilian clothes while questioning suspects, and following or observing dubious activities. I have the clothing at home of a clerk or young lawyer."

He leaned forward, gave Jean the address of his parent's apartment, and then said, "Tomorrow I need to investigate General Bonaparte's comment about recognizing DeVillars as one of the men following him. I need to discover who they are and where they live. I also need to ask around and find out where the men from Fontainebleau were staying, where DeVillars kept his horse, a distinctive black Andalusian stallion, and if he was practicing with his épée at any of the salle-de-arms in Paris. General, what time should I come to your house tomorrow morning?"

"Come for breakfast at seven o'clock."

FIFTEEN

April 27ᵗʰ

APPROACHING LYON, FRANCE

At eight o'clock Friday morning, the mail coach left the stage stop at Villefranche on the Saone River. They had been traveling all night down the Saone Valley. It had rained heavily, as a storm front passed through. The innkeeper at Villefranche had offered everyone hot toasted and buttered bread to tide them over until the next long stop in Lyon. The second largest city in France was still two hours away.

Riding in the conductor's box, Charles and Paul were both wearing their caped cloaks. Clods of mud from the hooves of the team ahead intermittingly pelted both men. Charles was discussing how they would handle the security of the gold shipment when they arrived in Lyon, when Paul suggested, "After we unload our passengers we can have the driver take us to the Divisional Gendarmerie Headquarters. You can show your letter from Bonaparte and request they keep the gold in their secure arms room until tomorrow morning. Have them deliver the gold to the Lyon terminus before the coach leaves in the morning."

As rainwater dripped from his hat brim, Paul admitted, "I miss the military life. I've been a coach conductor between Paris and Lyon for the last three years. Occasionally I meet attractive women, but I must go to work the next day. Mostly I drink too much after each trip and can barely get myself ready for work. If I could get my old rank back, I'd rejoin the colors and go with you." He turned away, embarrassed by his frank disclosure, took out his pipe, and lit it.

"At least it won't be raining there," Charles said. "I'll see what I can do when we get to Toulon. Right now we need to discuss how we're going to keep an eye on our suspects while we're in Lyon." He didn't want to discuss the war plans for Egypt even though the conductor probably knew where the gold was going. The rear channel of his bicorne was dripping water down his back. He rearranged it to drip on the shoulders of his cloak. His face was still getting wet.

"You know Alphonsine Say is going to arrange a dinner and a music recital for me tonight. I'm so tired I'll sleep all night after the entertainment. I don't think I'll be able to take one of the watches tonight."

"Let's get Lieutenant Faurie as well as Raoul to watch and let us know if either Commander Duval or Major Menou meets with anyone or goes out while we're unloading the gold," Paul said. "You take too much on your shoulders. They can take turns tonight watching from the public room. While we're at the Gendarmerie caserne, we can ask them to assign some gendarmes to watch the outside entrance to the inn today and tonight."

"That's a good plan. I want to take the time to buy some clothes and supplies while I'm in Lyon. I definitely need a rain cover for my hat and overalls to protect my breeches and boots."

Later that morning, the rain stopped and the fresh north wind started drying out the road. The coach entered the built-up area on the western approach to Lyon. They passed through Old Lyon, the ancient Roman town full of ruins on the slope of Fourviere Hill.

There were several aqueducts, a huge amphitheater in the distance, and several ancient graveyards. The Messageries Nationales Terminus in Lyon was on the Place Bellecour, which was located on the peninsula between the Saone and the Rhone Rivers.

The coach pulled up to the yard of the inn and a hostler held the lead horses. Everyone dismounted as Paul talked to the lieutenant and Raoul. Meanwhile Charles told Horace and Alphonsine that he would be back after depositing the gold.

"I'll return in an hour to take you to my tack shop for the saddle cover," Horace said. "Then I'll take you to my tailor's. I'll ask about the other shops."

"I will arrange our dinner party and recital and send the information with Horace," Alphonsine told Charles. "Don't forget, I want to see your drawings."

Charles entered the inn and paid for a room overlooking the square. Returning to the coach, he and Paul remounted and the driver pulled out and headed south to the Gendarmerie.

Pulling through the gates of the old fortress, the driver stopped in an area where the coach could turn around. The driver pointed to the headquarters building. Charles and Paul dismounted, walked into the orderly office, and told the gendarme on duty that they wanted to see the commander.

"Colonel Saint Just is in his office, may I tell him who is calling?"

After giving their names, they had to wait for a quarter hour. Finally, they entered the office of Colonel Saint Just. They both saluted and handed him their papers. Saint Just read the letter from General Bonaparte, with Paul Barras' countersignature and asked, "How can I help you, lieutenant?"

"The coach outside is carrying gold worth over 600,000 francs. Royalist highwaymen tried to rob the coach in the Forest of Fontainebleau. We would like you to secure the gold overnight and deliver it tomorrow morning to the terminus before the Avignon Coach. We also suspect two of our passengers may be British agents. We would like you to assign pairs of gendarmes in civilian clothing to watch and follow them until we leave. We don't know for sure, if the two men are agents. However, they are our only potential suspects on the coach. One is Naval Commander Renee Duval and the other is Major of Infantry Pierre Menou."

Colonel Saint Just called for his Adjudant-Chef and ordered a work party to unload the gold and store it in the arms room. As Charles, Paul and the colonel walked outside to supervise the unloading and two of the gendarmes were about to pick up the first of the boxes, Charles told them to wait while he checked the contents. Paul had all of the keys hidden in a pocket sewn into his boot. Charles and Paul opened each box and counted the contents, randomly inspecting the coins inside their paper tube wrapping. When the colonel realized what was happening, he ordered his sergeant major to count the coins in each box while he kept a running total on a scrap of paper.

Charles mentally added the totals in a few seconds. Each tube was marked VoC in ink and contained 50 coins. Most of the shiny gold British guineas were dated 1797 and struck with a "spade" shaped shield on the back. There were three levels of 15 rows in each box. That made 2,250 guineas in each of 10 boxes, or 22,500 total coins. Since a British guinea was worth about 27 francs, the strongboxes held 607,500 francs worth of gold.

Colonel Saint Just slowly worked out his mathematical calculations with a dull pencil. He then laboriously wrote out a receipt for his quantities and gave it to Charles. He and Paul then walked back to the inn, since the coach had already returned. When they got there, they picked up their baggage and went up to their rooms. Charles paused and asked the innkeeper to send up a pitcher of hot water.

Paul was staying in the regular conductor's room he used each trip. When Charles reached his own room, he took off his field uniform after removing his boots. He had been wearing these clothes for the past two days. His field jacket, waistcoat and breeches were dusty from travel, but the smell wasn't too bad. His greatcoat was filthy from the clumps of mud. Then, as he opened his portmanteaux, he realized why his mother had insisted that he carry a stiff bristle brush in addition to his hairbrush, shaving and toothbrushes in his *nécessaire* kit. He brushed the dirt and dust off his greatcoat and duty uniform. In Fontainebleau, he had tried to remove most of the blood spots using cold water. He took a damp cloth from the washstand, rubbed more blood spots, and polished the buttons. He spread everything out on the bed, and rubbed the specks of blood off the buckles, plates and the black leather straps. He had not been wearing his messenger bags, and his cartouche case had been at his back, so they were clean. That done, he dusted off his almost new riding boots.

Then he inspected his newly damaged field bicorne. There was a ragged hole near the tri-color rosette and his only aurore plume was now much shorter. He maneuvered the rosette and black straps to cover the hole. He dusted it and placed it on the pillow.

There was a knock at the door; his hot water had arrived. Withdrawing his sabre, he cleaned the blade with a warm damp cloth. He removed his water stones and his brass loupe, a ten-power magnifying glass, and inspected the cutting edge. He honed several spots that appeared to need sharpening. He checked each firearm and rubbed them with an oiled cloth.

Unpacking his rectangular kit bag and taking out his dress habit with the orange velvet lining, he brushed out the wrinkles. He removed his gold trimmed folding dress chapeau from its tin box for tonight. He would ask about new orange plumes. Removing his under-clothes, he took out his toilet kit and brushed his teeth. He then filled the basin with hot water to shave everything but the mustache he was trying to coax into life. He used some more water to scrub his crotch, legs, chest and armpits—the closest thing to a bath he could take on a trip. At home, he showered outside under the overflow pipe from the attic cistern. He used the remaining water to wash his dirty set of underclothes and hung them out to dry; he would need them tomorrow, since he had only one spare set.

He put on that set of clean underclothes and redressed in his damp field uniform. The cotton stockings wouldn't stay up. He had to tie two cords around their tops to stop them from sagging inside his boots. If he could have afforded a complete dress uniform back in Paris, he would have purchased a white silk pair of breeches and waistcoat, white gloves, silk stockings and dress shoes. However, during his time at home, he didn't have the money for them; or enough to buy horse tack, a riding coat, extra boots, or extra feathers. I am now rich, he thought, so I can buy a silk set here in Lyon to wear to the party tonight.

SIXTEEN

April 27th

SHOPPING IN LYON, FRANCE

A sudden knock at the door, jerked him from his thoughts. Answering, Horace was standing there with a grin. "Enough daydreaming, life awaits!" After dressing quickly, he accompanied his friend downstairs where they ate some sausages, roast pork and drank a glass of a local red wine, called Beaujolais. When they finished they walked to the main shopping district where Horace led him into a saddler's tack shop. Charles examined several saddlecloths and chose the recommended blue one with two gold stripes and custom made IG emblems. He asked about delivery and the shopkeeper said it would take three days. Horace promised him he would bring them with him when he came to Toulon next week.

Continuing to the next shop, he purchased a pair of dress shoes with gilt-gold buckles. He now had two pairs of riding boots, infantry hobnail boots and the new dress shoes. They left and went down the street to Horace's tailor. While there Charles bought a pair white silk breeches and a white silk waistcoat with matching silk stockings and underclothes. The tailor outfitted him with another set of under-drawers, a linen shirt and two wool stockings; the cotton pair was useless. When Charles asked about riding overalls the shopkeeper brought out two examples and pointed out, "Along with the heavy winter ones; there are two different regular styles. With the overall style, there's no need to wear a waistcoat since the extended bib and suspenders replace it. Most officers wear it with the longer waisted field surtout."

Charles noticed that the pocket flaps covered false pockets so he asked, "Can you add real pockets for my watch and prismatic pocket compass? Suddenly he remembered Paul talking about his utensils, so he asked for a top center pocket for the leather case with his folding utensils."

Told that he could have a set of overalls with real pockets in three days, Charles told the shopkeeper to go ahead with a tan color, natural leather facings and brass buttons and then asked Horace, "Will you also pick them up and bring them to Toulon? Also, I need an aurore colored plume." The shopkeeper asked a clerk to bring out one.

Charles asked about kerchiefs and large scarves. Turning to Horace, he explained, "My father told me the locals in Egypt wear fine silk headscarves to protect their nose and mouth from insects and the enormous sand and dust storms that arise with little warning."

The shopkeeper brought out several stacks of silk scarves. Charles picked out two large dark blue headscarves, several heavier ones of black velvet and two thinner white gauzy ones. He then selected half-dozen large headscarves in various bright colors. Each scarf was about six-feet by six-feet square. Charles gave one large blue scarf to Horace and said, "This is a token of thanks for your kindness. As for the rest, I'm going to send the six bright ones back to my mother to set aside for gifts this Christmas. When I get the time, I will reline my greatcoat with the black velvet scarves."

Their final stop was a narrow half-timbered shop full of wonderful and evocative odors, where Charles bought a sack full of Ethiopian coffee beans, preserved food and spices. Walking back to his room at the inn, he pulled his watch out by its fob and, saw it was near three o'clock.

"Are we still having dinner and music?" he asked Horace

Horace smiled and said, "'s best friend is a beautiful young girl. You will thoroughly enjoy this evening."

Horace gave Charles directions to his home and told him to be there at four o'clock if he wanted to practice with one of her brother's violins. Dinner would begin at five.

When Horace left, Charles opened his sketchbook and filled in the lines of the sketches he had started of Alphonsine and Horace sitting at a table outside the inn at Fontainebleau.

When he finished he dressed in his new silk underclothes, stockings, breeches, dress shoes, and silk waistcoat. Before putting on his dress tailcoat, he attached the epaulettes and hung his dress *épée de cour* from its shoulder sling. Checking in the small mirror, he put his dress chapeau-de-bras on his head, fore and aft, and left for the Say residence.

SEVENTEEN

April 27ᵗʰ

SAY TOWN HOUSE, LYON, FRANCE

Alphonsine and Horace watched as Charles McDonald walked into the reception room of their home. Once again, Alphonsine noticed that he looked both graceful and powerful. He was much taller than Horace was, with shoulders and arms that were more muscular. I hope that Helene likes him, she thought. He might lure her away from her infatuation with that Royalist groveler who has been courting her.

As Horace and Alphonsine greeted Charles, Horace's brother and his wife joined them.

"Charles, I would like you to meet my brother Jean Baptiste and his wife Julie. My brother and I spent several years in school together before the revolution. He can speak English much better than me. Now he's the editor of a newspaper. We served together in the Army of the North when your father was there. I went on to go to *L'École Polytechnique* and he came back to Lyons."

At that point, a stunning young woman with long wavy auburn hair and sparkling green eyes entered, accompanied by another young man.

Alphonsine took Charles's arm and said, "I would like you to meet my best friend, Mademoiselle Helene Grillion. This is her younger brother Auguste."

Charles stammered a greeting to both of them. Alphonsine smiled; she was quite accustomed to the effect that Helene had on men. Helene gave Charles a look of cool appraisal and said, "I have heard so much about your exploits, lieutenant, and I'm dying to hear more." Before she could continue, Horace's father came in and he introduced him to Charles. A successful silk merchant in Lyon, Citizen Say had an air of quiet confidence and a somewhat formal manner. He was a tall, lean man with penetrating dark eyes.

As one, they all moved over to the sideboard and each took a glass of champagne, a Moet of pre-Revolution vintage. Horace raised his glass and said, "To Charles, and my other great friends, and my family, I wish them health and happiness. I would also like to celebrate our new adventures in parts unknown. Finally, I wish to honor my new wife, Alphonsine. *Santé!*"

Alphonsine took Charles by the hand and led him over to Helene and her brother, saying, "We need to discuss tonight's planned recital after dinner. Charles says he knows the violin part of the new Beethoven piano Trio but claims he's not a good musician. Helene and I, however, have been practicing this work, with her brother playing the violin part. Helene plays the violoncello, and I play the pianoforte."

With a note of excitement in her voice, she added, "When Horace and his brother returned from London they brought back a Broadwood square piano, the same model used by Haydn and Beethoven. Since my family home is just three doors down the street, I came here for piano lessons every day — that's how I fell in love with Horace. Let's go into the music room before dinner and you can inspect the violins."

The four of them made their way into the music room next door and closed the two sets of closely spaced double doors that served as a version of soundproofing. Auguste went to a sideboard and opened two violin cases. Charles walked over, picked up the first violin, and peered through the *F* holes. In a tone of amazement he said, "It is signed Joseph Guarnerius and the label says fecit Cremone anno 1743 + IHS. It's made by Giuseppe Del Gesu."

"My brother inherited this and the older violin from our grand-father," Helene explained. "He was in Cremona in the 1740s, where he had this one made at the Guarneri shop to back up his principal violin made by Antonio Stradivari. Therefore, my brother now has three instruments; the newest by Nicolas Lupot of Paris and the Stradivarius that he plans to take to university with him. He's trying to sell this Guarnerius violin along with the case and the bow."

Picking up the bow and the violin, Charles began to play a simple scale. He tuned one string slightly and then started playing a more complicated piece, the opening solo from a Mozart Violin Concerto. Unfortunately, he hit more than a few wrong notes. Somewhat abashed Charles asked, "Do you think I should play with the three of you, or should you play for the family? I would love to just listen."

"Yes, why don't you just listen," Helene said. "We have prac-ticed this piece a number of times but even so we still make mis-takes." She was obviously trying to reassure Charles, who turned to Auguste and asked, "How much do you want for the violin? If I carry it with me I can practice every evening after dinner."

"I'm asking 2,000 francs. I will play it tonight so you can listen to the tone and quality of the sound. I'm sure you'll be favorably impressed." Charles thought that two thousand is a year's pay.

Returning to the reception room, they were just in time to join the others going into the dining room. At the table, Charles sat across from Helene and next to Alphonsine. Throughout the meal, there was a lively discussion of music, literature, and the latest Paris fashions. Charles had little to contribute about fashion since he had been back in Paris for only a few weeks. Alphonsine was puzzled that Charles had so little to say. While he didn't seem to have any trouble discussing politics with the men, he hardly addressed a word to Helene, who seemed to ignore him and spoke most of the time with her brother, sitting on her left. Alphonsine could not understand, Charles was so handsome. Why was Helene not engaging him in conversation? On the other hand, why did he sit there tongue-tied and not speak to her? She realized that Charles hadn't opened up and actually started talking to her until their breakfast in Auxerre. Maybe he was just shy around women.

The main course for dinner was a delicious *filet de boeuf en croûte* served with a wonderful red wine from a winery near L'Hermitage called St. Christopher's Hillside. It had a deep garnet color and an aroma of black fruits, berries and spices. After dessert, the gentleman removed to the reception room where they smoked and drank cognac. Charles discussed purchasing the violin with Auguste and agreed finally on the 2000-franc price for the instrument including the bow and cases. He excused himself and stepped into another room. Removing the seventy-four gold coins from his money vest plus a copper one, Charles returned and gave them to Auguste. After the men had finished their after-dinner drinks, they joined Auguste and the ladies in the music room. The three musicians moved to the end of the room, where the pianoforte stood. Auguste positioned himself at the far side of it and Helene sat in a chair on the near side.

Opening their sheet music, they began playing. All three players made small mistakes during the Allegro movement, mostly noticeable only to themselves. During the next three movements, they played with almost no missed cues. The audience of nine stood and gave a standing ovation. Charles was sure that he would have made a mess of the piece and was relieved that he had not played. The cook and two servants stood in a doorway clapping. At the end of the three-quarter hour's performance, the mental and physical effort caused the faces of all three musicians to flush.

The evening was ending. Charles packed his new violin and bow in their leather cases. Auguste gave him the fitted oiled-canvas covers that made each case waterproof. As everyone returned to the reception room, Charles overheard Hélène whisper to Alphonsine, "Charles is a pleasure to look at. He certainly fills his silk breeches, doesn't he?"

He peeked down and wondered. Do my new silk breeches show too much? The new silk underpants were skin-tight.

There was more champagne and brandy. Charles suddenly became aware that it was getting quite late, so he said farewell to everyone, explaining that he had to get ready for the next morning's journey.

He shyly asked Hélène, "Can I write letters to you? Will you write me letters in return?"

"I will answer the letters you send," Helene was somewhat surprised; Charles had not engaged her in any sort of extended conversation. She felt sorry for him and wanted to let him down easily. "I hope you have a good journey. Do take care of yourself—and practice on your violin!"

Charles walked back to the coach terminus, humming part of the Beethoven trio and fantasying what it would be like to be alone with *la belle Helene.*

Approaching the inn Charles looked around, but did not see anyone on watch. When he entered, he saw Lieutenant Faurie sitting in the common room. He walked over and asked, "Have you noticed anything unusual?"

Faurie said, "Sergeant Pelle reported that this afternoon Commander Duval and Major Menou walked down to the Gendarmerie fortress. He followed and reported they were inside for over an hour."

"Have you recognized any gendarmes or men who look like they might be watching?" Charles asked,

Faurie answered, "I've seen no one since I came on duty a few hours ago."

Charles wondered where the gendarmes might have positioned themselves. Going up to his room, he stopped at the doors to Commander Duval and Major Menou's rooms. He held his ear close to each door but he did not hear any sound. Once in his room, he opened his baggage. He rolled and packed his dress uniform, laid out his undress field uniform, checked his pistols and rifle, and set everything out for tomorrow morning. He then took out his sketchbook and did a quick drawing of Helene, relying on his vivid, still fresh, memory of her.

Before drifting off into sleep, he thought about how he had gotten several glimpses of Helene's breasts when she leaned over; her décolletage had amply displayed them. When Hélène tucked her cello between her legs, Charles had found himself wishing he were there rather than the instrument. From the way the silk and voile fabric draped around her hips and thighs, he imagined her wearing nothing under her dress but her gartered stockings.

EIGHTEEN

April 28ᵗʰ

LYON GENDARMERIE CITADEL

Charles was jolted out of sleep by Paul, who grabbed his arm and said, "Wake up, we've got trouble."

"What time is it? What's the problem?"

"It's just past three o'clock," Paul answered. "I woke up early and went out to check around. There was no one on watch, no one! Raoul was slumped in the corner banquette after drinking too much. Walking down near the fortress, I saw a number of men and horses at the corner of the street down from the gate. They're all armed and wearing scarves pulled up over their faces. They seemed to be waiting for someone. Get dressed and grab your weapons. I'll get my guns and meet you downstairs."

Charles jumped out of bed, lit his bullseye lantern, and pulled on his underclothing, dark uniform and boots. To cover his blond queue, he tied a new black kerchief over his hair. Buckling on his waistbelt, he slung the sabre on his back. Closing the shutter of his dark lamp to a sliver, he quietly moved downstairs and out the front door. Paul was in front of him, "Come on—let's hurry."

Rushing down the street quickly and quietly, they crossed several side streets. He noticed a group of dark horses tied at the corner, just short of the Gendarmerie fortress. There was a two-horse cart hitched next to the six-saddled horses. Moving up to the gate, he opened the lantern's shutter slightly and saw two guards lying behind the open leaf of the fortress gate with pools of blood around their heads.

With Charles leading, they entered and quietly crossed the courtyard to the headquarters building. The front door in the entrance to the orderly room was open a few inches. Charles quietly placed the shuttered lamp on the steps. He had carefully noted the layout of the place on his previous visit, instinctively considering how he would attack it—or how he would defend it. Someone was hiding behind the door; he had peeked out through the opening a few minutes ago.

He crouched, triggered the lamp shutter open, and then jumped forward forcefully, slamming the door open with his left shoulder as he shouted a war cry. He charged through the entrance to the orderly room in an explosive rush so his sabre draw would not hit the overhead doorjamb.

His speed of entry startled a masked intruder, who made a thrust with his sword but found no target for it. Charles was well beyond the doorway when he turned, and rising to his full height, drew his sabre with his right hand. Grasping the pommel with his left, he cut backhand down and across the bandit's neck. His head fell forward with a spray of blood while his body fell to the left.

Stepping back to recover, he glimpsed the movement of a second thief who was trying to disengage himself from the door that had slammed him into the wall. The light from the bullseye lantern was blinding anyone in the room looking out. He lunged almost six feet across the well-lit open doorway and thrust the tip of his sabre into the villain's chest and on through to his spine. He realized the robber was wearing a cuirass. The chisel point of his tachi blade pierced the steel breastplate with only a momentary hesitation.

He lunged so deeply that he had to drop his left hand to the floor in a *passata-sotto*. He continued his recovery pushing up with his left arm while he jumped up with both feet and hopped forward. He yelled to Paul, "Look out, they're wearing breastplates."

A third masked man was on the far side of the orderly desk to the left of the door. Charles jumped onto the desk and kicked the enemy in the chest, knocking him on his butt. He jumped down and stabbed him in the head with a two handed downward thrust.

Paul had followed him into the doorway holding a short-barreled blunderbuss in each hand. He aimed and fired the right and then the left into the arms room, just beyond the desk. Dropping both guns as he continued forward, he drew two horse pistols from his belt and fired a third and fourth shot. He then moved into the arms room. The four flashes had completely lit up the orderly room and filled it with smoke. There was no one left alive. Paul had fired at their heads.

Charles moved back through the entrance door to shout an alarm. Peering across the courtyard, he noticed the main gate was slowly closing. There was movement from two shapes in the narrowing opening. He suddenly knelt down to turn the bullseye lamp toward the gate while drawing his right pistol as he saw the movement. He suddenly saw sparks and the bright flash of a gunshot. He heard a crack and thump just behind his head and then the sound of a shot from the gate. He aimed and squeezed his trigger in one motion. He was peering through the smoke at the opening, just as the gate was slamming shut. The flint sparked and the pan flashed, but the charge did not ignite. His shot was a misfire.

Cocking the second lock, he ran to the now closed main gate. Something was blocking it from the outside. He noticed that the wood gate beam was missing from its normal position beside the gatepost slot. The escaping men must have carried it outside and braced it against the outer door. He could hear several footsteps running down the lane but no sounds of horses.

As he walked back to the headquarters building, a huge gendarme duty sergeant ran up. He said, "I'm Sergeant Leblanc, I was on a roving patrol across the courtyard when I heard the first shot. I turned and saw two masked figures in black only a dozen feet behind me. I was startled to realize that both were carrying daggers, about to stab me in the back. They turned and ran for the gate when they realized that they were too far away to attack."

Charles saw that dozens of half-dressed gendarmes were exiting the barracks. Entering the orderly room, he saw Paul, who told him, "There are six dead bandits here who are dressed like the six highwaymen we killed in Fontainebleau. One of them had keys to the arms room and the headquarters door." Paul held up a duplicate set to the keys Colonel Saint Just had shown them yesterday afternoon.

He turned to the gendarme sergeant who was entering the room. "Sergeant Leblanc, we need to get the gate opened. There are two dead gendarmes outside. There are also eight horses and a cart tied at the corner of the fortress. I want all of the bodies lined up so I can sketch their faces. Bring their horses and equipment here without touching anything. Also send for Colonel Saint Just."

NINETEEN

April 28ᵗʰ

AVENUE DE SAXE, PARIS

Tristan had worked all of yesterday and all of last night investigating the activities of the highwaymen who had tried to hold up the mail coach in the Forest of Fontainebleau. Today was Sunday and it was Décadi, the tenth day of rest. He was working, not resting as he approached the town house of General MacDonald to report his discoveries. He had not seen him since a chance encounter the previous afternoon at the Salle d'Armes of LaBoessiere & Son at No. 152 Rue Saint-Honore.

That same Saturday, the newly promoted captain of gendarmes had arrived at General MacDonald's house at seven o'clock. He was wearing the plain civilian clothing he had worn as an advocate in training, wool trousers, a waistcoat and a darker frock coat. He buttoned his unbleached shirt to the neck, and he was not wearing a fashionable cravat. He was carrying a smaller, 7-inch long screw-barrel belt pistol and he had a Spanish style long folding knife in his pants pocket, but there was no way for him to conceal a sword.

Jean answered the door and brought him into the family dining room. General MacDonald was sitting at the table with a number of items spread about before him. His wife walked in and sat down next to him. Scout was on the floor at his feet.

The general said, "My wife has been busy making a copy of Charles's sketches of the seven highwaymen for us to carry and ask people if they recognize any of them. My daughter Barbara will be home from school this afternoon and she can help us make several additional copies. As soon as Elizabeth finishes I think you should take your drawings, go to Bonaparte's house, and snoop around. Remain inconspicuous. Follow him to the *Palais des Tuileries* or any other place he goes. Look for places where a watcher or follower would wait and observe him. Pay attention to inns, public houses, coffee shops, and tobacconists. Are you armed?"

"Yes."

"Do you have a sword?"

"A sword would be out of character, I'm dressed as a law clerk."

General MacDonald walked into the hallway where there was a brass stand with walking sticks. Choosing one by feel he turned and said, "You can borrow this plain blackthorn walking stick. It has a hidden release concealing a sword blade. Are you any good with a sword?" As he asked, he demonstrated how the sword released from the stick.

Tristan said nothing but it affected him when General MacDonald did not stop or hesitate when he went into the hall to retrieve the cane. One would never know that he was blind.

"I've had lessons and some practice with other gendarmes," Tristan replied. "I'm average, not an expert. I am good at street fighting and have strong arms. Of course, I have trained with the musket and pistol."

General MacDonald nodded and said, "While you are investigating anyone following Bonaparte, Jean will drive me to a number of Salle d'Armes and we can ask if the fencing masters have seen any of the men in our sketches. Most of the masters will know Colonel DeVillars. First, I'm escorting the twins to La Boëssière's for their regular lessons where I will ask Nicolas Texier if he recognizes anyone."

The general paused for a moment, "You do know that I was a colleague of Colonel DeVillars. He had an amazing reputation as a fencer but he was extremely cautious with me. He was aware that I never dueled with fellow officers. DeVillars had killed nine inept Republican assemblymen in duels over the last decade. But, he knew that I had killed a considerable number of men in real swordfights. He bitterly resented Maître Nicolas LaBoessiere, Sword Master of the Royal Academy, saying I was one of the best swordsmen in France. In '90, we did have one secret bout at LaBoessiere's using épée's with fleurets. I touched him on five straight passes to none for him. I helped force him into exile, because of what he was doing."

A fleeting expression of anger passed over the general's face before he continued to brief Tristan, "This morning, Jean sent a messenger to my farm in Bougival to give instructions to Mahamoud. He and his helper will be here tonight to take the early morning mail coach to Fontainebleau. Later this afternoon I need to be back here to meet with the two officers General Bonaparte is sending to help us. If our investigation involves a number of men working out of this house, I may send Elizabeth and the twins to the farm, particularly if there's any danger. Barbara's school is fewer than four miles from Bougival and she can go to the farmhouse on the weekends."

After a hasty breakfast in General MacDonald's dining room, Tristan made his way to Bonaparte's house. It took him over an hour. It would have been quicker riding a horse but the General-in-Chief or his mounted guides might see him if he were on horseback. Enemy observers might notice a horse too. General MacDonald had warned him that the guides would be looking for possible trouble.

He crossed the Seine on the *Pont de la Révolution* and took up an observation position at the west end of the newly named Rue de la Victoire, almost a block away from Number 60.

During the first hour of his surveillance, he saw a number of messengers and officers arrive and depart from Bonaparte's house. He also noticed vendors pushing their carts up and down the residential street. There were farmers with fruit and vegetables for sale, a grinder to sharpen knives, and a tinker offering to mend pots. About ten minutes after he arrived, he noticed a bearded man take up a similar watch down the block on the far side of the general's house.

At about half past nine o'clock, Bonaparte, several staff officers and two dozen guides in their buff doeskin breeches, scarlet waistcoats and green coatees rode out of the gates, turned right and rode down the street in the opposite direction from his position. After the riders rode past, the bearded watcher turned and followed them. He was strolling on the right side of the road. Tristan had already started to follow on the left side. The platoon of cavalrymen around the general turned south on a street that led to the Rue de Richelieu and continued toward the *Palais des Tuileries* where Bonaparte had an office. As the two of them followed the guides, the cavalry platoon finally entered the courtyard of the Palais des Tuileries compound. Bonaparte and the staff officers dismounted. A dozen guides collected the reins and led their horses to the stables while they entered the building surrounded by the remaining guides.

Tristan, who had kept his distance, suddenly saw the bearded man reverse and walk toward him. He turned east on Rue Saint-Honore and walked along the left side. This district was a noisy quarter made up of shabby five and six story buildings crowding the street. Among them were a riding school, stonemasons' yards, dingy hôtels, and alleyways choked with traffic. There were a few carriages, a lot more handcarts, horseback riders and people walking about.

When the bearded man reached a six-story, four-bay building across the street from the abandoned Oratory chapel he crossed the street and entered the ground floor stairway.

Tristan watched the outside of the building for a few minutes and then followed the man into the entrance. He noticed a small wooden plaque numbered 152. Walking up to the first floor, he realized from a hallway sign that this building housed the famous Maître LaBoessiere & Son, Salle d'Armes.

He entered the door and immediately saw Jean standing inside. General MacDonald, with his dog Scout, was talking to the sword master, who must be the younger LaBoessiere. The bearded man had walked the length of the salle and was passing into a dressing room at the far end of the training room. Eight pairs of men and two young boys were practicing on the sanded wooden floor. Tristan walked over to General MacDonald and told him quietly that he had followed the bearded man to the academy.

Fencing Master Antoine Boessiere nodded and said, "That's the Irishman who came here to practice fencing with DeVillars. He practiced with him and one or two others almost daily. For the past few months, he has been fencing with another man, an American who arrived a few minutes earlier. They both are changing."

"I'll go back outside and follow when they leave," Tristan said.

"The twins have another hour of fencing with foils followed by an hour upstairs with pistols and then two hours down the street for equestrian training," General MacDonald said. "Jean can pick them up. I don't need to go to other schools since they've been practicing here, right under my nose." Jean took General MacDonald's arm following Tristan back down the stairs and outside. A hostler was holding their horses and carriage across the street on the church's sidewalk. While Jean, General MacDonald and Scout got into the carriage, Tristan walked up the street and entered a tavern. Ordering a *cidre doux*, he sat at a table near the window to wait for the bearded man to emerge.

After about two hours, the man he had followed, accompanied by a slender man with a noticeable limp, came out and turned west, heading back toward the Tuileries. After a few blocks, the two men turned north and went into an outdoor café in the Palais-Royal. They took a table looking down the cross street where anyone coming from the Tuileries, would pass their sight. Tristan took a seat two tables over, close to the back wall. Both men were talking in English. Tristan believed that they were Americans because of their accents. The second man, who also had a tuft of chin hair and a full mustache, drank a glass of wine, then left the bearded man at the table and proceeded north. Tristan decided to follow the second man with the limp; the bearded man was obviously trailing the general. He walked north on Rue de Richelieu, where many of the French aristocracy had houses before the Revolution. It also had been the location of foreign embassies until *la Terreur* drove most diplomats further away from the center of violence. *Monsieur Moustache* turned and limped past the Theater de L'Opera. He continued northwest toward the Clichy barricade, past the entrances to a number of large town estates. He finally reached the northern wall of the *Ferme-Générale*, about 500 meters east of the Monceau Rotunda. This private tax-collecting company had erected a twenty-four kilometre long wall with 62-toll barriers at which the ten percent *Octroi* tax on all food and material entering Paris was paid. The wall had been one of the major causes of the French Revolution, and the Jacobin's executed most of the rich tax-farmers. During the revolution, the National Guard had used the wall to control movement into and out of Paris by aristocrats and foreigners. The Directory, the current five-man executive of France, had reinstated the tax last year.

He paused and watched *citoyen la moustache,* as he turned right at the tax barricade. Tristan decided that since he was American he should think of him as Mister Mustache. As he moved further away from the barrier, he allowed the space between them to increase. The subject of his surveillance was limping down the *chemin de ronde,* the raised defensive walkway running around the inside of the stone perimeter wall. On the outside of the wall was an open meadow running around the entire perimeter of Paris. The man with the limp was now just passing a right-angle zig in the wall.

Tristan watched as he walked another dozen strides east of the northern point in the Farmer's General tax wall. He started after him as the man turned into a large walled property before reaching the Blanche barricade. Walking past the entrance gate, he realized that it was the old Montmartre Benedictine Convent, closed and abandoned during the revolution. He walked on to the Blanche barricade and asked the national guardsman on duty if he knew the man with the limp.

"No, I don't recognize him, but we get almost no traffic here, so I'm only here on relief once a week," he told Tristan after viewing his police warrant card. He pointed to the barricade and then down the street. "The barrier opens at eight and closes at five o'clock. The Rue Blanche is in terrible shape, too many holes and ditches for wagons. The path is for carts and donkeys only. I do know that there is a unit of the 2nd Division of the National Police, you know the secret police unit, which uses the old nunnery buildings. My sergeant said that some of the spies, the *merde-mouchards,* are Americans, Irishmen and Scots. There are even a few from Switzerland."

The property appeared to be run-down and neglected. After the National Assembly had abolished religion in '90's, and taken control of all church property, half the clergy left France and abandoned countless abbeys, convents, churches and other religious facilities. In

'94, the guillotine took another half of the remaining celibates. The rest quickly got married, or joined the army. Standing beside the guardsman, he watched the mustache man limp across the property to the stable wing.

"The property was once over 250 acres, before the perimeter wall divided it into two sections," the guardsman explained as he pointed outside the wall, "The larger outside portion of the convent was at the foot of Montmartre and their church of Saint Pierre de Montmartre is at the top of the hill." Peering up the incline, Tristan could see the tower of the church. The Chappe semaphore télégraphe mast, "regulator" spars and wing "indicators" now occupied the summit of the church steeple alongside two windmill water pumps.

Six years earlier, Tristan had been in charge of an investigation into wine shops selling untaxed drinks. An informer of his had heard rumors there might be a secret tunnel under the perimeter wall. A tunnel, according to the informant, that was supposed to end in the basement of a church. He was never able to pin down the rumor or find the church. As he watched the former cloister, he tried to imagine where a secret tunnel would run. Could this have been the location of the rumored tunnel?

He realized that in a few hours, after dark, he could get inside the wall and take up an observation point concealed by underbrush. Until then, he moved across a ditch and into the cover of some trees near the main gate; he was watching for guard dogs or other signs of security. The religious property was roughly five-sided, with the two northern sides formed by the tax wall. The only entrance was the north-facing gate. A wall formed the southern perimeter, between the nuns paddock and a vegetable farm while beyond it was dirt track between more walls around estates fronting on the cobblestoned Rue de Clichy. He could look left down the unfinished Rue Blanche toward Paris. He observed several riders and men on foot entering and exiting the convent over the next few hours. They all wore dark clothing; rode dark horses and almost all had facial hair. The beards functioned, Tristan suspected, as a form of disguise, protecting these men by concealing their true-identities.

After sunset, he climbed over a crumbling section of the wall, moved closer to the stable wing and continued to watch. There were a few lanterns visible from the back, but not visible from the street. During the night, he heard men speaking in English and he thought he heard the sounds of riders leaving the hillside on the other side of the Paris wall. He also heard horses walking, stamping their hooves and neighing in the barn, but none ever came out into the pasture. He watched almost all night. Just before dawn, two men released all the horses into a paddock behind the barn. They were definitely speaking English.

He made his way back to General MacDonald's house near the southern perimeter wall. When he knocked on the ground floor door, Jean asked him to join the general in the kitchen and gave him a cup of coffee. Tristan yawned and then described what he had observed.

"We need to start watching the convent full time," the general said. "No one is in the semaphore télégraphe tower at night since it operates only during daylight. The men staying in the nunnery could move in and out of the church basement or a crypt after dark without anyone noticing. Every morning I want a count and description of all the horses released into the enclosure. Maybe we can keep track of their horses. Are you sure that they were speaking English?"

"I speak it with an accent; but, I can understand conversations." Tristan replied in English.

MacDonald finished his coffee and said, "Yesterday afternoon, I met with the two men Bonaparte has assigned to us. One is the former Sergeant Major and now Adjutant-Sous Officier for the guides. He is not going to Egypt because his wife has consumption and he needs to find someone to help look after his children. He will stay here in Paris and work on this investigation."

"The other is an experienced officer in the *Sûreté Générale* of the Ministry of General Police, the investigative division of the Bureau Central. Bonaparte trusts him and he has no connection with the Minister of Police, and with the local Paris police and their secret police department."

"What's his name?" Tristan asked.

"Agent Marten Napier"

"I know him. He is a best friend of Jacques Henry, Chief of the Bureau de Sûreté"

"They will be here in just over an hour for breakfast. Since you've been up all night, you should take a nap on the cot in the room next door. Jean will wake you when they arrive and we can make our plans."

"Why don't you send a boy with a message asking Marten Napier to stop by City Hall and bring us the plans for that section of the wall, the convent, or anything else he can find," Tristan asked.

"I'll send both twins with a note immediately," the general replied.

TWENTY

April 28th

TURGOTINE TERMINUS, LYON

C harles and Paul walked beside the horse-drawn cart carrying the gold from the Gendarmerie fortress to the terminus in Lyon. They were carrying everything that they had collected from the six men they killed last night except the horses. The turgotine was behind schedule, and they would have to delay even more while Charles finished his reports to Paris.

Charles had drawn sketches of all six faces; they were so well done that they made the subjects look as if they were still alive. The six had been dressed and armed like the highwaymen who had tried to rob the coach in Fontainebleau. Paul sold the cart, horses, tack, and arms to the gendarme sergeant major for 6,000 francs. The colonel had no idea of what was happening under his nose. His senior sergeant usually handled things for him. The saddlebags of the leader's horse had a mixture of papers, including five coded letters and a small prayer book. It also had 600 gold guineas packed in paper tubes of 50, just like the tubes of coins they were carrying. The coins were worth a total of 16,200 francs so when the two of them divided the money, each of them got 11,100 francs in gold.

Charles had spent a fortune in Lyon buying his supplies, equipment and clothes, as well as the violin. Thanks to this encounter, he still had almost 13,000 francs left. Paul said, with a wide grin, "I may quit the mail coach service and go into killing highwaymen for the money."

Paul lit up his pipe while he supervised the gendarmes transferring the gold from the cart to the turgotine while mail-guard Raoul Pelle stood watch. Charles left and went up to his room to pack. When he finished he cleaned and reloaded his pistols, collected his baggage and carabine and returned downstairs.

He was handing his baggage up to Raoul when he turned and said to Paul, "I see Captain Say coming down the street. Why don't you go in and eat breakfast. I'll join you when Horace gets here. The two gendarmes can help Raoul guard the gold. I still need at least a half hour to write reports for Paris."

As he was talking with Paul, a postal messenger rode up at a canter and stopped at the hitching post. The hostler grabbed his reins as he dismounted, removed his mail pouches and went inside.

When Horace arrived, Charles told him about the attempted robbery several hours before. He was still describing what had happened as they entered. The terminus clerk called out for Charles MacDonald, Ingénieurs-Geographes. He went over and signed for a sealed message from the clerk. Returning to the table where Paul had ordered coffee, he opened the letter with his folding knife. Sitting down with Paul and Horace, he said. "General-in-Chief Bonaparte has promoted me to captain, Ingénieurs-Geographes 1st Class. Paul, he offers you the rank of *Adjutant-Sous-Lieutenant* in the guides, if you will sign-up and go with us." Horace jumped up and hugged him, while Paul almost choked on his coffee. Charles smiled and said to Paul, "I guess this cancels your idea of going into business killing highwaymen."

After Horace left, Charles asked Paul to make sure that the passengers were ready to leave. "While I write my reports, find out where Duval and Menou are right now, and where they've been all night." Charles hastily wrote a short report to General Bonaparte and he then dashed off a longer report to his father, describing the number, appearance and markings on the tubes of coins in the strongboxes as well as those in the saddlebags. He mentioned the weapons, the extra keys and a description of the bandits, enclosing his sketches. Then he carefully wrapped the tubes of guinea coins and the mixed bag from the gendarmerie. He was sending his father over twelve thousand francs from the coins he had left. This left him with almost 700 francs in mixed coins, more than two months pay. With his promotion and newfound wealth, he could afford to keep two horses and hire a batman.

Paul returned and said to Charles, "I talked to half-a-dozen regular workers at the inn and discovered two tidbits of information. I'm very close to one of the maids who told me that Duval didn't sleep in his bed last night; however, Menou was snoring like a pig this morning. A groom told me the second bit of information. Both Menou and Duval spent over an hour yesterday, and again this morning in the privately owned fencing salle that extends over the gatehouse entrance to the rear courtyard. Duval was already in the armory well before breakfast. He was fencing with the master Giorgio Castracani. My informer says that there is something odd about him. He doesn't believe that he's Italian; instead maybe he's German or from the Alps of Switzerland. Do you think it was Duval that shot at you from gate of the fortress?"

"There were only six horses and we killed six bandits. Somebody drove the two-horse cart. I think that there could have been two men running from the gate. The extra bandits had to be on foot or else they were in the cart. They could have been gendarmes or they could have been our suspects. No one was watching outside for Commander Duval or Major Menou last night. Is there a British agent here in Lyon that I don't know about?"

"I fell asleep at five o'clock yesterday afternoon," Paul admitted. "I woke at two o'clock this morning. When I went down for a drink there was no one on watch inside or outside. When I went downstairs, I listened at both their doors, and there was no noise from Duval, but there was loud snoring from Menou's room. Then I walked down toward the Gendarmerie to check if everything was OK and noticed the horsemen."

"In my report to my father, I mentioned there could be a conspirator in the Gendarmerie of Lyon since the bandits had a key to the strong room," Charles told him. "I'll add our suspicions about the fencing master. He and Tristan can investigate."

He stuffed the coins, papers, coded messages, prayer book and the package of silk scarves into a pair of strong leather saddlebags. He sealed the eleven-pound container with a wax seal, gave it and the smaller letter for General Bonaparte to the clerk and paid to send it to Paris by Postal Messenger. It would arrive early Monday morning.

After finishing his reports, Charles went outside the common room and saw Horace standing beside the coach with Alphonsine. "You're out of uniform," Horace said, as he removed the epaulette on Charles' left shoulder and the contra-epaulette on his right. Borrowing his small penknife, he removed the thin red lieutenant's stripe from the contra-epaulette. He then replaced the left shoulder board with the more elaborate fringe worn by a Captain and kissed him on both cheeks. Alphonsine shook his hand and wished him a safe journey.

With all of the passengers and baggage loaded, Charles and Paul mounted the conductor's box and the coach pulled out for the bridge over the Rhone River. As it left, Charles stood and waved goodbye to his friends. Turning south, the coach moved along on the old Roman road that ran south alongside the Rhone River. Most of the fields were turning green with the rising winter wheat and other early crops. There were drifts of budding flowers in the peach orchards and vineyards. It was a beautiful spring day.

The coach continued down the Rhone River valley, changing horse teams at every post stop. In the afternoon, they stopped for dinner and then continued through the night. When coach pulled into the inn in Avignon about nine o'clock the next morning, Charles decided not to stop for longer than food; they needed to make up the lost time. They changed teams and took on a new postillion driver, after waking him up. While waiting, Charles noticed Commander Duval leaving a note with a stranger.

Normally the coach would have returned to its terminus of origin after each leg. This coach, however, was one of the newest in the system and they were taking it all the way to Toulon. It would return to Paris after they delivered their load. Since Paul would not be accompanying the coach back to Paris, he would have to make sure it returned and one of the local routes didn't steal it. The trip from Avignon to Toulon usually took 16 hours. They pulled into Toulon after ten o'clock on Monday evening. Charles asked for a room for the night at the company inn. "You'll have to share with two other officers." The innkeeper told him. Once again, Paul took the conductor's room but he had to share it with Raoul.

After leaving their baggage in the care of the innkeeper, Charles, Paul, and Raoul accompanied the now almost empty coach from the Toulon terminus to the army headquarters in the main Arsenal Building. Even though it was well after dark, the streets were clogged with traffic and drunken men. After the coach arrived at the arsenal, Charles and Paul went into the orderly room and asked for the duty officer. When a gorgeted artillery captain appeared, they informed him that they had more than 600,000 francs worth of gold to deliver. The duty officer said, "We've been expecting your shipment." He then called for several soldiers on duty to help unload the strongboxes and carry them into the armory. Paul handed over the keys to the chests and the duty officer opened and confirmed the contents matched the manifest. He then signed a receipt and released them to return with the coach to the terminus inn. In passing, he mentioned the gold shipment from Switzerland had arrived yesterday. It had come down the Rhone by boat and then the escort had transferred it to a coaster for the final leg to Toulon. Charles acted nonchalant, but he didn't know about a second shipment. Was General Bonaparte using him like a cat's-paw to misdirect the enemy? He, Paul and Raoul rode in the coach back to the inn, entered the common room and ordered a drink. They raised their glasses in celebration of a job well done, drank up and went upstairs to bed. The fatigue accumulated during the long and tension-filled journey had finally taken its toll.

The next morning Charles was still sleepy when he woke up, poured cool water in the basin and brushed his teeth. Then he washed, shaved, and dressed in his clean set of underclothes, using the water that remained in the basin to wash his dirty things. He wore his summer uniform, slinging the sabre from his waistbelt after removing both pistol holsters. Going down to breakfast, he sat with Paul and Raoul. Both were smoking their first pipes of the day while they had their coffee. Charles greeted them and said, "I need to report in to headquarters today. Can you continue to keep an eye on Commander Duval and Major Menou?"

"Major Menou took the morning coach on to Genoa to join General Menou," Paul told him. "I'll watch Commander Duval."

"Do you need to collect your belongings in Paris?" Charles asked. "If not, I can write my father and have him arrange to have anything stored until we return."

"I carry all of my belongings in my bag. For the past three years, I've spent only one night in Paris or one night in Lyon. I haven't had the time or money to collect any belongings."

Turning to Raoul Charles asked, "Would you be interested in re-joining the Army. I can ask if there are any openings in the guides."

"I have wife and children in Paris," Raoul replied. "If I escort the coach back, they may make me a conductor. Paul has offered to write me a recommendation. But thank you for the offer."

TWENTY - ONE

April 28ᵗʰ

AVENUE DE SAXE, PARIS

S aturday morning at breakfast, Tristan met the two new officers who were to help him with the investigation. General MacDonald introduced Adjutant-Sous-Lieutenant Henri Dumas to him. "The second-lieutenant was a former sergeant major serving with General Bonaparte for the last few years. He has his complete confidence. General Bonaparte recently promoted him to Adjutant Officer. He started in the Artillery with Captain Bonaparte. After the action in Toulon, he served with the Guard of the Directory in Paris until the general asked him to join him in Italy. There he moved up to the Squadron of Guides that protect General Bonaparte. He is a native of Paris, but for family reasons he can't go to Egypt."

Tristan asked Dumas, "Do you know Paul Forgeron?"

"He was our sergeant major at the start of the revolution. During the battle for Toulon, he was the senior artillery sergeant. That's where Captain Bonaparte had his first victory, which led to the Directory's promoting him to Brigadier General. The general later asked the sergeant major to fight in the Vendée and keep an eye on General Menou."

General MacDonald then introduced Agent Marten Napier. "As you know, Citizen Napier is a longtime detective in the Sûreté of the Ministry of General Police. I gather that this division is the investigative section of the Bureau Central. Agent Napier has been in the national police for almost twenty years. Before the revolution, he served in the *Lieutenant Générale de Police de Paris*. He was one of the four *inspecteurs* responsible for dealing with crime, reporting directly to Citizen Henry, chief of the bureau. General Bonaparte trusts *Citoyen* Napier because of the many different and highly confidential services he's rendered."

During breakfast, as the general and his four men discussed their plans, Martin Napier pulled out the drawings and plans he had brought from the Paris Police archives showing the construction of the *Ferme générale* perimeter wall. He also had a set of plans from the Archdiocese showing the construction of the sewer down the center of Rue Blanche from the high slopes of Montmartre to the Seine River at the Tuileries gardens. He said, "When I got your note, I knew that we had a set of plans in our files. It only took me a few extra minutes to bring them with me."

"You three go to the convent." General MacDonald ordered. "I will stay here and wait to meet with Eliza Rossignol, the codebreaker from the cabinet noir." After breakfast, Charles, accompanied by Napier and Dumas, left for their assigned observation spots on horseback.

Tristan led the two men to the Blanche barricade to view the abandoned religious community's gates that ended at the perimeter wall around Paris. "Anyone leaving the nunnery gates will turn either left to the northwestern districts or right to the northeastern districts," Tristan pointed out to the two officers. "Anyone going to the center of Paris will turn south at one of those barricades. The closest road to downtown runs west to the Place Clichy and then south down Rue Clichy to the center of the city. Rue Blanche may be a shortcut south, paralleling Rue de Clichy; but it is a rough path and not in good shape. It follows the construction route of the sewer and the edge of the original abbey," Tristan asked if anyone had questions before giving them assignments. "Dumas, you will wait beyond the Blanche gate and follow anyone going east from the old convent. Hide your horse in the trees. Napier and I will wait at the Place Clichy roundabout to follow anyone going into the city. We can rest and meet at the inn on the far side of the square. We'll change places every four hours so one of us can relax at the inn."

Over the course of Saturday and Sunday, they followed only a few men each day. Both evenings, they split the night watch among themselves and rented a room above the kitchen of the inn. Tristan showed them how to use the broken section of wall to enter the retreat grounds unobserved at night.

Each day, a different person would shadow the spy who was following General Bonaparte. Each night the person on early duty reported faint noises from the back of the convent and from the church on top of Montmartre. Although they had started out as professional acquaintances, they quickly became friends.

Early Monday morning, before sunrise, all three officers met at General MacDonald's home to discuss progress and their plans for the week. Tristan said to the general, "We need more watchers. Our section needs at least a dozen more men."

Marten said, "My friend Jacques Henry can get three more experienced agents assigned to our investigation for the next week. I wouldn't trust any *mouchards,* the secret informers from the 2nd Division. We call them flies because they are attracted to shit."

"You and General Bonaparte will have to use your influence to get more men assigned to us," Tristan told General MacDonald

"We can afford the pay for at least a few dozen more men," the general said. "Tristan, you need to hire some trusted gendarmes. They must be men you know and have experience working in civilian clothes during gendarme investigations. Henri, you need to find some good retired military sergeants who we can bring into our section. I will help as much as I can. Jean drives me to General Bonaparte's office at the Tuileries every morning after I integrate your new information with news from my other sources. I have prepared signed identification papers for each of you, countersigned by General Bonaparte. It gives you a warrant-*carte de la police* for your investigations, good anywhere in France. It also allows you to travel armed."

The general added, "Every afternoon, I walk down to the Military Academy. It's now the offices for the various specialists from the War Depot and the War Commissioners, where my friends give me the latest news from abroad. One of my best friends was born in Ireland before coming to France for his schooling and officer training. He maintains extensive contacts with the Irish republicans and he says that there are some unusual international situations developing. The British are fomenting disturbances in Ireland, Western France, Northern Europe, and the Netherlands. They are supporting Russian armies, using the Kingdom of Naples as a surrogate. He says that they want to reverse our victories in northern Italy by using these armies. Finally, their agents are hard at work in Austria, trying to cancel the current peace treaty. He thinks the British are forming a second coalition to crush France."

The general concluded by saying, "I have received a note from Eliza Rossignol that she is decrypting the coded messages discovered by Charles. She writes that she will meet us here for dinner Tuesday night with her information. I understand that some of the messages are in English. My wife, Elizabeth, is helping her with those."

Tristan and Henri left for their watch positions just after seven o'clock and Marten departed to meet his friend Jacques Henry and ask for more men. When they changed watches, both Tristan and Henri Dumas would go to their respective contacts and ask about more men.

In the late morning on Monday, a uniformed National Messenger rode into the nunnery carrying a dispatch bag. A few minutes later, he departed and turned out of the drive, heading in the direction of downtown Paris. Fifteen minutes later, an individual limped out and turned left at the main road. Tristan started following him after he left the roundabout toward Paris. It was the same man, Mister Mustache the American, whom Tristan had previously followed to the Montmartre Convent. This time the man's destination was the dirt track that ran between Clichy and Blanche. The narrow track included stable entrances for farms adjacent to the religious compound and entrances to several estates on its southern side.

He watched from the corner as the man walked down the path and stopped near a gate in the southern wall. Mister Mustache lifted a wooden crate lying next to the gate, took an envelope from his coat, and hid it in the box. Peering in both directions, he continued east on the track. At the end of the track, the man turned back to the north along the rough path down the center of Rue Blanche.

Tristan ran along the track to the far end and watched as the man limped toward the Blanche barrier, where he turned left as if to return to the convent. He decided to wait and see who recovered the envelope. At one o'clock, a man in the livery of a butler came out the back gate from the estate. He picked up the envelope and returned inside. Tristan walked back to the Rue de Clichy and down to the main entrance for the estate. He noticed a distinctive flag flying over the main house; he immediately recognized the red and white stripes and blue starred field of the national banner of the United States. He realized that this house was the legation of the United States. Tristan now had to consider the possibility that the Americans were somehow involved with the British Secret Service. Did the Jay Treaty between the United States and England and the current unofficial quasi-war between the United States and France mean that the Americans were secretly working with the British?

The three officers continued to watch throughout the day on Monday. They took turns following different individuals to various locations around Paris during the day. Getting together late in the afternoon they divided the night and the next day into three watches with two men always on duty. That evening, Tristan rode to the general's townhouse and discussed the possibility that the Americans were working with the British Secret Service. MacDonald asked, "Is Mister Mustache, a former loyalist working for the British? Or, is he an American Federalist working for the government in Philadelphia?" He didn't know.

Every day two watchers from the nunnery left to follow General Bonaparte to work and then practice at the salle d'armes, alternating between two pairs of operatives. Another half-dozen men practiced in the courtyard between the barn and the kitchen. The detectives on lookout didn't bother to follow the daily watchers since they knew their destination, but they did follow other operatives emerging from the convent and going to many different French government offices. On Tuesday morning, they agreed to meet at General MacDonald's house for dinner that evening. The last two men on afternoon watch would stay in place until relieved by the new detectives assigned to help them. After his early morning watch and their meeting, Tristan left to have breakfast with the general. There was a new package of papers from Charles. He read the report and letter out loud to General MacDonald. He was amazed to hear Charles and Paul

Forgeron had killed another six bandits. Unfortunately, he's spent his extra money on an old violin. As Tristan was getting ready to leave for his afternoon watch, General MacDonald sent a message about the new coded pages to Eliza at the cabinet noir. He also had some questions about the source of the gold in the shipment Charles was guarding. The general told Tristan, "The VoC marking on the rolls of coin in Charles's shipment is the cypher used by the Dutch East Indies Company. I thought the stolen gold shipment from Holland was the only source of VoC marked coins. The coins Charles seized from Colonel DeVillars saddlebags were also "spade" guineas." Tristan left to meet with Marten Napier as Jean was reading the rest of the documents from Charles to General MacDonald. Neither officer had come up with a way to discover if the Americans were involved with the British.

On late Tuesday afternoon of the 1st, Tristan and Marten rose from their lookout positions near the nunnery when the new watcher appeared. Three experienced Sûreté officers were taking the night shift, with two at the inn and one on watch. After reviewing everything that they knew or suspected, Marten asked him to come back out to the street to guide his relief into position. Tristan and Marten left to walk back to the maison on the Avenue de Saxe, pausing at the inn to brief the other two new watchers.

TWENTY-TWO

May 1ˢᵗ

ARMY HEADQUARTERS, TOULON, FRANCE

After breakfast, Charles left for the Arsenal Building on the Place d'Armes to report for duty. Horses, wagons and soldiers clogged the streets and thoroughfares. The streets were filthy and full of potholes. At the operations room, he asked to report to General Caffarelli, the Chief of Engineers. An orderly escorted him to the outer office of the general where a harried Adjutant-Chef was sitting at one of two desks. He gave his name and said he was reporting for duty. He heard someone shouting in the inner office. While he was kept waiting for half an hour, the sergeant major, carrying papers, rushed into the inner office several times. He assumed the second desk was the one Horace Say would use when he arrived. He was glad he didn't have his job.

His watch showed almost ten o'clock when the Adjutant-Chef told him that the General would see him. He stood, straightened his sabre, placed his dress chapeau under his arm and entered the inner office. The general officer sitting behind the desk was a portly man with short, curly hair, a prominent sharp nose and chin. Charles formally reported for duty and handed the general his papers, including the letters from Bonaparte.

General Caffarelli stared at Charles and chuckled, "You must be an amazing officer to be promoted so often in one month, from sous-lieutenant to full lieutenant and then to captain. What did you do?"

"General Bonaparte has confidence in my fighting abilities," he replied.

General Caffarelli nodded and said, "I have received dispatches from General Bonaparte, first informing me that you were coming, then you were escorting the gold shipment and, finally, that he was promoting you for your actions in the Forest of Fontainebleau. What were your actions?"

Charles briefly explained what had taken place since he had left Paris. He described the sequence of events. "First there was the attempted robbery in the forest and then there was a second failed attempt in Lyon."

General Caffarelli informed Charles that he had worked with his father when he had served with the Army of Sambre-et-Meuse. "He is one of our greatest pathfinders."

Charles then told the general of his suspicions about two officers who had accompanied the coach from Paris. General Caffarelli said it would be difficult to follow a naval officer who was joining his ship or to follow the cousin and assistant to General Menou who was now in Genoa. "General Bonaparte will arrive in about a week; we can then discuss ways to investigate these two officers. In the meantime, you should report to Colonel Testevuide, the Chief of Ingénieurs-Geographes, who has an office down the hall. Since General Bonaparte has assigned you to the guides as their geographical engineer, you should also report to Colonel Bessières with the guides' cavalry near the Gate to Italy. They will house and feed you until embarkation. Food and lodging are almost impossible to find, or to afford, here in Toulon. People are sleeping in stables and in the hallways of public buildings." Charles replied that he had already found out about the shortage of rooms.

General Caffarelli shook his hand and dismissed him. Charles reported Colonel Testevuide, who was almost as old as his father was. The colonel had also received several memos about his arrival and said, "Since you are under the direct control of General Bonaparte we will have little contact. Please let me know if you need any assistance. I only have one map of Egypt, the 1665 by Johannes Vingboons, and my only information is based on the book *Travels through Syria and Egypt* by Constantin-François Volney."

"My roommate from *X*, Horace Say, is bringing all of the maps and reports he collected from the Topographical Bureau in Paris," Charles told him. "I have all of my father's maps, journals and reports from his expeditions to Egypt, Sinai, Syria and India. In 1749 and '50 , he helped survey the Vaugondy map and he accompanied Volney for a part of his trip through the Sinai and Egypt. General Bonaparte has asked me to study the journals in preparations for the landing in Egypt."

"I didn't realize your father was the geographer," Colonel Testevuide said. "I served with him several times over the years and have a great respect for his experience. If you are anything like him, you will make a fine topographical officer."

Colonel Testevuide asked if he needed any equipment or supplies. Charles told him that his father had completely equipped him with every necessity, "He gave me such things as a pocket chronometer, a small sextant and a cased Borda reflecting circle. While with the Bureau of Longitudes I copied the tables required to calculate longitude from the Paris meridian."

"I would like to see your equipment when you get a chance," the colonel said and then gave him directions to the headquarters of the guides.

Charles walked east through the city of Toulon to the fortifications designed by Vauban. He continued walking along the fortified wall to the Gate of Italy on the eastern fortifications where he found the headquarters of the guides in the adjacent bastion.

Entering the guides' brigade office, he asked the orderly for Colonel Bessières. The orderly told him that the colonel and his officers were outside the gates, mounted and practicing with sabres. Walking outside, Charles saw a number of officers on horseback watching as each one charged a wooden post with an apple on top. While at a full gallop, each tried to slice the apple. He noticed most either missed the target or hit the post. It must be painful on their hands and arms when they hit the post, he thought. Most of them miss on purpose to avoid the post. There were a number of broken gourds at its base, leading Charles to conclude that the officers must be moving down in the size of their targets.

He walked up and asked the nearest rider for Colonel Bessières. All of the officers were dressed in field uniform, but they edged their horses to the side exposing the only officer wearing two epaulettes. He asked, "Who are you?"

Charles gave his name and assignment to the thirty-year old man with braided blond hair and curled cadenettes; assuming he was speaking to Colonel Bessières. Bessières smiled, introduced himself and said, "General Caffarelli sent me a message half an hour ago letting me know you were on your way. He told me about your recent adventures."

Charles showed the colonel the promotion letter from Bonaparte and described what a great help Paul Forgeron had been. He praised his fighting abilities and his intelligence. Colonel Bessières, after explaining that the Brigade of Guides needed an experienced adjutant since their existing one was staying in Paris with his sick wife, told

Charles to go back to the inn, pick up his baggage along with the new adjutant and return.

"We are having a formal mess dinner for the officers this evening. Our quartermaster will issue you hammocks for use in the casemates and later onboard the ship. We're sleeping three officers per vaulted chamber." The colonel told him.

Arriving at the Toulon inn, he discovered Paul in the common room drinking from a mug. "Where's Duval?"

"He's left and reported in to his ship. There is no way I can follow either of them now."

"Pack your bags and let's go to the Brigade of Guides lines," Charles told him. "Colonel Bessières is expecting both of us for dinner tonight. They have a casemate room for us. You are now a Sous-Officier and will dine in the Officers Mess."

When they reported for duty, the Chief of Staff said to Paul, "Your first duty as the new Adjutant-Sous-Officier is to start a pay book for yourself and fill out the promotions in Captain MacDonald's pay book."

At dinner, he and Paul met most of the officers in the Brigade of Guides. They were still waiting for the 1st squadron of the *Chasseurs à Cheval* who were on service with General Bonaparte in Paris. Charles had taken special notice of one the officer mounted beside the colonel that morning. He was Captain Joseph "*Hercules*" Domingo, a free man of color. He was massive; an exceptionally strong black man who was born in Cuba and moved to French controlled Saint-Domingue as a young man. He later arrived in France and became a citizen who supported the revolution. Bonaparte had promoted him and awarded him a sword of honor for his bravery on the battlefield of Arcole-Veronese in Italy.

After speaking with Domingo, Charles looked around and realized that he was the only officer not smoking in the officers' mess.

Even worse, he thought wryly, they would be even more upset when they discover that I don't gamble.

TWENTY - THREE

May 1ˢᵗ

DINNER AT THE MACDONALD TOWN HOUSE, PARIS

Tristan and Marten arrived at General MacDonald's town house shortly after five o'clock. Everyone was meeting upstairs at the round table in the family room for dinner. The general's housekeeper had already brought platters and bowls of food upstairs. After greetings all around, General MacDonald began by saying, "We have important information for all of us to discuss, so I hope that everyone will be comfortable with eating as we share our news. First, I would like you to meet Mademoiselle Eliza Rossignol, who will read her decryptions of the first three of the eight messages we have captured."

Eliza Rossignol was an attractive unmarried girl in her early twenties. She was wearing the plain sensible working clothes of a modern woman. Tristan particularly noticed that she had short brown hair and a trim figure. The young lady was nervous when she stood and started to describe how she had deciphered each message, "Hidden inside the end page of the common prayer book is a thin copper *Alberti chiffrer disque* — the English call it a cipher disc. You have to turn the end cover almost backwards to allow removal of the disc." She demonstrated by removing two pieces of copper with the smaller one riveted to the larger at its center. "Each agent has a special code word that allows them to set the wheel based on a page number and line number in the prayer book identifying the word that denotes the setting for the wheel. These two numbers change in the first line of each message. Since a special character is used to mark the end of each tenth word, and some letters are used much more often than others in each language, I deciphered the messages based on the frequency of each symbol," she explained in a halting tone. Tristan didn't understand and asked her to help him comprehend how all this encryption worked.

She showed them how to rotate the smaller wheel by lining up letters against the key symbol on the outer wheel and then transpose each old letter or number into a new one. Then she wrote out a three-word message and encoded it. "The first three messages found in Colonel DeVillars saddlebags were from Mandrake to Sword Master at Picardie d'Fer. I have not yet assigned real names to the coded agent names they are using in their messages."

She continued, "The first message is in French and dated the 24th. It orders them to prepare to rob three special mail coaches coming to Paris in a week. The first would be a special diligence stage coming from Holland with over a ton of gold guineas. He ordered *the Picardie d'Fer* to ambush the coach in the Forest of Chantilly south of Senlis. The second would be a regular turgotine mail coach from Frankfort through Reims to Paris carrying 750,000 marks in gold from Hessia. They were to rob it in the forest and finally they were to be prepared to hold up the third, a coach carrying gold guldens from Brussels to Paris. It was one day behind the first two shipments. Sword Master was to meet the Falconer south of Senlis for further instructions from London."

"The second and third messages are also in French and both are similar but involved the gold coach in Fontainebleau and instructions for the men in Lyons and bribe payments to someone there. The message strangely refers to an Academy rather than the French word, Salle. This leads me to believe that man in Lyon is an English agent. He is probably the resident British agent in Lyon and not one of the émigrés."

"We just got a new report in from Lyon, sent by my son Charles," interrupted the general. "He reports that there is a suspect sword master calling himself Giorgio Castracani. He runs a salle d'armes above the gatehouse of the turgotine terminus on the peninsula."

"The third message also warned him that the jail escape from Temple Prison would happen on Tuesday the 24th." Eliza Rossignol reported.

The General said, "Of course you are all aware that on the 24th English Naval Captain Sidney Smith escaped from the Temple Prison in Paris," the general continued. "I suspect that he was also an agent of the British Secret Service. Of course, the old Templar headquarters housed the King and Queen before the Revolutionary Tribunal had them guillotined. For over five and a half centuries, until the 24th, no one had ever escaped from the Temple enclosure."

"There is something odd about the format and wording of some of the messages," Eliza said. "The words seem unusual, almost as if someone coded the message twice, first in English and then reciphered it into French. Of course, they are using code names for the identity of all of their actors. When they repeat words or places multiple times within various messages, it helps me to decode them."

"Colonel DeVillars must have subdivided his men into geographic sections," General MacDonald said. "They must be referring to the various Black Horse Cuirassier units when they use the term d'Fer-of Iron, as a code name. There are five coded messages captured in Lyon and we are still finishing their decoding. Mandrake coded all the messages in English and addressed them to his resident agent in Lyon. The agent was to translate and forward them to the men in Lyon. They apparently contain more instructions including the names of some supporters in Lyon, Dijon, Geneva, Bern, and Zurich. There are also references to d'Fer units in Normandy, Brittany and Death Hussars of the Damascus Legion in Province and Aquitaine."

The general continued, "If Sword Master is Colonel DeVillars and if the Black Horse Cuirassiers are men from his old regiment, there may be as many as four hundred royalists spread around France. We need to find out more about the Damascus Legion along the southern coast. The royalist Roger de Damas used to command a legion of almost 2,000 men. We will act on this information after we finish our operations here in Paris. The information in these messages may allow us to discover where the leak about the scheduling of gold shipments is coming from. Using the date sent, we can find out who knew what was planned and when they found out."

General MacDonald asked Henri Dumas if he could send a message to the Army Paymasters in Holland and confirm what type of gold coins were in the Amsterdam shipment. In addition, he should ask how they were packaged, were they in *rouleaux* with a company cypher on the *papier* tube. "Get a response as quickly as possible."

Tristan DuMayne then described how many people were occupying the Montmartre Benedictine Convent. He also detailed their appearance. "By my count there are between ten and fifteen men in residence," Tristan said. "But, there are additional men appearing unexpectedly every morning and disappearing each evening. They must be coming in and out through a secret tunnel and traveling to other cities. I based our count on a chart of all the horses pastured next to the convent each day. All of the men at the nunnery speak English when they are inside the compound. I recognize American, Irish and Scottish accents in addition to English. I did wait outside the Montmartre church complex one night. Riders emerged from the cemetery and went north, east and west along the tax wall. They are sending messages to other units in at least three directions. We have followed individuals to the legation of the United States, the Turkish Embassy, and the Tuileries Palace and across the river to the Luxembourg Palace. One also visited the offices of the Minister of War and another went to the Minister of Marine. We do not know whom they visited at any of these locations."

General MacDonald interrupted, "We need additional men to follow them inside the Palais des Tuileries and the Luxembourg Palace. However, it is highly likely they are meeting with members of the Executive Directory, the War Ministry, the Assembly and the Council of Ancients."

"Three local people, a café worker, our national guardsman and a hostler, have reported that these men were posing as officers of the secret police," Tristan said.

"I will start dictating a report to my wife Elizabeth, for me to deliver to General Bonaparte tomorrow morning," General MacDonald said. "I believe he is leaving for Toulon next week. Before then, we need to find a way to inspect the interior of the convent, without them knowing we have been inside. Is there any time they are all gone or is there any way to get inside at night?"

"Although we made a thorough search of the grounds, we have only done a cursory look at the building," Tristan reported. "It's too dangerous to search inside. A few of the structures are empty and abandoned. An unknown number of people are always there. If our plan is to enter occupied buildings, we must be extremely careful and it must be well after midnight so everyone is asleep."

"Let's meet tomorrow at dinner to review our progress," General MacDonald suggested. "Between now and then, please think of any way we can investigate inside the convent buildings. We need to set up an exploration of the religious property for tomorrow night to see if there are any guards on duty. Our men can check and confirm which buildings are in use and which are empty. I know Marten Napier has asked three officers that he trusts, to take turns watching the grounds tonight. Have you or Henri been able to talk to any additional men?"

"I have privately talked to the men who worked for me here in the Ile-de-France province," Tristan replied. "The colonel commanding the 17ᵗʰ Military Division of Gendarmes has them assigned to other duties. I know that Henri is talking to several old sergeants and a couple of old Directory guards. We need written orders from General Bonaparte."

General MacDonald then asked the group, "Who can we use for an exterior patrol to follow anyone using the tunnel? Tristan, can you get some trustworthy gendarmes to handle following their messengers outside the city limits? I realize that they have no jurisdiction inside the city."

"Colonel Ackler is watching my old section too closely; my men can't leave their new duties." Tristan said. "However, I could ask a few friends for some unofficial help. I know the commander and the sergeant of the *flying squadron* of mounted gendarmes that patrol the roads north and east of the city walls. The caserne de gendarmerie just inside the *Barrier de la Villette* at the northeast corner of the tax wall is not only the headquarters of the 17ᵗʰ Division. The mounted squadron and all the gendarmes in the Saint Dennis and Marne departments also work out of the fortress. It's about four kilometers from the nunnery, straight east along the tax wall."

TWENTY-FOUR

May 2^(nd)

THE MACDONALD TOWN HOUSE, PARIS

Early the next morning General MacDonald got a note from Bonaparte to meet him and formulate new plans since he wanted to leave a few days early. James dressed in his uniform and Jean took him to the house on Rue de la Victoire. Napoleon met him upstairs in the office.

"Over the last few nights during our investigations of the compound, we have not entered any occupied buildings," General MacDonald told him. "But, we have watched their movements and the horses. We have followed their messengers and spies to other locations but we don't have enough agents to go everywhere. My wife wrote out our observations and prepared a report for you. They're going to attack you when you leave the city. You and your Guides need to take the southern route through Orleans. They'll assume you're going through Lyon and set up an ambush before you cross the Seine River. Lets work on a plan using any ideas you come up with about what is going on there."

"Seize the compound," the général-in-chief said. "I'll get you all the men you need from the 17^(th) Gendarme Division, both for that and any fighting that may come up."

After he got back to the townhouse General MacDonald sent a note to Tristan telling him that Bonaparte was leaving first thing tomorrow morning. He told him to be back here with everyone for an early dinner. Make sure to bring your two friends from the flying squadron.

When Tristan arrived he told him, "Since the British agents will only have a few hours warning, they must leave tonight to ambush Bonaparte's convoy. This morning I warned General Bonaparte of the threat and worked with him on a plan to launch a raid against the convent at first light. The fifteen men at the convent won't be enough to attack the column, since Bonaparte will be taking the duty squadron of his guides-a-cheval with him for protection; he'll have a hundred and fifty experienced cavalrymen as bodyguards. The British operatives will have to ask some of their émigré cavalrymen to help."

Wednesday afternoon while the investigators met for an early meal, General MacDonald began to outline the plan he and Bonaparte had prepared. Nodding in the direction of the gendarme lieutenant and sergeant he said, "Tristan has arranged for an elite troop of mounted gendarmes, the Flying Squadron, to be available to follow the British agents and foil their plans to kill Bonaparte. He has approved their use in combatting the terrorist."

The convent attack force will shut the door behind the British and secure the perimeter of the nunnery while our men search the buildings." Motioning his arm in the direction of Tristan and Marten he continued, "Use only highly experienced detectives to search the convent and try not to disturb anything. Make copies and return everything into its original position. Of course, if you take any prisoners everything will change. They'll know we were there. In that case, bring everything back here for evaluation."

"General Bonaparte is carrying all of the remaining gold from the War Ministry with him," General MacDonald said. "It's all new

British guineas, about 750,000 francs worth. Over 650 pounds of old gold coins are missing. Someone has stolen over 1.25 million francs." General MacDonald paused for their comments.

"If it wasn't Major Menou, we may be looking for another British operative." Tristan said, "Since the British cannot pay bribes using only the new shiny gold coins, they have probably mixed the old coins into their payoff fund. Meanwhile it's vital to discover if they are using the convent as the British Secret Service headquarters or only a staging post for royalist action groups. Also, be on the lookout for any information that mentions the United States government. After the raid we need to watch the movement of messages into and out of the convent."

"I have decided to send my wife and children out to the farm for the next few weeks," the general announced. "If the British discover that the team is operating out of this house, an attack on it is a distinct possibility. My best friend, Artillery Colonel Ryan Murphy has agreed to accompany them to the farm, keep an eye out, and act as the boys' tutor while they are away from Paris. Some of you may have seen him around the house; he is missing half his left hand. He is taking a few weeks leave from the *Commissaires des Guerres d'artillerie & du genie* to help us. Elizabeth has been a great help to Eliza in her work decrypting the English parts of the British Secret Service coded messages. She's also been a great help in writing reports, letters and reproducing extra copies of the sketches of our opponents. In the housekeeper's absence, Ex-Sergeant Major Dulcos will do all the cooking. He and Scout will help guard the house at night."

TWENTY - FIVE

May 2nd

BRIGADE OF GUIDES LINES, TOULON, FRANCE

O n Wednesday morning after breakfast, Charles went for a long walk around the town of Toulon. It was the 2nd of May and a clear cool spring day with the flowers and trees just at full bloom. After returning to his shared room, he unpacked his father's first of four journals and went out to the Vauban sea wall to read. He was amazed to realize his father started this journal over 50 years ago as a student requirement for the French Royal Engineering School. His own first assignment at X had also been to start a journal. Bound in wine colored leather, his father's volume had 312 numbered pages that were each eight by ten inches. He had made the earlier entries with a feather quill and iron gall ink. Later field entries changed to a wooden graphite pencil or a metal dip-pen nib with India black ink. He hand tinted the scores of drawings and sketches with a set of watercolor paints. Charles still had the small wooden paint box with its twenty-four compartments, a dozen on each side for pans of colored pigments and half-dozen brushes.

The notebook began with his father's first eight years at the Jesuit College in Douai where he received a Bachelor of Arts in Mathematics at the age of fourteen. His mother and father had taken him to France hoping that he might become a priest since he enjoyed reading and studying. His older brother liked to fight and bedeviled him constantly. He transferred to the University of Edinburgh to study for a Master of Mathematics. Fascinated by the *Enlightenment* and its humanist outlook he joined a literary society that supported the Jacobite political cause. He also became a Scots Master Mason in the Blue Lodge of Edinburgh even though he was a Catholic and younger son of the future Chief of Clan MacDonald of Keppoch.

After the disastrous eight-month Jacobite Rising of 1745 his father was killed in the first wave at the Battle of Culloden Moor. As a young aide to the Duke, actually horse holder; James saw his father fall and moved to cover him with his kilt while collecting his weapons; the silver pistols, dagger and claymore. After the loss he spent months evading the English before finally escaping to France. The English armies were pacifying the highlands by executing all Jacobite officers. Under the *Auld Alliance* James was automatically a French citizen and because he had graduated from college there he spoke French fluently. Joining the Garde Écossaise-Scottish Guard as a private soldier he became a heavy cavalryman. The Scottish Guard Carabiniers carried basket-hilted claymore style heavy swords and carabines along with a pair of pistols. At the Battle of Lauffeld in 1747 he was one of the fifteen thousand horsemen charging the English-German cavalry. In order to enroll at *L'Ecole Royale du Génie de Mezières* he had to excel in the mathematics entrance exam and prove he was an aristocrat.

Engineering school was spread over six years. The first year was in the classroom and continued with another in the field. Then there were two more as an apprentice engineer. He joined the field exploration team mapping the Nile River in Egypt. Charles already knew that the third volume concluded with his two years of advanced study back in *Mézières* under the tutelage of Charles Camus, a famous mathematician and astronomer. He also knew that his father had help develop many astronomical surveying techniques.

The 1750 expedition in Egypt for the cartographer Robert de Vaugondy was split into two sections. The navy section explored and surveyed the 250-league coast of Egypt and Palestine while the military expedition, with his father, traveled inland up the Nile. They had measured both entrances to the Nile River all the way to their joining north of Cairo and south on up the Nile to beyond the cataracts and Ethiopia. Later, the land expedition followed the inland routes from Aqaba to the Dead Sea and on to Jerusalem. They then traveled through the holy land to Damascus, finally rejoining the naval survey in Beirut.

Reading the journals taught him some new lessons. From the notes and calculations, Charles realized that his father was attempting to solve the puzzle of calculating longitude. For two years, he recorded the angles between the moon and selected planets and stars every night. Over the next decade, Camus and Charles de Borda, one his later student at Mézières, used MacDonald's lunar distance observations to develop spherical trigonometry, one of the two procedures for calculating longitude. His father's description of the weather was extremely disquieting. In June, it became extremely hot and dry for months.

Charles put a slip of paper into the journal, closed it and walked back to the guides' cavalry lines for dinner. That evening while talking to Paul, he said, "Reading my father's journal, I discovered that we might not have enough water between June and August. Since you are in overall charge of equipment and logistics, you need to make sure we have plenty of water containers; not just canteens, we'll need barrels. You can't discuss our problems with anybody, because so few know our final destination, or at least are supposed to know. I need to talk with General Caffarelli about the water plans for the army."

On Thursday morning, he walked down to the City Hall for a meeting with the savants who were accompanying the expedition. Gaspard Monge, who had been one of Charles's professors at X, was one of General Bonaparte's friends and in charge of the scientists who would be on the expedition. A small number of them were aware of their destination but most were not. The sergeant major called the meeting to order and then General Caffarelli introduced a number of distinguished scientists, intellectuals, and technicians at the front of the meeting room. Among them were almost twenty military engineers, some geographical engineers, civilian engineers and cartographers, artist, poets, writers, manufacturers, wine merchants, printers, bakers, mathematicians, orientalists, geometers, chemist, astronomers, antiquarians, zoologists, mineralogists and a number of aeronauts who planned to ascend in their hydrogen-filled balloon, *L'Entreprement*.

The general reviewed the few simple rules that they must follow as members of the expedition. "Space is at a premium and most you will be sleeping in hammocks, hanging directly over your baggage. The quartermaster will issue rations and pay civilians as if they were officers. Each soldier and civilian now has an account for accrued pay as well as spoils of war with the Army quartermaster to reduce theft, drunkenness, gambling and whoring. Each of you must turn in your cash, spoils of war or treasure; anyone caught with valuables is subject to discipline. They must credit their quartermaster account with anything they liberate." A number of other specialists then discussed additional subjects. Finally, he told the assembled men that they could contact him, Captain Say or his Adjudant-Chef for assistance. The expedition would sail on the 12th of May and all of them would be sailing on the flagship, *L'Orient*. When the meeting concluded, the general went over to Charles and said, "Horace Say will be here late tomorrow night. I can hardly wait to have some additional help."

"I'll be busy for the next week studying my father's journals and maps," Charles replied. "I would like to set up a confidential meeting to discuss my findings. I have already discovered one issue that could be critical."

"What is it?"

Charles explained how necessary it would be for the expedition to carry an adequate supply of water in June, July and August. "The water in the Nile does not rise until late August, which lifts the ground water level in the wells and cisterns. In addition to extra canteens for each man, we need to build water wagons. We may need as much as 50,000 gallons of water each day. That much water weighs over 200 tons. Since each wagon can carry only six tons with a six-horse team, we will need over 30 wagons pulled by almost 200 horses, to give us enough water for one day."

"We are only taking 1,300 horses," General Caffarelli told him. "The cavalry, artillery and officers need at least 7,000. We are planning on acquiring more in Egypt."

After the general left, Charles continued to worry about the problem of water logistics. Perhaps his father's journals would give him some clues about how to deal with the problem. He decided he would bring it up for discussion with Bonaparte when he arrived on May 9th. Maybe Paul would have some ideas or advice, Charles concluded; he must have faced this problem as a sergeant major.

TWENTY-SIX

May 3rd

MONTMARTRE BENEDICTINE CONVENT, PARIS

Captain Tristan DuMayne was in charge of the raiding party waiting outside the main gate to the old Montmartre Benedictine Convent on the north side of Paris. Shortly before first light, he could hear men and horses moving around in the stable. As the sounds faded, he imagined the horses moving through the tunnel to the far side of the Paris perimeter wall. They must be on the way to attack the cavalcade of coaches, wagons and the squadron of guides in General Bonaparte's caravan. He immediately sent Henri Dumas to General Bonaparte's home to warn his guides that there would probably be an assault on his coach in the rising daylight and they should change his route.

Thirty minutes later, he heard distant sounds of clinking metal and numerous hoofbeats as the men from the nunnery mounted and rode off to the east, coming down off Butte Montmartre. He followed their sound walking quietly along the tax wall as they rode east. They were staying at least a kilometer north of the wall. Reaching the gendarmes posted outside the Saint-Denis barricade on the northbound Rue Nationale to the east of Montmartre, he told his friend, the lieutenant in command of the gendarme cavalry, "I heard a dozen enemy horsemen leave the convent and later sounds from the church on top of Montmartre. They are just crossing the Rue Saint-Denis north of here. As we discussed, use a disguised scout to follow them at a distance. Have him stay at least a half-league behind the riders."

"I already have my man watching the road," his friend said. "I hear him coming now."

The scout ran up, saluted and said, "Three dozen cavalrymen crossed the road followed by two howitzers and a dozen more men dressed as workmen."

"Mount up and follow them at a distance," the lieutenant told the scout, then turned to Tristan and said, "Where did they get the extra men and two artillery pieces. I hope the guides have changed General Bonaparte's route."

By five o'clock in the morning when Tristan got back to the convent, everyone was in place for the clandestine raid. At the worst, there would be only one or two lookouts and they might well be asleep. At half past five o'clock, he gave the word and the raiding party quietly rushed through the main gate. Marten had unlocked it an hour earlier with his picks. Tristan led Henri, Marten, and Jean, and half dozen additional agents followed them. While the four men ran down the drive to the eastern wing of the convent, the others spread out around the property.

As he and Marten charged into the kitchen of the residential wing, Henri and Jean ran into the attached stables. Beside the coals of a dying fire, they were surprised to find a sleeping watchman. They grabbed him and tied his hands behind his back and then his feet. Marten dumped him into a chair and then bound his arms and his chest to its back, making sure the chair faced the fire. He placed a poker and a set of tongs into the coals to heat up. After that display, Tristan covered his head with a sack. The two SIS agents then thoroughly searched the building. They brought everything of importance they found to the kitchen for inspection, a separate pile for each room. There was no longer any need to conceal their search. Tristan stepped outside and waved for one of the sûreté detectives to come in and start an inventory of what they discovered. Removing the hood from the first prisoner, Henri and Jean brought a second hooded prisoner into the kitchen, lashed him into another chair, and then moved the second prisoner into the next room.

Tristan started to question the kitchen prisoner, a tall muscular Germanic-looking man with a long blond queue and face hair flowing from in front of his ears to his mustachios. Tristan pulled the red-hot poker from the fire and moved it closer and closer to his face as he described what he was doing; *Citoyen la cuisine*-"Mr. Kitchen"-refused to talk. Marten grabbed a cherry-red coal with the tongs and carried it into the next room as it popped and flamed, followed by Tristan replacing the first prisoner's blindfold. Moments later it sounded like Marten thrust the burning coal into the face of the stable prisoner. You could almost image the smell of burning hair and the aroma of seared flesh as his scream sent chills up and down their spines. Although he knew that Marten had burnt his arm or leg, Tristan pulled away the hood as he brandished the red-hot poker a second time and whispered that his partner had burnt out the eye of the other prisoner. The kitchen prisoner started talking as soon as he felt the intense heat against his face.

He mumbled, "I don't know any British agents. I'm the Swiss footman for a rich international gentleman. He ordered me to take care of his houseguest when he left on a trip. When the authorities confiscated his house, his friends joined a few others and we moved here to this abandoned property."

"When did your employer leave on his trip," Tristan asked him.

"He left a few months after the massacre of the Swiss Guards in August of '92," the prisoner replied.

"You are lying," said Tristan. "You say he left six years ago implying that you have worked for no pay since then or that he's still in contact." This opening led to numerous additional questions and a few more threats. Finally, the frightened man admitted, "Over half the men staying at the convent are Americans and they report to an official of the United States government who lives nearby." The rest were Scotsmen and Irishmen, guests of the French since they opposed the British. The bearded man said he was a former Swiss cook who lost his job when the Jacobins beheaded his employer in '94. Tristan and Marten asked both men alternating questions for the next half hour.

Finally, Marten muttered, "Merde!" He grabbed the red-hot poker and jerked the younger prisoner back out of the room, shutting the door behind him. He began a muffled scream, and then began begging for mercy in a rising and then lowering voice. Marten came back into the kitchen a quarter-hour later and said, "He's been lying. Citoyen la stable was a former infantryman in the Swiss Guard Regiment and Citizen Kitchen here was a sergeant in the Hundred-Swiss, a personal bodyguard to the king. All of the men staying here are British Secret Service agents. If he doesn't immediately tell me about his chief, I'm going to blind him. Then Citizen Stable will tell me everything when he regains consciousness. The kitchen prisoner finally admitted that the Englishman, Quintin Craufurd, was the head of the British Secret Service in Europe. Marten dragged the second man back into the kitchen and started asking rapid-fire questions. He would occasionally slap one or the other while asking more questions. Marten picked up the glowing poker, touched the chin of the ex-sergeant and asked, "What are you protecting? Where's the gold from the Amsterdam shipment?"

The kitchen prisoner moaned as his flesh sizzled and then gasped, "It's hidden in a *cave*. The nuns had a group of cellars on either side of the tunnel to the sewer that runs under the Paris wall. The entrance to the tunnel is under the floor of the first stall in the barn."

Marten untied the prisoner from the chair and released the ropes around his feet. Leaving his arms tied behind his back, Tristan, Marten and Jean walked him out to the barn.

There was a tack room and a workroom on either side of the entrance. At the end of the barn was the entrance to a paddock, with a fenced pasture along the entire southern side. Tristan walked down the length of the barn and looked out into the paddock. Glancing back into the barn, he realized the ten stalls on the north side of the barn had wooden plank floors while the center aisle and the stalls on the south side had paving stone floors. Carefully inspecting the first and second stalls on the north side, he noticed there was a metal eye, bolted into the top board of the short sidewall between the two stalls. A rope was running over a beam-mounted block and tackle set with a hook. The men had tied it to the wooden column at the end of this short wall. When he hooked the rope to the eyebolt and lifted, the entire wall rose upwards in slots cut into the columns. The wood floor of the stalls, hay, feed troughs and wall sections rose up together, revealing a stone ramp running down toward the Rue Blanche under the remaining eight stalls on the north side of the barn.

TWENTY-SEVEN

May 3ʳᵈ

TUNNEL UNDER MONTMARTRE, PARIS

Tristan went outside to where he had left his bullseye dark lantern near the gate. He relit the lamp as he walked back to the barn. He and Marten Napier went down the ramp into a stone-lined tunnel. It was six-feet wide and eight-feet tall with a vaulted roof. There were closed doorways to underground rooms on both sides of the tunnel. The nuns must have used these cellars to age their cheese or their wine, he concluded.

Based on the number steps he took, the tunnel must go under the paddock and the convent walls to where it joined with the main Paris sewer under the Rue Blanche. There was an iron lock hanging loose from the door and ramp at the entrance to the sewer. The main sewer was twelve feet wide with a five-foot walkway on each side of the deeper channel. It was ten feet high with an arched ceiling. The bottom of the sewer was a good five feet lower than the beginning of the ramp to the stable, one foot of drop for every thirty feet of tunnel.

The builders had used limestone blocks to construct the entire tunnel, caves and sewer system. The city sewer, which smelled remarkably clean, had a two-foot wide by two-foot deep channel of water running down the center. Since the closure of the religious properties on Montmartre, there were almost no residents at this northern end of the sewer. The top of Montmartre had several windmill pumps to lift water and charge the water pipes of the northern suburbs. Overflow water must flush the northern sewer. Further south the main flow of the entire right bank of Paris would enter this sewer flowing into the Seine.

Turning and scrutinizing the tunnel from the sewer back up to the ramp, he noticed a locked, ironbound door fifteen feet from the entrance to the sewer, recessed into the wall of the tunnel. Marten walked up and checked the padlock securing the door. He then took several steel picks out of his pocket and unlocked the door in less than a minute. When he opened the door to the cave, there were eleven columns of eight-high ironbound strong boxes stacked inside. To the side were several crates of weapons and half a dozen barrels of gunpowder.

Tristan walked over and lifted one of the strong boxes. He estimated that it weighed almost fifty pounds. He had a sudden realization. This must be the gold stolen from the Amsterdam turgotine. Counting the boxes, he saw there were 88, too many boxes. The Amsterdam robbery involved 58 boxes of gold coins. It must be the British Secret Service treasury for all of France. Tristan and Marten walked back and opened the unlocked doors to all of the caves on both sides of the convent tunnel. There was another room with weapons and gunpowder. The rest of the rooms still held aging wheels of cheese or dusty bottles of wine. The room closest to the stable ramp had large wooden fermentation tanks, empty bottles and unused corks. The cave across the passageway had a pair of ninety-liter copper pots, wooden-hoop molds and rolls of cheesecloth.

He left Marten on watch while he returned to the stables and asked Jean, to join Marten on lookout at the sewer entrance. He then sent Henri Dumas to find a heavy-duty wagon to transport the almost two tons of gold. Tristan returned to the tunnel with four other officers. While Jean stayed on guard, Marten and the four agents started moving strong boxes up to the center aisle of the barn.

Tristan took the bullseye lantern and searched up the sewer. There were no wheel tracks from cannon carriages. Several hundred yards north of the first intersection, he discovered a second tunnel intersecting the sewer from the west, to his left. He walked up this steep tunnel. It ended in an empty room with stonewalls and large double doors. He could see light through the doors and two sets of wheel marks on the dusty floor. There was a simple latch on the inside and he opened the doors. He was standing in an old cemetery outside the tax wall; to his right was the Church of Saint Pierre de Montmartre. He could hear the creaking and clacking of the sema-phore arms rotating and swinging and the squeaking of the rotating windmill sails further across the hill. Turning around, he realized the double doors and room was a mausoleum for the remains of mem-bers of the Conté family. However, he saw no remains; the place was empty. At this point, Tristan's two gendarme friends had to leave to go on duty. It took the next several hours to recover the hidden treasure, arrange for a heavy freight wagon, and load the almost two-tons of coins and other lighter items before they were ready to return through the crowded streets of Paris to the Avenue de Saxe. Placing the still bound prisoners in the back of the wagon on top of the double layer of 88-strong boxes, the driver whipped his four-draft horse team out the gate, surrounded by six horsemen. Two Sûreté officers stayed to keep a watch for the return of anyone who might have escaped from the ambush force that was chasing General Bonaparte.

After several hours fighting traffic through Paris during the day-time madness of carts and delivery wagons, the gold-laden wagon arrived at the front of the MacDonald house. The six riders dismounted and helped unload the wagon. The men carried all of the material into the ground floor storage rooms and secured the two still tied prisoners. They placed the gold in the wine cellar, which had a sturdy metal clad door with a strong lock. General MacDonald was there with Scout, asking questions about everything that had happened. Two of the men went into the wine cellar and counted the gold.

There was well over 5.3 million francs worth, about 1.95 million francs in new British guineas and an additional 3.35 million francs in mixed gold and silver coins. There were dozens of coded messages. The papers included many different identity documents and passports as well as military plans and notes. The agents also found the copies of confidential minutes of hundreds of Directory meetings.

Leaving a man downstairs as sentry, the general called his investigators up to the dining room while Jean Dulcos put together a meal for everyone. After locking the front door and carrying several bottles of wine, they all went up. As each man started filling their plates and glasses General MacDonald said, "Tristan, please make notes. First, Jean should go and ask Eliza Rossignol if she can work here for the next few days until we review all of this new information. Second, Marten must make sure we have one of our officers on watch at the convent for at least the next week. Third, Tristan, you set up a shipment for the gold to Toulon. You will be responsible for chaperoning it all the way. Take any gendarmes you can trust with you. I will sign a letter to the Gendarmerie colonel ordering him to assign the men you need. You should take any information we have about agents at the Mediterranean ports and the traitors in Lyon. Start investigating them. When you arrive in Toulon, give General Bonaparte and Charles any information we have in addition to delivering the gold. If you leave tomorrow morning, you should arrive a day before they sail."

"Fourth," he continued. "We need to write out everything we know or suspect about any potential agents or Frenchmen receiving bribes and try to tie this information together. Fifth, starting right now and working all night, we need to make copies of everything we have collected including the earlier reports, and send the copies with Tristan to give to Charles. Don't copy anything he already has, but do send him copies of the newly decoded messages."

He turned and asked, "Jean, is the wagon still outside?" When Jean told him it was, General MacDonald said, "Go down and pay the driver, but have him come back tonight at midnight. Tell him it is worth a Louis d'Or for his work tonight. Continue on and bring back Mademoiselle Rossignol."

General MacDonald then asked, "Tristan, which gendarmes you can trust? I know that two friends helped you last night."

"I trust both of them—and there are two others who have worked for me over the past few years," Tristan replied. "They were all on my team investigating the British bribery."

General MacDonald dictated a letter, as Tristan wrote it out; he addressed it to Colonel Ackler, commander of the Gendarmerie Division of the Île-de-France. In it, he reiterated his authority based on the appointment by General Bonaparte, and confirmed by Paul Barras, and requested the permanent assignment of the listed gendarmes to Captain Tristan DuMayne for special duties. He ended the letter with the statement, "The above-mentioned activities are secret and confidential. A special section of the National Gendarmerie under my command is investigating this activity. He signed it as *Général de division de la République.*"

"Do not let the colonel know that we have discovered the gold," the general told Tristan. "Do not let him know that you are taking a turgotine to the coast. Also, can you hide the prisoners for the next few weeks?"

Tristan went downstairs with Marten and hoisted each prisoner onto one of the horses tied outside. He left with the letter, leading both prisoners. Crossing Paris from the far southwestern tax wall to the far northeastern corner, he arrived at the Caserne de Gendarmerie Headquarters before dinner. There, he met with Colonel Ackler and got his four trusted gendarmes assigned to the new section. He then went down to the mess hall in the barracks and took his friends aside. "Be at the turgotine terminus at two o'clock in the morning with your weapons. You need to bring extra pistols and blunderbusses for each of you and two pistols for me. I left two tied prisoners in the orderly room. Go and ask Jacque Henry to put both men in La Conciergerie prison and question them, but don't allow them to communicate with anyone else until we return. Don't tell anybody where you are going."

He then rode back south to the Messageries Nationales. Entering the manager's office, he showed him his orders. "I need a sturdy coach and team for a special trip, all the way to Toulon. I will be furnishing five gendarme escorts. I also need an experienced ex-military conductor. Is conductor Raoul Pelle available for a special trip?"

The manager answered, "Yes, but you will have to pay him for the special."

"Send him a message," Tristan continued. "I want to hire him for the trip. The coach will be carrying almost two tons of cargo in addition to the guards and their baggage. You are not to discuss this special cargo with anyone other than Conductor Pelle. If the information leaks out, I will arrest you for treason. I want to leave about a half hour before the regular mail coach so we will get the freshest horses at each stop. You need to send a messenger immediately to warn each stop of the need for extra teams and additional postil-lions." When he finished giving his instructions, he left and headed back across the river to the Avenue de Saxe. On the way, he stopped at his parent's apartment and picked up his bag. "I apologize for this brief visit," Tristan told his parents and sisters. "I'll be back in a few weeks."

When he got back to the Avenue de Saxe, leading two horses, it was already past nine o'clock. He went upstairs to the dining room and was amazed at the progress the group was making in copying the information. Tristan mentioned that he had hired the same conduc-tor that helped Charles and Paul escort the original gold shipment. General MacDonald took him aside and said, "There's too much for us to copy everything, so I had Marten and Eliza split it into the most important details. Meanwhile, Jean and I took the silver and worn gold coins, 350,000 francs to my bank, Perregaux & Cie where I deposited it in the name of the Section d'Investigation Spécial, the SIS. I gave the chief bookkeeper, Jacques Laffite your name as an alternate signatory. When you return we must go and show your identification and give them a copy of your signature. My wife Elizabeth is the co-signer for our personal account with them, so I used her signature as the temporary alternate."

Eliza Rossignol was at the table reviewing the content of dozens of new decrypted messages. While watching her as she explained the decoding method, Tristan had found her an intriguing young lady who was extremely intelligent and attractive. He decided that he would like to get to know her better. That would entail calling on her properly at her home and meeting her mother. General MacDonald had told him that a few revolutionaries murdered her father in '92 during a British-created incident.

Before midnight, he packed copies of most of the papers into a second traveling bag. General MacDonald insisted that he carry one of their extra prayer books with an Alberti disc and 10,000 francs for the coach and travel money. He went outside to where the wagon had just arrived. The men loaded 82 strong boxes into the wagon and then started for the terminus. Before loading the wagon, Tristan peered up and down the Avenue de Saxe and determined that no one was watching.

Tristan sat on the wagon seat next to the driver and rode to the terminus, accompanied by three outriders. At the terminus, they loaded the mail coach. The hostlers brought out three teams of horses as two postillion drivers exited the stables. Tristan knew that the heavy load would require three teams of horses and two drivers for the entire trip.

As he came out after paying the fare, Jean gave the promised Louis D'Or to the wagon driver and thanked him. Then Tristan and three of the four gendarmes' boarded the coach, while the fourth took his place on top in place of the mail-guard. Conductor Raoul Pelle took his place in the box and two postillion drivers mounted the left lead and wheel horse of the six-horse team. It was Friday morning May 4th as the coach began its journey through Lyon and on to Toulon.

TWENTY-EIGHT

May 4ᵗʰ

TOULON, FRANCE

After meeting for breakfast on Friday morning, Charles, Horace Say and Paul went into Toulon to a wainwright's shop. A shop that specialized in building wagons, field cannon carriages and ships' gun carriages. They were there to inspect the special wagon that Paul had asked the wainwright build to Charles' sketches. It was a water wagon with two big wheels and six woodstave naval water butts. These 400 litre water barrels were stacked in two pyramids behind the seat directly in front of and behind the single axle. "I got the idea for this cart from father's notebook," said Charles. "He drew a picture of long-horned black and white spotted oxen and he wrote that the locals called the castrated draft animals, either *zebu* or *brahma* depending on the color. Most were large and pulled extremely heavy loads. Even though we're not carrying many oxen, I thought that we could get a few here and a lot more in Egypt."

There was a cradle under each pyramid of barrels, and a strong oak frame with cross members and a steering pole. Hitched to the wagon was a team of two oxen with neck yokes. The wainwright showed them all six barrels were full of water and then started the team. The oxen slowly pulled the wagon down the crowded street, around the three corners of the block and back to the shop. The wagon was able to maneuver around the traffic in the street.

"The loaded water cart weights over three tonnes," Paul told Horace and Charles. "That's enough water for the Brigade of Guides for one day, without horses. With 200 horses, we would need six times the number of barrels. While a man drinks 4 litres per day, a horse needs over 60." Turning to Horace, Paul said, "Using this shop and two more, another in Toulon and one in Aix, we can make about twenty wagons before we leave. You should send drawings immediately to the other three ports and tell them to fabricate as many of these carriers as they can. With 100 wagons, the army could march two days without drawing water from wells."

"I still don't know how we're going to unload oxen from the ships to the shore," Charles said. "In addition, the sergeants must inspect the men's canteens and make sure they're full of water and not wine. My father's journal warns that wine and extreme heat produces more thirst, not less."

Down the street from the wainwright's workshop Charles had spotted a malitier, a trunk maker for ships officers with several chests in his window. Horace and Charles went there after they finished their inspection of the water wagon. Inside the shop, Charles asked about the item that had caught his attention, a small flat-topped half-trunk that nestled inside a slightly larger trunk. Charles said, "I'm interested in their size. Will my 39-inch long dress sword fit the diagonal across the top tray? It also needs to carry the 30-inch bow case that goes with my violin. They look like they are the perfect size to strap on either side of a donkey as panniers."

"A sea chest maker from London, J. Merriman and Sons, made them for a ship's officer," the owner answered. "The English sized inner trunk is 36 inches by 20 inches by 17 inches and the outer trunk is one inch larger all around with a tray on top." Taking out one of the new meter sticks, he measured the diagonal. "You can see that it is more than one meter across, about 41 English inches. Each one is water resistant and has a strong lock with two leather straps to keep the lid from springing open. When stacked at 35 inches they make a perfect table or writing desk." He pulled Horace to the side and whispered, "In Egypt, I plan to carry my field equipment in both shoulder bags. I hope to get a cart to carry my cookset, food, one change of underclothes and stockings in my leather portmanteaux, and new saddlebags. I have heard that the Nile River fleet of shallow draft boats will carry officer's trunks and extra horse tack, along with the heavier cannon. I would like to pack my violin, bow, épée, dress uniform, epaulettes, extra journals, drawing and writing supplies, extra underclothes, and wool greatcoat in the stacked trunks. If I acquire more possessions, I could use both trunks."

Horace Say had arrived on Thursday and immediately plunged into a whirlwind of activity; before he reported for duty he had stopped at the Brigade of Guides lines and delivered the items Charles had purchased in Lyon just the week before. General Caffarelli and his staff were overwhelmed with the amount of work required to satisfy the civilians. They also had to arrange accommodations for the dozens of businessmen who were going with the expedition, including the wine merchant from Dijon who supplied General Bonaparte with pipes of Bordeaux, as well as the officers' uniform manufacturer and a hatter from Paris. All of this added up to a massive logistical headache. Captain Say had to straighten out Caffarelli's staff and make things run more smoothly.

Later that morning, Charles changed into the new tan overalls Horace had brought from Lyon. They were made of a strong linen canvas; the bib at the front had real pockets with buttons and looked somewhat like a waistcoat. Charles planned to wear them in Egypt over his short under-drawers and linen shirt. He could reach his knife by loosening a button or two on his right leg. They matched his brown-topped riding boots.

He borrowed a horse, saddled it with DeVillars tack over his new saddlecloth and went for a ride in the hills. He had been borrowing a horse and going out every day for the past week, leaving and returning by a different route each time. He would dismount at one of many clearings overlooking the harbor, hobble his horse and read his father's journals. Some days he would practice with his new violin. He smiled and thought that he was chasing all the cats away with his screeching.

Every day at noon, he duplicated all of the measurements that now knew he should be entering in his journal. He practiced with his portable tools and his larger surveying and navigation instruments, using the tabulae that he had copied during his summer at the Paris Observatory. He had developed a formula to modify the annual tables for each year into the future. When he could, he used the lunar distance method to adjust the accuracy of his chronographic watch. It usually ran a minute fast each week. Extensive mathematical calculations were necessary to convert his sightings into actual coordinates.

After lunch, he would practice with his weapons. He made sure he could trot, canter, gallop and still be able to draw his sabre, his horse pistols, his carabine and his belt pistols. His carabine had a 30-inch barrel. The new Manton pistols had 12-inch barrels while his LePage over-and-under belt set had six-inch ones. The longer barrels fired the same ball much faster and further than the shorter ones.

Because of Paul's comments, he started practicing with his father's tomahawk. He could swing it in a much smaller space than the sabre so he practiced both with his knife in his right hand and the hawk in the other and vice versa. He sharpened it until it was like a razor. His could still use it for splitting slivers of firewood but not chopping heavy logs. From time to time, he would observe the ships in the harbor with his erecting telescope. The four-draw spyglass measured just over seven inches at its smallest, and twenty-three inches when fully extended. His father had it built by Jesse Ramsden of London in1791 and smuggled into France by a friend.

Charles kept a special watch for activity from the *Peregrine*, the warship commanded by Frigate Captain Duval. He had seen Duval on the deck of his ship a number of times. He had also sighted him taking a ship's boat to shore or to the flagship several times. He watched him when he went ashore and could follow him with his telescope to shops and to *L'Auberge du Oyster*, the higher-class inn used by naval officers. He made inquiries about a younger officer who often accompanied Duval. One of the port officials told him he was Lieutenant Louis Duval, his younger brother. Charles kept watch after dark several nights but there was almost no boat movement in the evening. If an officer was on shore, he stayed all night. Commander Duval, however, did not stay on shore overnight.

On Friday May 4th, Charles had dismounted in his favorite clearing on the top of Mount Caire, overlooking Point l'Eguilette and the inner harbor. He was late because of an earlier meeting with Horace and Paul. He had just finished setting up his pocket sextant for the noon sight. As he bent over his hat flew off his head with a huge crack as the bullet passed his ear. He knelt and pulled his carabine loose from its scabbard sleeve, cocked it and stared in the direction of the sound, which had arrived a moment after his hat had left.

There was a large expanding cloud of smoke about 150 yards due west. It came from some bushes where the ridgeline extended down toward his meadow. A gust of wind revealed a dark clothed man hurrying to a hobbled horse. Charles flicked his long-range leaf up, took aim leading the target for movement and fired as he slowly squeezed the trigger. His vision had narrowed to the target, the front sight, and the fuzzy rear notch. He was concentrating so intently on the front sight, that the flash of the priming charge did not distract his aim.

With the explosion, he immediately started running toward his target. As he ran, he pulled another cartridge out of his cartouche giberne, bit off the end of the paper, poured the powder down the barrel, manually pushing the paper and patched bullet into the muzzle. He drew his ramrod, and drove the new charge home. He slowed after about a hundred yards to prime his frizzen pan and then forged ahead as he withdrew and reseated his ramrod.

He had fired, reloaded and ran over 150 yards in well under a minute. He could hear a horse galloping away in the distance—the assassin was escaping. Charles caught a glimpse of the horse and its rider as they moved further away. He once again raised his carabine and fired at the escaping form, almost 200 yards distant. This time he saw the rider flinch as the ball struck his back. He slowly dropped off the horse, which slowed and stopped.

Before running to the body, he reloaded his carabine as he studied the signs on the path left by the sharpshooter between his shooting position and the horse. Charles spotted a disturbance and spots of blood where his shot hit him. The assassin sprawled forward as he was running full speed. He had dropped his rifle when he fell.

Reloaded, Charles ran to the downed rider and checked him for signs of life. He was dead with two wounds, one in the center of his back and the second in his side. He looked like a hard-bitten soldier with queued hair, side curls and numerous scars from fights. When Charles whistled, the black horse nickered and walked over, hoping for a rubbing. There was a Hungarian light cavalry sabre strapped under the bock-saddle skirts. The dead man was wearing a black hat and farmer's clothing, but his breeches under the brown coveralls were silver-decorated medium blue, hussar style. Looking at his boots, Charles concluded that he must be a hussar since they were black with silver tassels; an armored cavalryman wore taller plain black boots. Slinging and strapping the man into his saddle, he led the horse back to the shooting position in the bushes.

The rifle was an elegant German made Jäger rifle about 43 inches long, which indicated he had probably served in Germany. Charles carefully gazed in all directions for additional assailants. He searched for any more signs and found only the ashes of the man's burnt pipe tobacco, balled up paper and several used beer bottles, which were now full of piss. It looked like his assailant had been in this position for the last day or two. He returned to his overlook with the German rifle, packed up his equipment, and rode to the Brigade of Guides lines leading his new extra horse. After hearing his story and viewing the body, Colonel Bessières said, "Someone is obviously out to kill you. What do you make of this fellow?"

Charles replied, "He's dressed like a hussar. He had a letter, addressed to *Légion Damascus* in his pocket with a complete description of what I looked like, my clothing, and my normal routine. What's the meaning?"

"The letter refers to the royalist regiment of the Count of Damascus, Roger de Damas. I have heard rumors that his unit moved to the southern coast with the breakup of the Army of Condé after the Austrians surrendered. I also heard a rumor that the British are now paying them."

Searching the assassin's cantle bag he discovered a pair of dark blue coveralls with black metal buttons. The new overalls fit along with the boots so he kept both while he also kept the new horse; it would save him the trouble of borrowing one each day. Charles gave the rifle to Paul to add to his blunderbuss and pistol set

Late on Sunday afternoon May 6th, Charles was at his alternate overlook just packing his father's fourth journal when he noticed a ship's boat with the captain's crew rounding the side of the *Peregrine* to the entry port. The sun was just dipping below the hills, and Commander Duval was going ashore with his brother. Charles packed up his things and rode back to Toulon. He stopped several times and watched Duval through his telescope as the officers made their way to the Oyster Inn. As Charles was riding down the quayside road, dodging the traffic and ever-present reeling, drunken soldiers, he saw Commander Duval and his companion mounting horses outside the inn. Charles was still several hundred yards away and decided to keep his distance in order to avoid letting Duval know someone was following him.

The sun had finally dropped behind the western hills as Commander Duval and his brother Louis rode their rented horses toward the Aix gate in the northwest fortifications. Charles turned his black horse and headed for the city gate. He suspected where Duval was going since he had ridden that way several times. The road went up hill for about two and a half miles before it reached a level area with a public house. Local workmen, peddlers and others who did not want to pay the tax to bring their goods into Toulon waited there for customers; dockworkers also went there to buy untaxed goods that they would then smuggle back into town.

Charles stopped about a hundred yards short of the disreputable looking tavern and tied his horse under a tree well off the road. He watched as Duval and his brother tied their rented horses and went inside, through the low doorway. During his earlier visits, he had noticed that the right side of the building had a path that ran around to the *pissoir* in the rear, but the left side was overgrown, rocky and the hillside rose from the wall. Studying the candlelight flowing out of the building, he realized that the mountainside window was open.

Un-loosening his surtout buttons, he hung all his equipment on a rock near the hobbled horse including his two golden shoulder boards. Tying his dark stock around his neck, he also tied a dark kerchief around his head, replacing the bicorne. He slid his pistol holsters to the back of his belt, just under his dark blue waistcoat. His only other weapon was the Japanese bladed sabre, which he slung over his shoulder. Jumping up and down to ensure that there was no noise, he realized that the new leather saddle patches of his overalls made a swishing noise when he walked. Luckily, their tan color almost matched the color of the local boulders on the hillside.

Running across the road, Charles quietly approached the open window, bowlegged. Commander Duval was at the bar retrieving two pots of beer, while his brother was arranging three more chairs around the table just beside the open window. Charles dropped to his belly and crawled for the last few feet, crossing the rectangle of light escaping out the open window. Taking the pots, they sat at the table where they had a view of the road through the open window. "This beer is disgusting," Duval said to his brother. "It tastes like horse piss." Charles was stuck, stretched out along the wall. He couldn't sit up or look into the room without them spotting him. However, he heard most of what they said.

Three men dressed in dark traveling clothes, not work clothes, rode in from the north crossing his view of the road and tied their horses at the post and entered the inn. Charles could hear them as they went to the publican and paid for cups of wine. Walking over to the window, they joined Duval and his brother at the table. Charles could hear the rattle and noise from their sabres. One of the new men, probably the leader said to Duval, "I got your message in Avignon. Who's your friend?"

Duval answered, "This is my brother. Call him Goshawk. Why haven't you killed the young inquisitive IG officer like I asked?"

As they sipped the acidic wine, another of the royalists whispered, "Our man is missing. We sent him to ambush the officer you wrote us about several days ago. He's never failed an assignment." Charles had to strain to hear the words. The first voice said, "In addition, we were not able to intercept the gold shipment from Switzerland. My hussar unit is staying in the empty church of Sainte-Anne-d'Évenos. I've told the mayor we are a unit of the Secret Police protecting military activities in Toulon."

"I warned you that he is extremely good with his weapons," Charles recognized Duval's voice. "If your man got too close, he's dead… I want you to kill General Bonaparte when he approaches Toulon Tuesday night." Although he said it in a low voice, Charles understood what Duval wanted. "The best way will be a large bomb next to this road. There is a perfect spot just up the road another league toward Aix. Here's 10,000 francs in gold and his route. There'll be no more money until you hear from the new man in Paris. You should collect some bomb making material to attack his coach. I think that a barrel of gunpowder, some scrap metal and fifty feet of fast fuse should do the job."

Charles heard the scrap of chairs as the men rose to leave. He froze when he realized that one of the new men was poking his nose just outside the window looking up the road toward Aix.

While Duval and his brother left, one of the new men put the bag of gold into his saddlebags while the other two went back inside. They came out with three bottles of wine a short while later. They all mounted their horses, and rode back to the north. After waiting for them to get ahead, he followed.

The riders paused about two miles up the road. He watched as the leader pointed out a level spot off the road. Four hundred yards further, he once again pointed out a spot where dozens of large boulders had tumbled down near the road. At that point, the road made a sharp turn, because of the old rockslide. They have selected the exact spot I would choose to set up an ambush, Charles thought. The lower flat section is where I would hide my horses. He also realized that he needed to dye his spare linen shirt to a darker color if he needed to disguise his appearance. With no coatee, a headscarf and his loose shirt bloused over his overalls, he would look like a farmer.

Early the next morning, he went in to see Colonel Bessières. He explained what he had observed. He then reviewed his suspicions about Commander Duval. Bessières said, "Yesterday it was announced to a few officers that General Bonaparte will arrive late tomorrow night. I agree with you that they may attempt to assassinate him somewhere on that road as it nears the city. I would like to assign Paul Forgeron, and at least six guides to help you keep that location under observation."

TWENTY-NINE

May 6ᵗʰ

AVENUE DE SAXE, PARIS AND TERMINUS, LYON

General MacDonald held a meeting at his home on Sunday night May 6ᵗʰ. Present were Jean Dulcos, Henri Dumas, Marten Napier, Eliza Rossignol and two of the three new agents from the Sûreté.

MacDonald opened the meeting with, "I have heard from the Gendarmerie Flying Squadron. They followed two cavalry units east and watched them set up an ambush on the far side of the Bois de Vincennes, beyond the eastern barricade of Paris. The huge loop in the Marne River squeezes travelers down to one route just beyond Saint-Maurice. The first formation was almost three-dozen armored cavalrymen. The second unit was the dozen or so men from the convent. The cuirass-wearing cavalrymen were all mounted on dark horses and wearing dark cloaks."

"The second group was on mixed color horses including two grays and a piebald." The general said, "Much like the horses spotted in the convent paddock. Teams pulling two six-inch howitzers and ammunition limbers accompanied the Englishmen. All of the men must have assembled at the top of Montmartre mountain. After our warning, General Bonaparte changed the route of his coach to avoid this threat. Later in the morning, the Flying Squadron crept up and fired into the rear of the ambush. They managed to wound or kill four of the royalists."

"The insurgents split into two formations and headed north and east. There were too many to do anything other than fire into their position. If the gendarmes followed, they would be counterattacked. The ambushers abandoned the two howitzers, their limbers and four dozen exploding shells. Our watchers have reported that two Englishmen came back to Paris and entered the secret tunnel. They hurriedly left as soon as they realized that someone had removed the treasure. The sûreté detectives were not able to follow the two English agents, since they were on foot. They did report one strange occurrence. They were above ground when the bell and string that we rigged to warn them if someone opened the sewer door alerted them. Hurrying down to the locked sewer door, they stuck their head into the tunnel and heard a scuffling noise coming from further down, toward Paris and not upstream toward the tax wall… Eliza Rossignol will now report on her findings."

She stood and announced, "I have deciphered the old messages we collected. The new trove of messages will take our section another month. Unfortunately, as you know, we had identified only a few of the code words used for the identities of their agents in the transcripts. As an example, Mandrake is the code name used to describe the head of British espionage in France. The director in England is code named Belphegor, while their code for the head of all activities in Europe is Prince. Falconer is the code used for the number two leader and Castracani, Diamond and Dagger designate senior British agents. Sword Master is the code used to describe the man who we believe was DeVillars, leader of the Black Horse Cuirassier Regiment. Knight describes who we believe is Lieutenant Colonel Étienne DuBois. He's the second-in-command of the Black

Horse regiment. There are at least twenty additional code names. However, there are some clues. They use names from the works of Machiavelli to describe actual British born agents and they use descriptive names to identify Frenchmen receiving bribes. Here in Paris they have different names for members of the Executive Directory, the War Ministry, the Police Ministry and members of the Council of Ancients and the Council of Five Hundred.

General MacDonald nodded and said, "Thank you, Mademoiselle Rossignol. You can go back to work at the cabinet noir tomorrow, but please be available if we discover any additional information."

"We have discussed the content of the messages," Eliza replied. "We haven't discussed how they were sending them from one location to another. We need to discuss that after this meeting."

MacDonald nodded his head in agreement and the continued, "We need to put watchers on the US legation and the Turkish Embassy and discover who is picking up the messages left outside their gates. From the code name Mandrake, I suspect there is a British agent working inside the US legation."

"There are three code names for Directors, and thirty for what we believe to be legislators," the general said. "In addition there are three names for the War Ministry, two in the Ministry of Marine and two for the Police Ministry. I suspect the Minister of Police is one of the individuals in that ministry. Major Menou may be one of the War ministry code names. My suggestion would be for me to have a meeting with Paul Barras and brief him on our discoveries."

"I do not trust Paul Barras," Jean Dulcos said. "He may be one of the Directors in the pay of the British Secret Service."

General MacDonald agreed, "If he is innocent, he will give us all the help we need. If he is one of the people receiving bribes, he may try and deflect our investigations by shifting the blame to other people. Either way we should stir up some action."

The general stood up, indicating that the meeting was over, "I will meet with him tomorrow. I will need to have multiple agents inside and outside the Luxembourg Palace. When I finish my meeting with Barras, our agents must follow any suspicious people leaving his offices. I expect Barras will immediately fire the Minister of Police based on our reports. On Tuesday we need to start watching the legations."

After dismissing the rest, General MacDonald, Marten and Jean Dulcos remained to talk with Eliza Rossignol. "I suspect the British are using the French Chappe télégraphe system to rapidly transmit their instructions to the various agents and action teams," she told them. "The British are using their De Gray version of the code and an Alberti cipher disc. The French royalist still encrypt télégraphes using the old Vigenère cipher that my father improved for the King." General MacDonald asked her to explain why she was suspicious.

"Someone messed up and used the same paper used by our Chappe operators to send one short message. The paper has a grid of boxes printed on it. They erased the Chappe signs and wrote out their ciphers in the British encryption system. The number of arm positions in the Chappe is fixed from one to ninety-two, while the British use a different type of code. A bribed operator could deliver raw Chappe gibberish but use their arm position numbers to be decoded using the British cipher disc code."

"Eliza is there anybody from the Bureaux de Poste who would know more about this?" MacDonald asked. "Who should we talk to?"

"My sister and I discovered the code anomaly," Eliza said. "I would like to discuss this with my boss, Postal Inspector Jean Lacroix. He will know what to do."

"Get back to me as soon as you have information. You can work with Tristan on this problem after he gets back to Paris."

On the 7th, Tristan was in the public room of the Lyon terminus having breakfast. Sitting at the table with him and Conductor Pelle were two of his four gendarme shepherds. All four were friends who had worked for him in Paris. The third policeman was on watch outside and the fourth had walked down to the fortress barracks to see another of their gendarme friends. Within the hour, the two gendarmes arrived at the inn from the fortress. The Lyon policeman was Sergeant François Leblanc. He had been one of Tristan's best friends when they joined the Gendarmerie together. Tristan and François were directly involved in investigating the British bribery in Paris and the Amsterdam mail coach gold robbery. When they started to get too close to the British Secret Service, the Minister of Police had transferred both of them. Their new orders had sent Sergeant LeBlanc to Lyon and Tristan to Fontainebleau.

Tristan and François sat together in a corner with a pot of coffee. Tristan shared his suspicions about British Secret Service activity in Lyon. He showed François the transcripts of the decrypted messages from the Prince's Palace to the Lyon d'Fer, as well as the references to payments to the Colonel. He then asked, "Have you seen anything suspicious since you've been here?"

Sergeant Leblanc answered, "Yes, I've felt I was being watched ever since I arrived. Colonel Saint Just and his Adjutant-Chef ignore me. They have only assigned me to menial duties. I've been on no patrols; I haven't done guard duty on any of the checkpoints into the city. They've not let me leave the fortress while I've been off duty." Tristan asked him to explain.

"My first sentry duty inside the fortress was as sergeant-in-charge on the night of the attempted robbery. I was on a roving patrol checking back with the gate guards every hour. At the first sound, I turned and saw two figures in black a dozen feet behind me with open blades in their hands. I thought that they were getting ready to stab me in the back. I'm sure my real assignment from Colonel Saint Just was to get myself killed." Tristan nodded for him to continue.

"I'm aware that one of the six bandits killed by the two officers had keys to the arms room. There were only two sets of keys, one held by the Adjutant-Chef and the other kept by the Colonel. Both of those sets were still in their possession. However, no one checked with local locksmiths to see if a spare set of keys had been made. The last few days we have been on alert and several patrols went out toward Beaune. We had heard rumors that General Bonaparte was coming through. However, nothing happened. I do not know where the information came from. The Colonel does get regular messages that are not delivered by an official Messageries Nationales courier."

Tristan asked, "What did you think of Charles MacDonald? You know that I am working for his father, the general. He has been put in charge of the investigation by General-in-Chief Bonaparte."

"He is smart, quick and he moves like a dangerous tiger," François said. "When we were writing the report after the fight in the orderly room, I accidentally knocked the inkpot off the table. He reached and caught it before it hit the floor. I was still trying to turn around. I am taller and much heavier than he is but I would lose a fight with him. He is an expert in savate, kickboxing. He kicked one bandit in the center of his modern steel breastplate caving it in over six inches, and shattered his breastbone. He drove his sabre completely through another bandits steel cuirass.

"We are going on to Toulon in a few minutes," Tristan told him. "I have more information about British agents there and in Marseilles. I will be back in a week or two. Please start keeping a watch on Colonel Saint Just and look into this fencing master, Giorgio Castracani who works over the stable gate. Find out if any locksmiths have made copies of the arms room key. Do you have any of the local gendarmes you can trust? If so, get them to help you. Please send me reports to the Gendarmerie in Toulon for the next few days."

He rose, hugged, and kissed François on both cheeks. He then walked out to the mail coach and mounted for the continuation of the trip to Toulon. They were following the same route as Charles had taken the week before. They were not stopping overnight at any location. They should arrive in five days rather than six.

THIRTY

May 8ᵗʰ

OUTSIDE TOULON

Captain Charles MacDonald, Adjutant-Sous-Lieutenant Paul Forgeron and six scouts of the Brigade of Guides were waiting a hundred yards off the road to Aix, northwest of Toulon. They were high on the slopes of the western hills overlooking the mountainous coastal road. The moon was one day past the first quarter and cast enough light to see his shadow; but, Charles realized that it would be setting sometime just after midnight. No matter what route he takes, General Bonaparte's coach has to pass this point to get to Toulon.

There were a number of twisted cypress trees and boulders on the mountainside of the road right at a hairpin turn offering good cover and concealment. The mountainside dropped off on the outside of the turn, limiting escape. There was a short path from the ambush location, around the hill, to a spot further down the road.

As the moon raised higher, a group of mounted men rode up to what Charles now thought of as his ambush spot. The men dismounted and one took the reins and rode back down to the escape location, where he tied up the horses. Charles was able to count six of them. Five men remained at the boulders and started making improvised shooting positions. They stacked rocks in the spaces between boulders. One of the men went out to the road carrying something. It was a shovel. He started digging a hole beside the road directly in front of a boulder. Another man joined him with a pick. The pick man cut a shallow trench from the rock back to their ambush position, a distance of about fifty feet. The third and fourth man brought out two barrels and a coil of fuse. Charles watched as they placed the first barrel in the shallow hole on its side and then inserted the fuse into the bunghole. The second barrel they placed upright but in front of and leaning against the first barrel. The two barrel-men started stacking fist-sized rocks around both barrels. The pick man unrolled the fuse in the trench to their ambush position, while another placed brush he had cut from a nearby cypress over the trench. All five then settled into their concealed waiting place.

Charles turned to Paul and whispered, "They are going to detonate a bomb when the coach drives past and then shoot into the escort. We can't let that happen. We must slip down right now and attack them from the rear. Tell the men not to cock their weapons until we're down there. Then shoot them in the head." Paul turned and went to each man to give them instructions, telling the last man to watch the horses and keep a lookout.

Charles drew the skean-achlais from his boot and used his left hand to lift the tomahawk from its strap on his shoulder bag. He advanced quietly down the goat trail that ended behind the boulders. The other guides followed. Once again, he was wearing his tan coveralls and unbuttoned coatee with his head and collar covered by dark kerchiefs. He had dyed his white linen shirt a darker vegetable brown. The guides were wearing green surtouts with their scarlet breeches and waistcoats; both colors looked dark in the moonlight. He reached the flat area behind the boulders and motioned for his men to spread out. They quietly moved forward. Suddenly the closest attacker heard something and started to turn around. Charles leapt forward and drove the hawk into the back of his head. He pulled the handle down to lift his chin, while he drove the blade of his black knife into the murderers neck and ripped it forward, cutting his throat. His blood spurted outward and did not get on Charles.

Paul and the other five guides raised, cocked and fired their muskets and blunderbusses at almost the same time. The bright flashes illuminated the four remaining assassins. They fell forward or dropped like empty sacks. Several were still moving and groaning. Two of the guides went from man to man to check. Inspecting his man, Charles realized that he was wearing a black civilian jacket over brown coveralls. He told Paul to question any living men and find out the name of their unit and who had paid them. The last man died within a few minutes under Paul's questioning.

Charles walked forward to make the bomb safe. He removed the fuse from the keg, and then tried to pick them up. One had a hundred pounds of black powder, while the other weighed almost two hundred fifty pounds. He needed Paul to help to carry the second. While Paul relayed the dead hussars' last words, they opened the unwieldy keg and found it was full of iron nails and pieces of chain. He heard a horse gallop away from the area downhill where the sixth man had been watching their horses. Suddenly he also heard metallic clinking noises coming down the road from Aix. Paul lit his pipe while concealing the spark with his hunched body and then turned around to peer at the oncoming caravan.

Charles stepped out and saw General Bonaparte's troop of mounted guides leading two coaches and two wagons. He and Paul both raised their arms as the lead officer came to a halt. Recognizing the guides' uniforms the *chef d'escadron* asked, "What is it? I saw the flashes and heard gunfire from around the hill."

"It was an attempted ambush by British agents." Charles told him. "We've killed five and disarmed a bomb." Bonaparte was dismounting from the lead coach when he heard. He was startled to recognize Charles MacDonald and then his old sergeant major, Paul Forgeron. The squadron commander had no idea who he had been talking with.

"Captain MacDonald, how many did you kill this time?"

"Only one, your guides killed the other four. One escaped. All of them were probably Death Hussars from Roger de Damas's, Damascus Légion. Before he died, the one Adjutant-Sous-Officier Forgeron questioned said that a French naval officer paid them British gold guinea's to kill you."

The guide left on high lookout was just approaching the road, leading all of their horses down the hill. General Bonaparte said to Paul, "I'm glad that you're joining us. Bring the bodies and everything they had down to the Arsenal Headquarters Building. I want to question the gate guards about who has ridden down the hill within the past quarter hour." Charles mounted his black horse and fell in behind the two coaches with the rear escorts.

At the city gate, the sentry told General Bonaparte that he hadn't recognized the rider coming through the gate a few minutes before. The soldier said that he had been wearing a cape, had on a wide brimmed hat and was clean-shaven. It was too dark to see the color of his hair or the clothing he was wearing under his cape.

General Bonaparte then went to the *Hôtel de l'Intendance*, the house of the Vice-Admiral of the Arsenal, where he was staying. Before leaving, he told Charles to report to him for breakfast at eight o'clock in the morning along with Colonel Bessières.

Wednesday the 9th, or Décadi started out as a hazy, humid and overcast day. It was a holiday and scheduled to be a day of parades, reviews and music. Colonel Bessières and Charles walked to the

Admiral's House at three quarters past seven o'clock in the morning. Arriving and entering the dining room they were surprised to meet two Admirals, six Generals and four distinguished civilian savants. There were also a number of staff officers. Sitting down to breakfast, they were twenty-four including the general and Josephine Bonaparte. At first, Charles was sure he was the lowest ranking officer at the table, until he recognized a young lieutenant sitting next to Josephine as her son, Eugene Beauharnais. The conversation around the table ranged from political discussions to speculations about the chances of an encounter with the English fleet. As Charles listened to the senior men at the table, all of them came to the joint conclusion that the English fleet was still blockading the Tagus River in Portugal after they had withdrawn from Corsica and Elba.

General Bonaparte then stood and announced the schedule. Today there would be a parade by the Brigade of Guides and several other units including artillery on the Place d'Armes. After the parade, he would inspect all the troop-carrying ships in the harbor. It was his understanding the majority of the army was already loaded. Tonight there would be food, music, and dancing and then fireworks in front of the Arsenal Buildings. Tomorrow and Friday, they would complete the loading of the rest of the men, animals and material into the ships.

They would sail on Saturday morning the 12th of May. Bonaparte still could not reveal their destination at that point. Charles noticed about half of those present looked amused or raised their eyebrows, as if to say, I know. As everyone was finishing breakfast, Colonel Bessières left to join the guides. Bonaparte motioned to him to come closer and said, "Stay near me during the parade and review. If we get a moment we can discuss your findings."

The rest of the day was like a whirlwind. General Bonaparte was involved in every activity. He wanted to see everything. He made a mildly critical remark to Charles. "Your hat is ragged and torn. It looks disgraceful and there is no plume."

"It has been shot off my head twice in the last two weeks," Charles explained. "I will ask around for someone who can sell me an extra field hat."

During his review of the loaded ships, Bonaparte recognized at least a hundred old soldiers and greeted many of them by their names. He introduced Charles to numerous officers including all of the geographical engineers embarked. He usually described Charles as his *Américain* Pathfinder. During the day, they had no time to talk. That evening after dinner, during the music, he noticed a mail coach pull up to the Arsenal Headquarters building and watched as Captain Tristan DuMayne stepped out. He hurried over and kissed him on both cheeks.

Tristan, in answer to Charles' inquisitive glance, said, "I have brought the gold from the Holland shipment plus a lot more. We recaptured it and the British Secret Service treasury six days ago. I also have numerous reports and other information from your father. He is in good health. The clarity and sharpness of his mind amazes me. I would never have been able to get this far without his guidance and leadership."

Bonaparte turned and noticed what was happening in the street and walked over to the mail coach. It now had seven heavily armed men surrounding it. Tristan repeated what he had said earlier and suddenly the general's face broke into a huge grin as he asked several questions.

"How much gold do you have?"

"1.9 million francs remain from the Amsterdam shipment and I have another 3 million from the British Secret Service treasury. General MacDonald kept 350,000 to pay for the continuing investigation."

"Take the coach to the back of Hôtel de l'Intendance "Napoleon ordered. "I'll have my finance administrator Etienne Poussielgue and Colonel Junot my ADC handle unloading and storing the gold in the strong room. When I finish here, I'll meet you in my office at the Hôtel."

Later that night, during a three-hour meeting, Bonaparte had hundreds of additional questions. He reviewed the copies of the documents Tristan had brought. He had questions about which Frenchmen had been taking bribes. He was interested in the Executive Directory, the Council of Ancients, the Council of 500, the Ministry of War, and the Ministry of Police. He also had questions about the legation of the United States and he was worried about the Embassy of Turkey. He mentioned that Talleyrand, the man in charge of France's foreign relations, had warned him that the Turkish Ambassador knew about the invasion of Egypt.

He gave Tristan specific instructions on continuing the investigation and directions for sending him secret messages in Egypt. He said to Bourrienne, his secretary, "Write out expanded warrants— cartes de la police, giving General MacDonald, Captain Tristan DuMayne, Lieutenant Marten Napier and Henri Dumas authority in Paris, any French province, district or foreign country to investigate the British Secret Service and all French traitors in their pay. I guess you had better add warrant cards for Captain Charles MacDonald, Lieutenant Paul Forgeron and Eliza Rossignol. Also, write out a letter of authorization, with several copies, that the Section d'Investigation Spécial d'Gendarmerie Nationale is an official unit reporting directly to me. In my absence, War Minister Scherer and Interior Minister Neufchâteau can approve actions higher than the level of Major General." He signed them as the General-in-Chief. Tristan told him that no one in Paris, other than General MacDonald and his men knew about the gold. If he left with the mail coach in the morning, he should get back to Paris on the afternoon of the 15th.

Unknown to all in the late night meeting, the small French privateer *La Pierre*, was leaving the *Rade* of Toulon, the largest anchorage roadstead in Europe. The wind was light and the humidity was much higher; a fog was lowering over the *Rade*. It looked like there would be a storm in the next two days.

Earlier the ship had received a visit by Captain Duval and his brother from the frigate *Peregrine*. Meeting in the small cabin of the corvette, Duval passed over a strong box with 2,250 British guineas and a waterproof sealed letter. His instructions to the middle-aged captain were to sail to an area twenty nautical miles due south of Cape Sicie and search for the Battle Squadron of Admiral Horatio Nelson. The local privateer asked, "What fleet, the English are still beyond Gibraltar, aren't they?"

"Nelson's new Mediterranean squadron has six experienced men-of-war; his main firepower is from the 74-gun third-raters with extensive training in battle and fleet actions. The French have seven poorly trained first and second-raters leaving Toulon. Later, another six battleships from Italy will join them. When you turn the sealed letter over to Nelson, the admiral will arrange transport to Spain and hand you a matching box with the same amount of gold. I understand that your Spanish wife will join you there; she had little love for the French."

"What's Admiral Nelson going to do?"

"He will take *La Pierre* as a prize and disperse its crew throughout the British squadron. Then he will destroy the French battleships from Toulon before they can join into a larger fleet. More than a hundred freighters and transports follow the haphazardly loaded battleships."

The next morning in Toulon, the loading of the ships continued. During the afternoon, a wind picked up from the north. By late evening, it had developed into a mistral, a cold, penetrating strong wind from the north. By the morning of the 11th, the mistral had become so violent that longboats weren't able to row from ship to ship in the inner or outer anchorages. The harbormaster closed the *Rade* to traffic. Vice-Admiral Brueys informed Bonaparte the fleet could not set sail until the weather got better.

THIRTY-ONE

May 11th

BELLE-VUE-RIVÈRE, BOUGIVAL, FRANCE

General MacDonald was sitting in his 4-wheel calash with its rear top folded forward. He was going to his farm near Bougival. It was a fine spring morning and he could feel the rising sun on his face and hear the birds twittering. Jean Dulcos was driving and they were taking the country route rather than crossing the Seine twice and paying tolls. Scout was sitting beside him on the back seat. Jean had arranged for both old sergeants to guard the MacDonald home over the weekend. They went down the Avenue de Saxe, turned right, and proceeded to the Paris-Serves barricade gate in the tax wall.

The previous evening, the general had gotten a note from his wife Elizabeth. She wrote that she and the children missed him and wished he would visit. The property next door, Chateau Belle-Vue-Rivère was finally for sale by the Commune of Bougival. He knew that the National Convention had confiscated the entire estate early in the revolution under the Forfeiture Act. A royalist baron had previously owned the property. Before the revolution, a tenant ran his ten-acre home farm, the dairy and vegetable garden to the side of the abandoned estate. In '91, the assembly had banished the baron, his relatives and seized all of the family properties. During one of the battles in '92, the baron died in action. In October of '92, a grateful legislature had split off the home farm and awarded it to the disabled general in gratitude. The next-door estate was slightly over 150 acres with a stone 24-stall horse-breeding barn and outbuildings. The baron had also owned 110 acres of uncleared hillside behind his property. In addition, there was a once elegant but now rundown country house. The chateau had been unoccupied for the past seven years and badly needed repairs.

The farm and adjacent chateau was about nine miles from the MacDonald town house using the two Seine River bridges to cut across the huge loop in the river. It took a little longer on the country roads south of the river. The general was bringing the gold coins Charles had sent him, and some additional gold he had collected from his secret hiding place in the town house. His son was not aware that he had any extra money. Jean had loaded the 60 pounds of coins into the light carriage.

When he arrived at the farmhouse, he heard his wife Elizabeth, and his twin sons calling to him as he pulled up the drive. As he and Scout got down, his wife and the boys hugged and kissed him and petted the dog. General MacDonald had keenly missed them for the past two weeks. His friend Ryan Murphy shook his hand and then said that he would watch the boys as they played with Scout before their first lesson of the day.

His wife took his arm and said, "Barbara is getting out of school and will join us tomorrow afternoon and all the next day. James, I would like you to meet Advocate Meyers, who is handling the purchase of the property for us."

He shook the lawyer's hand and asked, "What do we need to do to get a title in my son Charles' name?"

"You know that the estate has been stuck in the courts with ownership claimed by both the state and the local commune," Advocate Meyers explained. "The court has dismissed all claims by a distant cousin in England. Apparently, the commune has prevailed and is now selling the property for back taxes and other fees that they settled with Paris. We have to pay for the property along with the back taxes. They are offering to reduce the price if the payment is in gold or silver coins such as guineas, guldens, ducats, or the French Louis d'or. We must go to the City Hall in Bougival and pay 75,000 francs worth of coin to the Mayor and the Commune Treasurer. They don't want any paper money, but the price in French paper or bonds is quadruple, 300,000 francs. The town of Bougival is desperate for hard money. The economy is in terrible condition and they need cash."

"Where did they come up with the figure of 75,000 francs? No one locally has that much gold," the general asked.

"Using the new metric system the Belle-Vue-Rivère property is 62.5 hectares," Meyers answered. "I know that they were originally including the chateau, the boat and the adjoining 50 hectares of uncleared land behind the estate for 75,000 in gold. They withdrew the two extra items because I think they want a payment on the side——a commission, or they just want to haggle. If you propose buying all three items for coins, I think that they'll accept the offer."

"What's on the uncleared land?" was the general's response.

"Charles said that the back property includes a hilltop covered with slate, flint and building stones, maybe room for a new quarry," Elizabeth told her husband. "The rest is woods and natural glades that you could clear and turn into 40 more hectares of pasture. Both sections would give us a total of 278 acres to add to your 10 in the home farm; over 230 acres of it would be horse pasture."

Advocate Meyers said, "I have set up a meeting with a local builder to see about fixing the roof, doors, windows and the insides of the main building for this afternoon,"

Turning to Elizabeth, James said, "I'm here for three days, and I don't have to return to the town house until early Monday morning. Do you think that I should transfer the home farm into Charles' name also?" "Yes!"

After checking on the children, who were playing with Scout, Elizabeth took his arm, assisted him into the back seat of the carriage, and then sat beside him. Advocate Meyers sat in the front, facing the rear and Jean Dulcos started for the City Hall of the Commune of Bougival.

Later in the day, Jean drove the MacDonald family to the old chateau. Elizabeth described it to James, "It's a T shaped main building with two stories raised above the ground floor work space with a finished attic garret. The outside is clad in large cream-colored Paris limestone blocks from the quarry at Saint-Maximin."

She turned to Advocate Meyers and explained, "We have lived here at the farm for over five years. However, my husband has never been inside the chateau. We are buying it on our son's advice." Turning back to her husband, she continued her description, "Its copper roof is green with verdigris. The overall width of the ten-bay building is more than a hundred feet and the depth is over half that. A wide fan of curved stone steps leads up to the covered portico."

As Elizabeth led him to the front doors, she noticed both sets were open. The builder came out of the entrance vestibule, greeted them and introduced himself as Gérard Mayeux. As they entered, MacDonald could smell and feel the dampness. When the interior doors closed, he could hear the wood creak and the hinges squeak. Suddenly he heard birds flying about inside the house. Elizabeth mentioned the house was still fully furnished and muslin dust cloths covered the furniture and chandeliers.

Mayeux told them, "Some of the upholstered furniture now houses wildlife. You'll need to reupholster the furniture and everything in the house needs cleaning and repainting." James could feel a slight breeze coming from broken windows. The coolness of the stone foyer rose through his boots.

Elizabeth continued to describe the chateau and its situation. "The front of the chateau is on a ridge facing north, overlooking an island in the Seine. The baron named it *Belle-Vue-Rivère*—beautiful river view—because of the wonderful panorama from the front windows. There is a boathouse and landing on the nearside channel, half-a-mile from the front doors. A sailboat belonging to the estate is dismasted and upside down on the stone quay."

Advocate Meyers referred to his notes and read, "The estate also owns a Baltimore-built clipper with gaff-rigged masts. The Fells Point shipyard in America built it as a schooner. The baron fitted it out as a yacht and used it to visit friends. He also planned to use it to smuggle wine and brandy to England and bring manufactured products back to France. A master's mate lives on board and takes care of it. Since '92, he's anchored it above the floating bridge in Rouen. He wrote that it needs repairs and renovations and that he's not gotten any money since he sailed it upstream from Honfleur. He wants 1,000 francs to cover his wages and cost to date."

Builder Mayeux broke in and said, "I estimate it will cost 20 to 30 thousand francs to restore the chateau. I'm not including any new furniture or decorations.

"What needs to be fixed?" the general asked. "Why is there such a range in final cost? Are you including the cost of repairing the outbuildings."

Mayeux said, "All the buildings are included but there are a lot of repairs inside. There is one small leak in the copper roof, 8 windows and 9 doors are rotten and need to be replaced. I'll have to replace the glass in thirty or forty more panes, which are cracked or broken. Someone smashed one of the ballroom doors and shot out several windowpanes. All of the glass needs new putty and re-glazing. My men need to paint or varnish all of the wood and plaster. There are no keys for any of the door locks. My men need to clean and repair the interior, and then we need to re-finish the wood floors, particularly under the leaks. The two fountains no longer get water from the Machine de Marley and you will need to fix the pipes and plumbing. I don't know how much that will cost. I have no idea how much restoration of the furnishings will cost."

"Does your price include all the outbuildings and the horse barn?" MacDonald asked, "How long will the repairs take?"

"I can do everything we discussed including all of the buildings for 25,000 francs," the builder replied. "I will brush and clean all the upholstery and drapes, without replacing anything. You still need to hire a *plombier* to clean and repair all the pipes. I can finish before the autumn rains."

James told Elizabeth to give the lawyer 1,500 francs to pay for his work and for the ship in Rouen. Give the builder Mayeux 5000 francs as an advance with the balance due upon completion.

After returning to the farmhouse, James and Elizabeth had a wonderful time sitting out in the garden with their friend Ryan Murphy, as the two boys finished their riding lesson with Mahamoud. The weather was so pleasant that Maria served them dinner outside.

After dinner, General MacDonald brought the family as well as Ryan, Jean, Mahamoud and Maria up to date on the latest developments. "Charles is now the co-owner of a horse stud farm, a quarry and a ship. I want to develop the estate into a profitable operation to support anything that he wants to do in the future. Mahamoud, I want you to breed all our mares to the new Andalusian stallion," the general continued. "His Barbary background will bring much needed stamina and speed to our French riding and jumping mares. When our builder finishes repairing and re-opens the horse barn on the estate property, we can start keeping more mares there. The original builder designed its larger stalls for foaling. We now have fourteen mares and the new stallion. I think we should plan on buying half dozen light-cavalry mares and six more heavy-cavalry mares at the next national horse sales. Until they get pregnant, they can run loose in the paddocks."

"Next summer we should have around twenty-five adult horses and over two-dozen foals. Our newly combined property can easily support up to 350 horses after we clear the new pastures. Over the next five years, we can build the herd up. The farm could sell up to 100 horses per year starting in five years, an income of almost 200,000 francs per year. You need to start building stone cross walls to divide the pastures this summer," the general told Mahamoud. "Clear a road down from the new quarry to bring fieldstone for the walls. You also need to plant a hedgerow along the back property boundary until we can clear the new fields. We need to start by dividing the property into at least eight paddocks."

General MacDonald had obviously given long and careful thought to every aspect of the family's future. "Charles will want to repair the schooner *Eagle* and put it into use. Last summer he told me in confidence that at some time in the future he wants to sail it back and forth to America, not as a yacht, but as a blockade-runner and privateer. He thinks that it is faster than any boat in France or England and several summers ago, he worked on the sailing plan and hull re-designs with one of his marine engineer friends and the master's mate. Last Christmas, Charles and I spent his entire vacation with Colonel Murphy and Captain Dobenheim discussing, calculating and drawing gun mounts. I think that Colonel Murphy also talked with a foundry master in northern France."

"All of his new designs use the proposed new French naval gunnade," agreed Murphy. "Its shorter barrel can fire different exploding shells in addition to shot or canister. For the last five months I've been helping Captain Dobenheim calculating and drawing inlaid brass tracks from the center pivot to add port and starboard firing positions for each new gun. You're going to have to pay a bribe to Minister of War Scherer to get him to approve the brass foundry casting the modified howitzer barrels and the parts for the sliding-pivoting gun carriage. Charles will have to dock his ship in Le Havre or Honfleur and send his goods upriver in shallow draft bateaux."

That night James and Elizabeth made love in the upstairs bedroom. They had to be quiet to keep noise from carrying to the twins in an adjacent bedroom. Maria and Jean slept in rooms in the attic, Mahamoud slept in the groom's room in the barn and Colonel Murphy had taken over the small farmworkers' cottage on the far side of the barnyard. James opened the windows and let in the sounds and delicious smells of a blossoming spring filled the night.

On Saturday morning while Ryan was teaching mathematics to the twins, Mahamoud and Jean walked the general down to the small pasture behind the barn to greet the new horses. The Andalusian came up to him and ate a piece of apple out of his hand. Feeling his neck and muscular shoulders, he was impressed. He asked, "How tall?"

"He's 16-hands tall, black with a white star." Mahamoud said. "I've been calling him Sirius for the brightest star. He's proud, intelligent and cooperative. I've taken him for long trail rides. He can canter at twelve miles-per-hour. He has the endurance to canter for one and a half hours and then walk for a half-hour. In twelve hours carrying a cavalry load cross-country, he could ride a hundred miles before he needed to rest."

Later that morning after Jean left in the calash to pick up Barbara, General MacDonald had a long private conversation with Elizabeth. "We are going to turn this decrepit estate into a model horse farm for Charles," he informed her. "We went through the revolution in America together and you know what people can do when they work for a common goal. The letters we both receive from friends in America talk about how the United States is getting stronger and everything is improving. However, I am not happy with some of the things happening here in France."

"Everything here is about personal ambition. Most of the politicians and many of the military officers are taking bribes. Those who aren't would take them if offered. I think that Napoleon Bonaparte is a great military leader. However, I am not sure that I trust his brothers and sisters. I think France will be at war for the next decade and everyone will suffer from shortages of food and manufactured goods. A horse farm will be worth a lot of money. A fast blockade runner could be worth a lot more."

"Last week I had a private meeting with Paul Barras of the Executive Directory to discuss our findings about British Secret Service bribes to French officers and politicians. One of the reasons we met was because I suspected that he was also guilty of taking bribes and I wanted to scare him into actions that reveal his guilt. I may have made a huge mistake."

"I should be finished with this investigation for General Bonaparte in less than a year. After that, we should take the children and leave for the United States. I've talked with Ryan Murphy and he's ready to leave too. The two of us, with help from the boys, could protect the family under most conditions. If I die before you do, go ahead and leave."

Elizabeth said, "I don't like to hear you talk about dying."

"Let's be practical. You're thirty-seven while I'm sixty-eight years old. I'm going to die before you do. I just want you and the family to be safe. Our friend Ryan has agreed to escort you to Virginia if the English or the winter weather manages to kill me. He's gotten several letters from America offering him the rank of Colonel in the United States Army. He's only forty-two and they are desperate for trained artillery and engineering officers, and he is both. You do know that at the end of the American Revolution, the Continental Congress made him a citizen, just like me.

"He courted me before I fell in love with you," Elizabeth said to James. "Since then his wife had become one of my best friends before she died in childbirth, and of course I will forever be in his debt after the both of you were wounded by the explosion at Valmy and he led you the hospital in Metz. I think that he loves both of us, and the children."

"I am leaving you the extra 5,000 francs in gold for emergencies," the general changed the subject. "Hide it in the safe place in the springhouse, down in the well. I showed you the false oven where I concealed the mogul diamonds, our other jewels and gold at the town house. I am hiding the new SIS papers in the same place. I already set up a new account with 350,000 francs for the SIS at Perregaux & Cie. You know that I'm not as sure about Jean-François Perregaux but I have great faith in his partner Jacques Laffite, both are brother freemasons and I trust them more than I trust any other banker in France. I am taking Tristan there as soon as he gets back to identify him and make him a signatory on the new account. You and Charles are already cosigners for our joint account and I told them that you had temporary co-authority on the new account. You'll have to write him a letter, Charles still has no idea how much we really have." He paused to make sure she understood.

"You know about my prior history with the British Secret Service and the East India Company," he reminded her. "It they discover who I am, they will want to search the town house. If they find out about the farm, they will want to investigate it too. I brought a case of six of the rifled Versailles carabines for Ryan to start teaching the boys to rapidly shoot and reload. He began training them yesterday, and with their thirty-inch .54-caliber barrels, both can easily use the smaller patched balls. You and Barbara also need to learn how to reload, aim and fire. If anything happens, you should go to the United States Legation and make sure everyone has current passports. Right now, because of the Franco-American quasi-war the safest way to reach Virginia is to take our road coach north of Holland to Emden in East Frisia. Cross the channel to England by the regularly scheduled mail-packet. Then, take an armed ship to Virginia from either Liverpool or Bristol." He then explained his calculations.

"There is almost no chance of naval interference and little danger from privateers until you sail into the Caribbean," James told her. "If you can, try and book passage on a well-armed full-rigged ship. You and the children should each carry several weapons to protect against bandits."

Elizabeth was thoughtful and did not dispute the advice. She did ask, "What about Charles?"

"I want Charles to have everything here in France. He is starting a wonderful adventure that suits his abilities. He will rise to great heights. He may even become a general. He will eventually recognize the corruption that exists here in Europe and if he survives, he will leave to join us in the new world."

He put his hand on her arm and said, "We need to find out what is most valuable in the United States. I'll talk to our bankers and go to the diamond bourse here in Paris. The lightest way to carry our wealth is in notes of demand calling for gold or silver from banks in the Americas, next would be the jewels. The only overseas notes valuable here in France are for payment in produce. Notes priced in things like hogsheads of sugar or rum from our island colonies. We need notes on Spanish or British banks requiring payment in gold or silver." Elizabeth then asked about the possible value of the jewels versus the gold or their bank account.

"The items that we should leave here for Charles are the bank account, then the schooner, followed by the horse farm. The House of Perregaux has invested our bank holdings in various long-term projects. They are carrying over half-a-million francs in them. However, they will not be able to give us much cash on demand. We need to take any foreign paper notes, some gold and most of the smaller jewels. We need to leave the large gems behind; the East India Company can identify the large stones too easily. Make sure you leave the aurore colored ruby ring for Charles' future wife."

"Please bring me the three wooden boxes, the package and the long cases next to my bag in the bedroom," he requested. "Before you leave, would you please open the bottle of brandy from Cognac and pour me a large drink."

When Elizabeth returned, he told her, "These contain the twins' twelfth-birthday presents. The last of them just arrived at the town house. I ordered one item two years ago when Charles started in graduate school at X-Ponts. I want you to set aside half for next Christmas, I plan to give them a brace of pistols for their birthday this summer. They can start practicing as soon as they open their presents. Don't give them the sabres, instruments or watches until later. They are duplicates of the equipment I gave Charles. The third carton contains two cased sets of small travel pistols for you and Barbara to keep near you for your protection.

Barbara came running around the side of the house and grabbed her father in a big hug as she chattered on about her day off from school. Meanwhile Elizabeth returned the gifts to their bedroom and hid them under the bed. Colonel Murphy followed the boys out from their temporary classroom in the parlor to greet Barbara who was the center of attention. When Colonel Murphy announced the whole family, including Elizabeth and Barbara, was going into the back paddock to practice firing the new carabines, the young girl innocently asked if she could wear long pants for the new activity. For the rest of that day and all of the next the family did things together. That Sunday everyone went on a long tour of the new chateau, followed by a picnic in the garden. Barbara spent hours drawing different decorating schemes for the new country estate before she went back to school on Sunday evening. She couldn't wait to tell Hortense about the new chateau. She knew that her mother, Josephine Bonaparte, was searching for the financial backing to buy the country estate called Malmaison, just a mile to their east.

On Saturday night and once again on Sunday evening James and Elizabeth quietly made love with the bedroom windows open to the overwhelming sound of the cicada's outside.

CHAPTER

THIRTY - TWO

May 14ᵗʰ

WORKWEEK AT THE MACDONALD TOWN HOUSE, PARIS

O n Monday morning, when the general returned to the town house on the Avenue de Saxe, Jean helped him down and then Scout led him in through the lower level door. The man and dog went into the kitchen, retrieved the SIS papers, and took them up to the dining room. Jean spoke to the old sergeant going off duty and told him to take tonight off, he would stand watch for both he and his partner. He then noticed Henri and Marten, riding down the street. He greeted both investigators as he helped them dismount. They all went into the kitchen where Jean started a fire and put a pot of coffee on to boil. They stood around talking until all three former agents from the sûreté générale arrived. They took the coffee, sliced ham, bread and cheese upstairs to the round table in the family room. After everyone started eating, General MacDonald began giving orders.

"For the next week I want our people watching the Luxembourg Palace, the Palais des Tuileries, the War Ministry and the Police Ministry. Also, we need to keep a man at the convent for at least another week."

Marten interrupted, "I learned this weekend the Minister of Police has been fired and will be replaced on Wednesday the 16th."
When asked who was replacing him, he answered, 'Jean François
d'Ardon'. I don't know him. Until he assumes his office we can
forget about the police."

"I guess my visit to Paul Barras is starting to have an effect on
their activities," the general said in a tone of satisfaction. "Since the
only investigator who saw the man at the United States Legation is
Tristan, we'll have to wait for him to come back before we proceed
to investigate them. However, I have learned there are several Greek
officers serving at the Turkish Embassy, men who have a reputation
for spying. We can start watching them this week." After a pause to
divide the duties, he continued.

"Since it is a long trip from the Right Bank to the Avenue de
Saxe, we should meet here every other morning at nine o'clock. I will
see all of you on Wednesday morning. If an emergency comes up,
please send a post messenger."

Later that day MacDonald listened while Jean Dulcos read and
reviewed each and every piece of information they had collected.
They had been putting notes with information, names, diagrams and
ideas on the dining room walls with pins. Until they left to go to the
farm, they had been leaving the papers lying around. Since the trip,
the general had decided to lock up their original information and hide
it in the secret compartment beside the kitchen fireplace every night.

Originally, the general had installed Franklin-type circulating iron
stoves in each of the fireboxes in the main house, except for the huge
kitchen hearth with its metal cranes and hangers. Two years after
that, he had a new French cast iron cooking stove installed in the
large kitchen fireplace. Installing the stove required raising the hearth
and modifying the flue. The new hearth closed off the exposed
entrance to the old brick beehive oven built into the side of the

original fireplace. It was no longer in use and not heated by the new stove. Jean had built a hiding place using this hollow space, creating an access to it by removing the last new hearthstone and swiveling the hinged stone pillar casing away from the stove. He had two metal strongboxes custom-built to fit snugly into the space. It stayed relatively cool in the vacant space.

The general and Jean ate a light dinner and then sat around the kitchen stove, drinking wine and discussing what Charles and Tristan were doing and what was going to happen in Egypt. Ex-Sergeant-Major Dulcos had been in India with then Colonel James MacDonald. They had traveled back through the Sinai, Egypt, and Malta to France, so knew what the weather in Egypt could be like. They knew what it felt like to face the heat of the desert without enough water. It was late in the night when the general went to his bedroom with the help of Jean. Jean went on to his room on the third floor after getting him settled into bed. Scout lay at the foot of the general's bed.

At four o'clock in the morning, Scout silently padded out into the hall and started a low-pitched growling. The sound woke both General MacDonald and Jean, upstairs. Both men got up and grabbed weapons from beside their beds. Suddenly, all three outside doors crashed in with the massive battering sound of sledgehammers. Over half-a-dozen, men rushed in the ground level service door while another eight came up the main front steps. Meanwhile, a third group entered the garden door and started up the narrow kitchen stair tower at the back. As the main group neared the second floor, the 130-pound dog from Rottweil launched himself at the leading two intruders. Both men tumbled back down the main stairs and knocked the next two back into the front hallway. Scout grabbed the lead man by the throat and fiercely ripped out his windpipe. Turning from the dying man, he bit through the calf and leg bones of the other man. The invader's shout increased to a scream when Scout released his leg and grabbed his groin. Whipping his head back and forth, Scout tore the assailant's private parts free.

The two diverted trespassers stepped around the chaos and started back up the stairs. Another two jumped over the tangle and followed them. One of the final two officers at the bottom shot the dog in the spine with a pistol. Scout scrabbled with his front claws trying to bite the leader, although his rear legs didn't work. The chief drew and fired a second pistol charge into the brave dog's still snapping head. The ball passed through the dog and killed the wounded man beneath him. At the head of the stairs, the front two men encountered Ex-Sergeant Major Dulcos who had grabbed his blunderbuss and sword when he heard Scout's warning growl. Killing the first man with a charge of buckshot and stabbing the second, he engaged the next two with his sword. They forced him toward the small *salle de bain* at the rear of the house. Stepping out of the kitchen stairwell, two more men surprised him from the rear. He turned toward them as the first two, disengaged and started toward the other end of the hall and the master bedroom. In the complete darkness of the main bedroom, General MacDonald had rolled out of bed after grabbing the duckbill blunderbuss pistol from his nightstand. Although blind, he also drew his sword and moved toward the partially open door.

Jean thrust his sword completely through the first man sliding out of the back stairwell and savagely kicked him into the bathroom's slipper tub. The second man was carrying a pistol in his left hand and a sword in his right. He pushed his left hand forward and shot Jean, who was turning after kicking the first intruder off his sword. Jean swung his sword backhand, slicing the neck of the second man. Hearing a scrape, he swung around holding his military épée with both hands as he thrust into the throat of the wounded man from main stairs. His sharpened blade carried to the bone. Jean then thrust through the other men's throats into their brains. All four intruders were dead.

One of the two that slipped by Jean, rushed down the hall and slammed open the master bedroom door. General MacDonald thrust his sword at the sound made by the man stepping through the door into the room. As his sword passed through the center of the invader's chest and struck into the opposite wall with a thump, he fired the charge of ball and buckshot into the body.

The second man, slowed by a limp, pushed the skewered body to the side, knocking the sword grip out of the general's hand. He raised a blunderbuss and fired at the shape backing up on the light colored carpet beside the bed. Buckshots and a ball struck MacDonald multiple times. His pistol had a spring bayonet. Even though severely wounded, he pushed the bayonet release lever and stabbed up as he heard the breath, and felt the touch of the man who had shot him. The bayonet drove home through the man's eye socket and into his brain just before the general collapsed to the floor. He was trying to reach a loaded blunderbuss beside the bed.

Jean rushed down the hall to the general's bedroom. Although seriously wounded, he knelt beside his friend's body. As he leaned forward to listen to a whisper, a ninth man stepped into the bedroom and shot him in the back. The ninth man was tall and slender, meticulously dressed as a dandy, an *Incroyable*. Two more men followed their leader into the room to check the bodies. As Jean Dulcos collapsed on to General MacDonald's body the blood of both men drained into the Persian carpet, a light blue silk prayer rug with a colorful 'tree-of-life" design.

THIRTY - THREE

May 15ᵗʰ

AVENUE DE SAXE, PARIS

On Tuesday afternoon of the 15th, the special coach arrived at the Paris terminus of the national messenger company. Captain Tristan DuMayne and four additional gendarmes stepped down and collected their baggage. They walked to the Paris gendarme armory to turn in their extra weapons, each keeping only a pistol and a sabre. This done, Tristan went into headquarters and asked for Colonel Ackler. When he entered the colonel's office, he showed him the new worldwide warrant from General-In-Chief Bonaparte.

Since he had seen the letter and warrant from General MacDonald only the week before and another from General Bonaparte two weeks prior to that, he showed Tristan some deference. Tristan respected Ackler since the newly organized SIS-Section d'Investigation Spécial was now the secret nationwide counterpart to his provincial gendarme division.

Colonel Ackler then let it slip out that tomorrow there would be a new Minister of Police. Tristan told the colonel, "I need my four men permanently assigned to the SIS gendarme section. I will need

more men later. I also need horses and equipment immediately."
Colonel Ackler agreed to his request.

Tristan went down to the stables with his four men; they saddled, mounted and rode to the Avenue de Saxe as a patrol. Entering the forecourt, Tristan dismounted, handed his reins to one of his men and walked to the ground floor door. He stopped when he realized someone had smashed it in at the handle, and then pulled it partially shut. He stepped back and gestured for his men to take arms. Drawing his sabre, he slowly entered the ground floor. All of the doors had been smashed open. The intruders had littered the ground floor with broken bottles. They had turned over all the shelves in the wine cellar. They had pried up all the ground floor flagstones and stacked them to the side. Someone had disconnected the cast iron sewer pipes and searched them. Going down the hall to the kitchen, food and utensils were all over the floor. He saw that they had turned over the heavy kitchen table. There was a trail of black drops leading to the back door; it looked like dried blood.

He slowly moved upstairs to the first floor and saw everything that had been on the walls of the family room was torn and missing. There were papers scattered over the room and at least one bottle of wine was broken. Whoever the invaders were, they had ransacked all the other rooms on this floor, sliced open the seats and backs of the upholstered furniture, and scattered the batting over the floor. Someone had searched each book and thrown it off the library shelves. The silver flatware, candelabra and jardinière were scattered on the floor of the formal dining room with its long mahogany table.

This was no robbery, he realized. The thieves did not even take the valuable silverware.

The dog Scout was dead, crumpled at the foot of the stairs. He had at least two gunshot wounds visible. There were also two large pools of dried blood near him. He went up to the second floor and saw four more pools of dried blood to his rear, not far from the doors to the bathroom, the water closet and the back stairwell entrance. He went to the front of the hall and slowly entered the master bedroom. There were blood splatters on the door and on the wall immediately inside the door. Then he saw the bodies, rushed over and checked the pulse of each. Both had been dead for some time, slaughtered like animals.

Tristan felt crushed. He did not know how he would be able to break the horrific news to Madam MacDonald or to Charles. He felt responsible for what had happened. He was short of breath and was on the verge of tears.

One of his men stepped into the room and reported, "There are no bandit's bodies, but it looks like at least two were killed on the main floor and four more at the back of this floor." The gendarme inspected the room and said, "I think they killed another two before they finally went down. Someone has obviously removed the attackers' bodies."

Tristan began thinking about what he had to do. He called his men down to the reception room on the first floor. Because of the brutality of the attack, he realized that each man must be ready for any challenge. Checking, he was relieved that all his men were armed. He examined the coat closet and discovered that the secret catch was unopened. A charged blunderbuss and two pistols were inside. His pistol was downstairs in a saddle holster, so he slid both horse pistols into his centurion belt and re-scabbarded his sabre. He put one man outside on watch, armed with the blunderbuss. He assigned a second to go to the Hôtel de Ville and report the murders and then on to the Gendarmerie to make the same report. He gave the third the home address of Henri Dumas and told him to inform him what had occurred. He was then to go on to the home of Marten Napier and tell him the same. He told the fourth man to search the stables out back. He started upstairs to search the house. All the men remaining at the town house, stayed alert, anticipating a possible surprise attack.

On the top floor, Tristan began his grim examination of the scene of the massacre in what must be Charles MacDonald's room. The front facing garret was a 48-foot long by 10-foot wide fencing salle with no ceiling, just the exposed rafters of the roof. The inside wall ran up to the rafters while the outside walls were shorter 6-foot knee walls. The room had seven dormers that added additional floor space and allowed for ventilation. Five of them looked out on the street while the two end dormer windows faced the neighboring houses and provided more space.

Charles had placed his desk and bookcase in the furthest dormer to the east, overlooking the street, positioned his built-in bed frame in the next, and a worktable in the middle dormer. The westernmost two dormers contained his washstand, basin and chamber pot, and a second bed. There was a small Franklin stove at each end, but nothing else intruded into the cleared space of the fencing salle. The floors in this room were parallel planks of smooth, unpolished, white oak. The invaders had scattered Charles' belongings all over the floor and broken into the attic through several sections of knee wall.

As he searched the house, he started to notice something strange. Starting on the top floor, the intruders had searched every room and they had thrown down or cut up everything during the search. There was soot scattered from the fireplace stoves. They had torn up the children's rooms during a thorough search. He had already checked all of the rooms on the first floor, including its water closet. Going downstairs, he realized the intruders had searched every single room. Stepping out the garden door, he asked the fourth gendarme what he had found in the stables.

"The killers have searched everything," the gendarme reported. "There is hay spread all over the stalls. All three horses are loose in the back garden. Several horse blankets have been cut open and someone has used a pick to pry up all the flagstones."

Tristan suddenly realized they had not found what they were looking for. He went back up to the family dining room and searched through all of the papers scattered on the floor. There were no original documents in the room. They were all missing. They must have been searching for the gold from the Benedictine convent, he concluded. They had combed through the stables, searched under the flagstones and behind the wine racks; they must have been looking for the documents among the books, upholstery, bedrooms and containers. However, they had not found whatever they had come for, he was sure of that.

They had not found the gold because Tristan had taken it to Toulon. They had not found the papers because General MacDonald must have hidden them. Tristan realized he would have to go to the farm to inform Madame MacDonald of her husband's death. He would also have to ask her where her husband would have hidden the papers.

It was already past nine o'clock when Agent Marten Napier arrived. A short time later Henri Dumas rode up. Tristan briefed both of them and voiced his concern about the missing papers, while one of his gendarmes straightened the kitchen and started a fire under a fresh pot of coffee.

"Did you check the fireplace?" Marten asked.

"What fireplace?"

Napier walked over to the raised fireplace hearth holding the iron range and felt around for the catch releasing the end hearthstone to slide out. He said as he worked, "General MacDonald told me that he was hiding his papers in this safe. Jean showed me how to open it." He then felt around behind the stone pillar for another catch, which allowed the casing to swivel to the side, exposing the old opening. He reached in and removed the metal box. To his great surprise, there was a second metal box behind the first. When he pulled them out, the bottom stones of the old beehive oven were loose.

Marten removed the loose stones and felt under the strongbox cavity. He found several leather sacks, hidden in a lower compartment of the raised hearth. The first sack was very heavy and probably weighed over fifty pounds. The second felt half-empty.

"These sacks must be full of valuables," Marten said. Opening the first strong box, Tristan found all of the SIS papers along with several personal items. The second box was full of leather pouches. When he opened the first pouch, he saw jeweled necklaces, rings, and bracelets. One diamond and ruby ring was bright red-orange in color with striking brilliance. The second included two-dozen white paper packets of unset jewels. Each folded paper enclosed more than fifty diamonds. One had forty huge jewels. Over two-hundred of them were large, while the rest were smaller. One diamond was a brilliant blue color and size of his thumb. There were two more pouches with white paper holding eighteen large rubies, seventy-five big sapphires and ten huge Mogul emeralds. "These belong to Madame MacDonald," Tristan said, "We need to go to the farm as soon as it's daylight, to let her know what's happened." He knew that this would be the most distressing thing he had to undertake in his entire life.

He heard several riders coming down the Avenue de Saxe. Colonel Ackler was leading a patrol of gendarmes. Following them were several Paris Commune policemen. It took the rest of the night to complete the reports on the savage assault on the house and its occupants. Tristan had to write a long letter to Charles and an even longer report to General Bonaparte. He put both into the same envelope and sent one of his men to the Messageries-Nationales to dispatch it via the secret route outlined by Bonaparte.

The General-in-Chief had instructed Tristan to send secret messages to a Corsican shipping company in Marseille. From there Bonaparte's agents would smuggle it in small ships to Corsica. From Corsica they would sail on to Sicily and then to Crete and finally south to Egypt. The messages would travel in small coasters, smuggler ships and fishing boats. Leaving Paris on the fifteenth of May, the packet should arrive in Marseille by the nineteenth and in Egypt about six weeks later.

In the early morning, Tristan and Marten left to ride to the MacDonald farm in Bougival. They rode up the drive, dismounted and knocked on the front door.

When she saw their expressions, Elizabeth knew what they were there to tell her. She asked, "What happened?" She then grabbed the doorpost and started to sway. Marten took her arm and led her into the sitting room. As Tristan stepped around the corner and asked Maria to fix something restorative for Madame MacDonald to drink, Colonel Murphy came in from the barnyard. They went back into the parlor and sat beside her on the sofa. Slowly, and painfully, Tristan described what had taken place at the townhouse, omitting some of the more horrific details, "Should Colonel Murphy know what the general was doing?"

Murphy responded, "I'm a Mézières engineer and Colonel in the Artillery. I served with James MacDonald during the American Revolution where I was his Aide-de-Camp. In 1792 during the Cannonade of Valmy, the explosion that blinded the general also removed half of my left hand. I collected two horses and led James over seventy-five miles to the hospital at Metz, where I knew and trusted the doctors. I am James' best friend and I know all about his SIS, in fact I was one of his main sources of information. I'm an Inspector of Artillery and Engineers for the Commissioner of War, working directly for the Directory, so I can't let anybody find out that I know about your secret gendarmes."

Tristan glanced at Madam MacDonald and after she nodded he said, "The intruders at the town house were searching for the gold from the Montmartre tunnel and for all of the documents the general had collected. They found neither. We recovered the documents in the kitchen fireplace safe. Marten and I brought all of the items of value with us this morning." He gave her the two bags of gold and the strongbox with the unmounted jewels, jewelry and keepsakes. She thanked him and said, "I will be returning to the town house later today. Will you help make arrangements? In addition, will you take care of Jean Dulcos' body? He must be given a proper funeral and burial."

Tristan asked, "Can you delay coming to the house until tomorrow morning since we needed to complete the investigation and to clean up the mess. The killers ransacked the house and it's in no condition for anyone to see. The murderers' threw all of the family's things into a pile in each bedroom."

Elizabeth, struggling to maintain her composure, told them, "On Saturday, General MacDonald discussed the possibility the British would try and kill him during this investigation. He gave me instructions on what to do. Barbara and I will come and prepare my husband's body," Elizabeth said firmly. "No one else is to view his body until it's prepared. The twins can stay at the farm, guarded by Colonel Murphy. When I get back to the town house, I want you to go with me to the Perregaux & Cie Bank. General MacDonald wanted you listed as a signatory on the SIS account. I am the only person who can now vouch for you. I also want you to send a message to Paul Barras informing him of my husband's murder. I want you to say I have insisted on meeting him personally within the next day to discuss this matter and the funeral arrangements." It was obvious to

Tristan that she was plotting her revenge. Suddenly, unable to hold back, her tears suddenly began to fall. Tristan put his arm around her and remained silent as she wept. Nothing he could say would comfort her.

T H E   E N D

TO THE READER

Thank you for reading this book. Please take the time to review my story on www.amazon.com. Reader responses are important to me as I continue to work on the upcoming books in the *Pathfinder Series.*

ABOUT THE AUTHOR

After four years at The Citadel, Frank Mitchell commanded infantry units in Vietnam in intensive combat for over a year. For the next forty years, he worked on construction projects all over the world. Initially a project engineer, Mitchell moved up  to project manager and finally International Project Executive. He built hospitals, laboratories, military facilities, industrial factories, office buildings, banks, and other high security facilities, like embassies and consulates. Mitchell spent time in Egypt building the International Medical Center in the Egyptian desert. While there, he got the idea for this book. Mitchell has visited the sites of most of the battlefields in this and subsequent books in his *Pathfinder Series*.